'*Rook* is an ... sounds, landscape, weather – a locality so precisely evoked that it rises up from the page as you read, and surrounds you with the fabric of the imagined lives which inhabit it. They are fascinating and compelling lives, and the plot delves into the layers of their past actions and secrets, delicately peeling them away ... an utterly engrossing novel' Lynn Roberts, *The Tablet*

'A mesmerising story of family, legacy and turning back the tides, from acclaimed novelist Jane Rusbridge, *Rook* beautifully evokes the shifting Sussex sands, and the rich stream of history lying just beneath them' *Living North*

'A powerful tale ... intensely written' *Lifestyle*

'Compelling, absorbing and beautifully written' Patricia Duncker, author of *Hallucinating Foucault*

'The Anglo-Saxon material is genuinely fascinating and the writing itself is really fine – often lush and ambitiously poetic, but always controlled' *Daily Mail*

'What a good novelist Jane Rusbridge is! I love the way she combines dexterous storytelling with deliciously descriptive, poetic prose. The people, the landscape they inhabit, even the birds in the air, are all vividly rendered in this mesmerising and multilayered story' Marika Cobbold, author of *Drowning Rose*

'A wonderfully written and atmospheric novel rooted in the landscape and history of the village of Bosham and its surroundings on the Sussex coast. The expressive and emotional power of natural, temporal, musical, interpersonal, and mental rhythms and relations permeate Rusbridge's narrative and prose' wordsofmercury.wordpress.com

'An affecting work, closely woven, beautifully tempered, and it bears out the promise of Jane's first novel, *The Devil's Music*, in fine style; it's a superb piece of writing' cornflowerbooks.co.uk

'Rusbridge's fine perceptions of the natural world, the way her writing is steeped in the landscape, history and culture of West Sussex, help define her as a talented new regional voice' Rachel Hore, bookoxygen.com

'A novel of complex relationships and the uncovering of buried secrets; the language is lyrical and the rhythm of the prose melodic, reflecting the music that is so much a part of Nora ... An exquisitely written, atmospheric and deeply affecting novel' susanelliotwright.co.uk

'A book to live in and to feel in all its textures and layers. Jane Rusbridge can do this because her lyric writing is excellent – accurate, potent and evocative. Definitely a book for the connoisseurs of language' litlove.wordpress.com

'A story of human fragility in the inexorable presence of the past, and of compassion that enables us to survive our own histories – an enthralling read' trishnicholsonswordsinthetreehouse.com

ROOK

JANE RUSBRIDGE is the author of *The Devil's Music*. She lives near the coast in West Sussex with her husband, a farmer, and the youngest of their five children. She has an MA in Creative Writing from the University of Chichester, where she was the recipient of the Philip Lebrun Prize for Creative Writing and is Associate Lecturer in English.

AUTHOR'S NOTE

THIS IS A work of imagination inspired by the landscape, wild-life and history of Sussex, and by the richness of local oral tradition. Bosham is featured on the Bayeux Tapestry. You can visit the ancient church, and The Anchor Bleu which occasionally floods when the tide is high, but you will not meet Steve the vicar or Jason the barman. Like all the characters, they live only in this novel. Bosham village itself is fictionalised here, though locals might recognise aspects of Dell Quay, West Wittering, the dunes at East Head, and the paths along the shoreline of Chichester harbour. Within these pages, where the story demanded, I have shrunk both time and distance.

ROOK

JANE RUSBRIDGE

BLOOMSBURY
LONDON · NEW DELHI · NEW YORK · SYDNEY

In memory of my parents,
Hugh and Jeanne Winchester

First published in Great Britain 2012
This paperback edition published 2013

Copyright © 2012 by Jane Rusbridge

The excerpt on page vii is from 'A Herbal', taken from *Human Chain*
© Seamus Heaney. Reprinted with kind permission of Faber and Faber Ltd.

The moral right of the author has been asserted

Bloomsbury Publishing Plc
50 Bedford Square, London WC1B 3DP

www.bloomsbury.com

Bloomsbury Publishing, London, New Delhi, New York and Sydney

A CIP catalogue record for this book is available from the British Library

ISBN 978 1 4088 3135 9
10 9 8 7 6 5 4 3 2 1

Typeset by Hewer Text UK Ltd, Edinburgh
Printed and bound by CPI Group (UK) Ltd, Croydon CR0 4YY

www.bloomsbury.com/janerusbridge

At walking pace,

Between overgrown verges,

The dead here are borne

Towards the future.

Seamus Heaney, 'A Herbal', *Human Chain*

Sussex, mid-eleventh century

THE BATTLEFIELD WAS churned to mud, air slugged with the smell of charnel. Late in the day they found his two brothers and, thinking he might be close by, sent down to the nearby camp for her, with Gytha, his mother. Like the others he had been stripped, mutilated. Edyth knew him immediately, although there was no head.

She knew the swell of muscle in his shoulders and the splay of underarm hair, the beady knots tangled there; the thicket on his chest – a few hairs, straight and white, around his nipples – and the dark line that ran off-centre down to his groin, now black with blood. She fell on all fours, fingers in the gawm, to kneel astride him, to press her nose and mouth to his chest where his smell was strongest, but even there he was cold, where the beat of his blood had always warmed her, his flesh lardy as a dead pig's. Her fingers kneading his shoulders slid away and she recoiled from the heap to face into the wind and lose the raw smell of blood. She thought of their children.

The year was dying: wind and wet leaves, a mist rolling in from the swan-rād. Her teeth began to chatter. The leech of fear must have sucked strength from him at the end of the day's fighting, dusk about to fall. Other women wept as they floundered in quagmire, searching, hands or bundled cloth clamped over their mouths and noses.

'Is it him?' His mother, Gytha, had never liked her. She gripped Edyth's arms and shook until her bones tumbled. 'We can offer gold,' Gytha whispered. A hand under Edyth's chin jerked her face to the watery sky. 'My son's body weight in gold so we may take him away and bury him.'

They will not allow it, Edyth thought, but she held her quiet and gazed down the hill towards the woods where smoke rose from the camps. Gathering rooks blackened the leafless branches of trees. Her body remembered his weight knocking the breath from her. He should have been exhausted after riding and march-ing for weeks, a battle and the slaying of his brother at Stamford. The days in London would not have provided respite. Thinking to soothe, she had brought aromatic salves and oils to his tent, ready to massage his lower back and rub deep into his hip where bone-ache made him grunt as he swung off his horse. He was no longer young but his body was broad and, a warrior since boyhood, his mind was tooth and claw. His feral pacing told of exhilaration at the thought of battle. He ignored her oils and potions, grasped her by the neck and kissed her. She felt the clash of teeth, her hands in his matted hair, his tongue opening her.

Edyth lifted her eyes and, seeing the clench of Gytha's face, turned to the other women. She told them she could not touch

2

him again, but they should look above the hard swathes of muscle at his shoulder to that tender ridge where the neck begins to sweep upwards. There, she told them, they would find an imprint of the crooked marks of her teeth.

May

West Sussex, early twenty-first century

IN THE HALF-LIGHT, a woman runs, her mouth snatching at air. Along Salthill Creek towards the sea, a rope of hair twisting between her shoulder blades, she ducks the salt-stunted branches. She has long limbs, strong lines to her cheek and jaw and, although she was born here on the Sussex coast, her colouring and build are more characteristic of the Scandinavian. She wears a simple sweat-wicking top, Lycra shorts, gloves, a canary-yellow cap pulled low to hide her eyes and the most expensive trainers she can afford.

At this hour, night has not yet become day. No one else moves in the fields and hedgerows, along lanes, down the ancient footpath or out upon the water. A mist ghosts the land.

Lack of breath woke her, the sensation of weight pressing, of Isaac's body plastered to hers, slippery. The smell of his hair came back to her, an oil he used, foreign, perhaps, and a little old-fashioned; black hair, silky as a pelt. She lay poised on the dream's edge, desire tipping her body like vertigo, but too soon her fidgety mind dragged her awake, alone in her childhood bed with a crinkled sheet beneath her.

Nora hates this time of year. Sap and dripping green; riotous birdsong and the sun's sudden surprising warmth; the bounce of new growth as her fingers raked the grass for scattered pieces of her wind chime, smashed to smithereens by recent gales. Apple blossom petals stuck to her hands. The old tree fooling itself it can still bear fruit.

The mud of the creek path is slick underfoot. Every time one of Nora's feet slips, muscle jolt and the flare of adrenalin disrupt her rhythm. Her weak knee twinges. She's too slow. The toe that's missing a nail rubs against the firmness of the new and very clean trainers. Before she left, the ibuprofen bottle, nearly empty, rattled as she tipped into her palm the extra two pills which now scrape like concrete in her throat. She can't even do this right.

Nora runs harder, thoughts spattering.

'Where would you be,' Ada's voice had crooned, her lips so close to Nora's body she jerked away in shock, hand instinctively pressed to her ear, 'if I'd done the same?'

The middle of the night, Nora was halfway through a virtual tour of a cottage in Norfolk and Ada should have been in bed, not there, leaning across the desk, her breath sweet as pear drops.

'Remember?' Ada pushed her face up close to the computer screen and for a moment seemed distracted, screwing up her eyes to peer at the image of a white sofa, a log-burner, alight. '*Cosy cottage for two*,' she read, then clicked her tongue and drew herself up to her full height. 'You came back from London so worn out from travelling Europe, so many concert appearances—' Her hand swept the air aside.

Nora tried to rise from the chair, but her mother's body was too close. She sat down again.

Ada's face was blank. Her fingers slid over the lapels of her kimono.

'Mum, you should be in bed.'

'Mother's Ruin,' Ada shook her head. 'And don't we know it.' Her voice dropped low. 'Such a waste, and your hair in rats' tails from the wind and rain, the dress sticking to you, sodden, skin and bone, your hip bones, my word, your ribs, one could have played the xylophone on your chest, like some little Orphan Annie you trailed through the village in the middle of the night, didn't bother to consider a taxi, or the worry you might cause –'

'STOP!' She gripped her mother's upper arms to move her away and Ada's head fell back like a puppet's. Horrified, Nora dropped her hands, pushed them down her sides. Bone showed in the set of Ada's jaw. 'Oh, I know what you did.' Her head turned from side to side, 'Don't think I don't.' She waggled a finger.

Nora drags her forearm across her forehead: the air is damp, her face wet. She should have said something. She will have to, soon.

She runs on. A few bars of the Martinů Cello Concerto, No. 1, bustle through her mind and her body reacts involuntarily, squaring up for the hurly-burly of battle with the orchestra but, with a jerk of her head, like dodging a blow from a branch, the music is banished.

Rachel, her star pupil, leaned in the doorway of the school music room yesterday, dwarfed by the cello on her back. A few strands of hair had escaped her plait and glistened across the navy school jumper. Rachel's talent is instinctual, fierce as a rage. 'I haven't had time to practise,' she blurted. Her face reddened as if the words were a lie, both hands running over and over her plait, one following the other in an unfamiliar repetitive gesture. She needs to find a way to help Rachel have more confidence. If she was a good teacher, like Isaac, she would be able to instil in all her pupils a faith in their own resources; the belief that the impossible does not exist.

Nora keeps running. She has run every day for almost a year. Even in the semi-darkness, this landscape is familiar, a part of her; she grew up playing here, fingers and feet in the mud at the creek's edge where the roots of misshapen trees are exposed more and more each year with the movement of tides and earth.

Perhaps Isaac has died. Perhaps the dream is his way of telling her he is no longer in the world.

The sea is close now, the air rich with the salty tang of rust. To the east of the creek path, the squat trees and hawthorns with their delicate twirls of new leaf-growth have given way to open grassland. Nora's muscles stretch and tighten. She is as lithe and strong as she has ever been, her lungs greedy for the pump and squeeze of her heart. She tastes the salt from her sweat and concentrates on lifting her heels, tilting her hips forward, pushing her elbows further back to get more benefit from her arms. In the silence of early morning, the only sound is her breathing. This she can do. She tugs off her cap, a hat from childhood, too tight and hot.

When she was small, the desire to be bigger and stronger and faster sparked like fuse-wire in her chest. The frustrations of being a child and the arguments with Ada and Flick often prompted her to run away. She'd sneak out from Creek House at night and race along the flint-walled lane to Bosham church where, in those days, her fist could fit inside the keyhole carved deep into the planks of the ancient door. The key was lost or stolen, no one knew when or how. Nora would wait, anchored in the shelter of the outer porch, fist jammed in the keyhole, until the thud of her heart quietened enough for her to listen beyond the percussion of the millwheel to the millstream's pianissimo ripple and the silted whisper of Salthill Creek.

The step down into the mussel-fragrant air of the church is worn; the door with its metal-studded planks impenetrable as a drawbridge. More than a hundred years ago, while working to lower the church floor, stonemasons uncovered a child's coffin under the centre of the chancel arch. It was roughly hewn in stone, Saxon, and buried in the position saved for those of high standing where, according to long-held village tradition, King Cnut had buried his young daughter. Later, children in the village marked the place with a memorial slab, etched with the words: *IN MEMORY OF A DAUGHTER OF KING CANUTE.* Today she will go there to light a votive candle for Noah, wedge the taper into the holder with care, so as not to snap any of the hardened dribbles of wax. The flame will smoke a little. She will stand and watch the wisps curl upwards to vanish between the rafters.

Nora has run a long distance. Her heart jostles her ribcage with exhilaration. A race, she's in the lead. She can run. She has run every day for a year.

My Saxon princess, her father used to call her, his hand on her hair.

★   ★   ★

By the time she's running up the drive to Creek House, several of Nora's fingers are white and numb, the blood gone from them to pump instead deep inside, to her muscles, her inner organs. She fumbles with the front-door key. In the hallway, Ada is halfway up the stairs with a cup of coffee. It's not yet seven o'clock.

'Early for you.' Nora shoves the front door closed with a foot.

Without turning, Ada flicks a limp hand in dismissal and continues to climb the stairs, her movements jerky and stiff as a puppet's. She's in another of her moods.

In the kitchen, Nora takes a long drink from the tap and notices that the pieces of the broken wind chimes, the shell fragments and salt-bleached sticks which she'd lain along the window sill ready to be untangled, have disappeared. Checking the clock, she does her stretches. She needs to shower and get dressed for teaching, but first she wants to find the broken bits and put them somewhere safe, so she moves around the kitchen, searching under newspapers and letter piles, coats and heaps of dry washing; she treads on the pedal of the compost bin and peers in at potato peelings and egg shells. Eventually, standing at the bottom of the stairs, she calls up. 'Mum?'

Ada has vanished.

Nora bounds up the stairs to rap on her mother's bedroom door. 'Mum?'

The door swings open and Ada stands in the doorway, her hands pressed either side of her face. 'Good gracious me, Nora! What on earth are you creating about now, and at this ungodly hour of the morning?'

'YOUR MUM SAID you won all sorts of prizes. A virtuoso, you were.' Eve wrestles with the barn-like outer door of the boathouse, struggling to fasten the latch and padlock because woody tendrils of ivy have jammed the hinges. Towering above Eve, Nora reaches easily to lift a clump out of the way. She leans a shoulder against the battered wood and shoves.

'All the exotic places you played. Like Russia. You never told me.'

'It was a while ago now.'

'She's very proud of you, isn't she?'

'Mum? God no.' Nora keeps her voice light. 'Mum thinks I'm the bad penny.'

'What do you mean?'

Nora looks down on the roots of Eve's mass of shoe-string plaits, the anchoring strands of hair like the aerial roots of ivy. She gives the door another hefty shove and the metal latch slots into place.

'I turned up again,' she says.

Eve snaps the padlock shut.

This afternoon, Eve has picked the theme of Special Occasions for their visit. From her plastic crate-on-wheels, she pulls a portable CD player, plastic flowers, a champagne bucket and photographs, arranging everything on a side table.

Nora can't get used to the silence and inertia, the circle of chairs with its jumble of occupants shut inside their own heads. Today the only sound comes from a woman slurping drink from a child's spouty beaker.

Come and play some of the old favourites, Eve had said, *They'll love it. Music and singing, it lights them up, please come, if you've got time.* Of course Nora has time; these days she has too much time.

Eve holds up a photograph, showing it round the circle of elderly people: a picture of the Queen's coronation. 'Peggy, do you know who these people are?'

She calls each person by their name, always. It's important, she says, because your own name holds a certain power. Peggy, dwarfed by the winged back of the armchair, grips the photo with both hands. 'Yes.' She smiles and nods.

Nora is very thirsty. Everything about this particular retirement 'hotel' shrivels her insides. On the window sill, beside a flowerpot of dried soil, lie the husks of three dead moths, while through the picture window blares the bright blue of the May sky; the blossom on a flowering cherry just outside presses against the glass. Nora turns back to the room. By the time they've finished here it will be dark, and will also be three hours since she last ate, so she'll be able to get out, escape for today's run.

'Do you know their names?' Eve is still asking about the photo, but Peggy's smile has vanished, her glance slipping sideways to the arm of the chair. 'I don't remember,' she mumbles.

Peggy did know, Nora can tell, she did remember the names, the occasion, and perhaps was even going to share a story of her own, but now she shrinks back between the enormous wings of the chair, the memory of whatever she was going to talk about having poured out of her like sand.

'It was such long time ago, wasn't it?' Eve coaxes.

Peggy places the picture face down in her lap, folds her hands together on top of it and stares at the floor. 'Not really.' Her voice is firm and tight. She is angry.

'When was it, Peggy? Can you tell me?'

A knot of tension tightens in Nora's throat. Eve's pushing too hard, she should let it go, but then Peggy looks up again, her face bright. '1953.' She gives a little toss of her head. 'That's some time now.'

'Yes, it is indeed. Can you pass that on for me now, Peggy?'

Nora's shoulders relax.

Eve looks peachy and ripe; she's put on a little weight. The air crackles with her *joie de vivre*. Those who were sleeping have opened their eyes and, one by one, each person in the room becomes aware of the others in the circle, passing photographs and red plastic carnations. Everything anyone says, anything at all, Eve conjures into some kind of conversation. She's very good at this.

'Shall we have some music now?' she says, 'from Nora?'

Obediently, the circle of faces turns Nora's way. She plays Saint-Saëns first, 'The Swan': lushly romantic. Some listen with their eyes closed. *Music has the power to speak straight to whatever is our human soul.* Nora remembers Isaac's odd, dramatic turn of phrase. He'd make a fist and knock his heart. *You must transmit the music's inner emotional message with simplicity. Speak for the composer.*

When Nora has finished playing, a hubbub erupts. The session has run out of time. While Eve moves around the circle of people saying goodbye, Nora zips her cello into its case. She can think of nothing to say to anyone here so she leaves the room and waits for Eve in the hallway, where posters, faded and small, hang too high on the wall. The front door is bolted and locked with a security keypad for which Nora does not know the code. From beyond a swinging door behind the unmanned reception desk, someone shrieks, whether in laughter or fear it's impossible to tell. To live in a place like this, Ada would require sedation.

At Creek House, Harry's red van is parked in the drive with the doors open, the ladder with a rag tied to the end poking out and his window-washing buckets and equipment lying on the gravel. Harry is bent over the bird bath with his shirtsleeves rolled up.

Harry, as Ada says, is a man of few words. The sort who turns his hand to anything: household repairs and gardening; window-cleaning. Someone in the village saw him with a canvas and easel painting in the ruin of the warehouse down behind the boatyard, Nora has heard, but his chipped knuckles and broad palms like a cowman's look all wrong for a painter.

In the bird bath are a few centimetres of dirty rainwater. Nora's body casts a shadow as she stands over Harry, but he doesn't look up or say anything.

'What is it?'

'A moth.'

Nora looks again, and sees the shiver of the water's surface. The creature's body presses a barely perceptible dip in the skin of surface tension as trembling ripples spread from the wings' vibration. The wings are patterned in different shades of brown, fine lines and swirls like calligraphy inked with a nib.

'It's drowning.' Harry pitches forwards, reaching with a finger.

Nora grabs his forearm. 'Don't! They die if you touch them.'

'Dead for sure otherwise,' he says.

She remembers something about fatal damage done if the dust on their wings is disturbed, but maybe it's an old wives' tale. She takes her hand from Harry's arm; his finger has already dipped in and out of the water. Wings closed, only the dull underside visible, the moth stands on his fingertip with the absolute stillness of death. As the two of them stare down, Nora can hear Harry breathing. Finally, the moth lifts a front leg, stiff and tentative; another leg, another and another, one after the other, as it unglues its feet from his skin. Front legs stroke along one antenna and then the other, uncoiling the entire length, then, apparently exhausted by all this effort, the moth is completely still once more.

They watch. The wings shift. Again, a rapid flutter followed by a pause. Finally, after a luxuriously slow fanning of the wings, spreading them wide, take-off is abrupt. The moth zooms skywards, veering to one side before righting its trajectory and heading straight into the blue.

THE BALL OF Ada's foot sinks as she leans forward to throw a chunk of bread into the water, mud squirting between her toes. The fresh ciabatta cradled in the crook of her arm is warm, doughy and alive. Saliva floods her mouth.

The chunk of bread sinks, disappearing from sight entirely before it looms, pale and ghostly, from the depths to bob on the surface. Again she leans forwards, to repeat the pleasurable ooze of mud between her toes.

The swans are a long way off, where the creek points a finger inland towards the Downs. They do not look her way. Ada flings the bread harder, her kimono rippling, the silk liquid against her skin. She lifts her arms high to allow the breeze to stroke the silk against her thighs and breasts and, when she does so, recalls the man who came to the house yesterday, a young man, who shook her hand and spoke her name as if he knew her. Tall, he was, and lanky, with a mop of hair and something of the eagerness of a puppy about him.

Was it his height, or his hand pushing the hair back from his forehead which reminded her, took her straight back to a party sometime that summer, the cacophony of voices and music, the crowded rooms. A blast of male laughter – and they were introduced across a throng of people squeezed into a hallway. Ada leans forward, glancing a little to one side to feign coyness, and places her hand in his. Someone says again, *meet Robert*. He stoops to catch her name and smiles as he looks down at her, his hand enveloping hers with warmth.

The way he looked at her. She had his attention, she could tell. His hands – Ada sees her hand stretched out over the water, grasping at air. It doesn't matter. She lets her arm fall. She rips another hunk from the loaf and drops it in the water. He said he would be back.

1954. That summer, she and Cicely had to air all the beds, beat the rugs and fling wide the windows. Creek House was full. They came down from London, the men in their snazzy suits, to look at the graves. Brought with them their canvas bags of equipment, tape measures, pencils and notebooks; took off their sports jackets, rolled up their shirtsleeves and drank Pimm's in the garden in late afternoons, before the shadows yawned across the lawn. Her husband was too busy getting overheated with his measurements and sketches; Robert was the one who carried the tray of glasses for her, back out on to the terrace where the others were laughing and excitement zipped the air tight.

Ada paused to dash some extra slugs of gin into the Pimm's as she refilled the jug. *Nothing* like gin on a hot day!

He came back in and closed the pantry door. The pantry shelf dug into the small of her back and his tongue tasted of mint. All afternoon Robert watched her as she crossed her legs, or leaned forward for him to light her cigarette.

Robert's body was so different, long and muscular, and his vigour took her by surprise. Under the macrocarpa, the smell of pine resin, the prick of needles on her spine and buttocks.

Simply for ever afterwards, ripping up the roots of mint that spread along the cracks and edges of the crazy paving, she'd think of Robert, of his huge hands tenderly cupping her face. The memories of him come to her only in snatches: Robert's head bent to the garden sieve, sifting the grit and rubble from the opened tombs, his hair falling forwards; his big, strong hands.

The young man yesterday had come about the graves. He ran his hands through his hair and asked for Nora. Eyes brown as a spaniel's, with the twitchy eyebrows one finds so appealing on a dog.

The ball of bread which Ada has squashed and rolled and stretched drops into the water. The white globule sinks and rises again, floating on the surface.

That time she met Robert in London.

Afterwards, whenever Brian was away, she went up to London to meet Robert – and Brian was always away on digs in foreign climes, leaving her waiting here, rattling around Creek House at the end of the long straight lane, no roads branching off, the last house before the water, looking out over nothing but mud and sky. But always those first days come back to her, the afternoons of that first summer. In a striped deckchair, Robert rests his forearms on his thighs and taps out a cigarette, offers the box to her, his gaze drifting over her ankle.

The number of years – and there were many – and the precise reason for their ending, she has forgotten. One time, near the end, when she announced her news, pulling off her gloves in Lyons' Corner House amid the clink of china and teaspoons, the waistband of her skirt so tight it hampered her breathing, Robert was gazing elsewhere across the room and, only reluctantly, when she touched his arm, looked back to her. *Why now?* he demanded, *Why now, Ada, when it's far too late!*

And it was. Too late for her to have another child, too long after the first, and it did cross her mind, as she said last week to the young doctor – whose name escapes her, these days one never sees the same doctor twice – after he'd asked her to breathe into a mouthpiece, when he placed his chilly stethoscope between her breasts and stared away at the louvred blinds covering the window, it did cross her mind. She said, I was nearly forty, you understand.

Someone had drowned the kitchen cat's unwanted kittens in a bucket.

The doctor's eyes met hers, finally. 'She knows, I assume?'

The presumption of youth! Barely out of his teens.

For a while she thought it entirely possible Robert would change his mind once the baby was born. Ada grabs at the loaf, tearing at what's left of it, scattering first pinches then fistfuls out on to the water. Empty-handed, she puts a hand to her belly and shivers.

'Mum?'

It's her daughter calling from the house, not Felicity, but the other one. 'MUM?'

Yelling like a fishwife.

Yesterday, the young man down from London – spaniel eyes and city shoes – his height put her in mind of Robert, but his handshake was a frightful disappointment. Limp as an unstuffed cushion. Not like Robert's, reaching for her across other party-goers in a crowded hallway, enveloping . . .

Above Ada, Nora stands high on the edge where the lawn ends in a sudden drop to the shoreline. Sunlight flares through her dress, blurring the edges of her silhouette and leaving the core of her body indistinct.

'Mum, why is Harry pulling up all the forget-me-nots?'

Nora wears her characteristic hectic look, shoeless, hair blowing across her face, looking for all the world as though she's about to run off again with the raggle-taggle gypsies-oh. Home she came for Christmas that year. Plain as a pikestaff what was going on, but not a word, oh no, not a word, and off she waltzed again, back to the high life in London. All over bar the shouting by the time she finally graced Creek House with her presence again.

'Mum!' Nora has her hands on her hips. 'It's past four o'clock. What are you doing down there?' There's criticism in her voice.

Well, what does it look like? But the loaf of bread for the swans has long gone and Ada stands by the creek in her scarlet kimono, holding nothing.

'What am I doing?' She assumes nonchalance with a shrug. 'I am thinking how headstrong and secretive you've always been.'

Rewarded by the fall of Nora's face, Ada slips her hands deep into the kimono's silky folds and turns back to the creek.

THE MUD AT low tide is alive with soft-lipped sucks and pops, the creek shrunk to a ribbon in the distance. Nora's wellingtons slop around her calves as she steps from one hump of eel grass to another, arms spread to counterbalance any slip on the silt. Far off by the sluice gate twenty or thirty swans are clustered, startling white against the bladder-wrack and mud. Every limpid arch of neck and fan of wing displays an orchestrated grace, reminding Nora of her mother.

'They're over. Dead. And they smother the other plants,' Ada said, when Nora asked again about the forget-me-nots. 'Though I don't know why it's any of your concern,' her mother added, 'you'll be up and off before the year's out.'

Ada was in the hall putting on her lipstick, about to leave for quiz night at the pub, her statement a question in disguise. Nora has no ready answer when her mother talks like this, as if with the turn of the calendar page to a new month the blank squares will be

miraculously starred or ringed in biro, the name of a country written in capitals alongside Nora's. Concert dates, gala performances,
a master class.

Ada patted her silver chignon and regarded herself in the hall
mirror. 'A little project for me,' she said over her shoulder. 'It is, after
all, *my* garden.' She closed the front door.

Since her return to Bosham, people stop Nora in the lanes or on
the creek path. *Couldn't stay away, then?* They smile knowingly. *How
nice for your mother to have you back home.* Ada, however, has never
seemed to need the company of her daughters, sending Flick and
Nora to board at a school only half an hour's drive away. Although
Flick was miserable, Nora loved it. She'd grab both suitcases and
shoulder her way through the front entrance door the moment
Ada dropped them by the wide steps at the start of each new term,
while Flick stood outside and chewed her hair as she peered down
the drive after their parents in the retreating car. For Nora, boarding school offered the chance to be fully engaged in musical activ-
ities whenever the opportunity arose; there were fewer distracting
undercurrents than at home.

Now, however, she and Ada have to manage living together.
With this in mind, Nora has brought the rake and sieve, thinking to surprise her mother with cockles. The drier mounds of the
cockle beds are further out across the gleaming mudflats, towards
the sliver of creek. As children, because of living where they did –
the lawn tipping towards the creek and ending a crumbling drop
ten foot or so above the shoreline – Nora and Flick were taught
early the pleasures of the mud; how to judge its character; not to
be unsuspecting of the dangers. Ada showed them the differences

in the mud's texture which could reveal where it was safest to walk, near the shore where buried flints lay just below the slip of mud, or where the root mounds of eel grass clumped. She taught them how and where to lay down planks, when to fling themselves on hands and knees and crawl, even to lie flat, if they should find themselves sucked into the slime that in certain places lurked, black and slick, below the surface, its stench of decomposition rising on hot summer days. After an afternoon on the mudflats Flick and Nora came home covered with mud, which tightened their skin as it dried. Before hosing themselves, fully clothed, under the outside shower by the back porch, they emptied their pockets of the buried treasures they had found and lined up their finds on a tin tray. Bits of bone, fire-cracked 'pot-boilers', Bronze Age artefacts, Iron Age hearths, a Roman helmet, Saxon pottery and a warrior's medallions – or so they pretended, both of them seeing their father, imitating the gentle probe of his fingers, his eyeglass, as they examined each flint or bottle top with a magnifying glass. They printed names and dates and numbers on to re-used luggage labels and envelopes. Flick was best at this, her joined-up writing flowing in the lilac Quink she used to fill her new school fountain pen.

One day, lying on her stomach – not because there was quicksand, but because in the glassy heat the suck of mud on sunburnt skin was seductive – the deep push of Nora's exploratory fingertips found something hard. She scooped and dug with her hands, manipulating whatever it was through the cloy of mud. As soon as she held the flint up and scraped the surface, she saw she'd found something real. She knew. The flint was tapered towards one end, the surfaces sharpened; the broad end fitted neatly in her palm. On each side of the tapered end were two slight indentations, notches, perhaps where the flint tool had been bound to a wooden handle. It was an axe-head, she was sure. Her father, cracking open a chalk boulder to search for the nodule of flint embedded in the soft, porous rock, had told her about Neolithic farmers who cut down forests to clear land for their crops, and the tools they made for their task.

Cradling the piece of flint in her fingers, she rinsed the mud off in the creek to reveal the colours of an English sky, grey shaded to white. Where the stone had been chipped away the blade was translucent and sharp-edged as glass, while around the notches at the tapered end the surface had been left uncut, chalky-soft and ingrained with dirt.

Nora knew she had to have this piece of history for herself, to make the axe-head her talisman. Flick was further along the shore-line, towards Creek House, wading knee-deep, her dark head bent as she picked through the contents of her net. Nora rubbed her piece of flint dry on the back of her shorts where they were still clean, and slipped her find into a pocket.

Back at Creek House she hurried to the lavatory under the stairs to wrap her treasure in a page of her father's *Daily Telegraph* left folded on the floor. She sneaked upstairs to hide her package in the mess of old tennis shoes, broken toys and salt-sticky flippers at the bottom of her wardrobe.

While having a clear-out the other day she found the axe-head, still wrapped in its bundle of newspaper and buried under heaps of clothes fallen from hangers long ago. There, too, was the bottle of gin: Bombay Sapphire. The bottle was heavy, almost full, and this fact took a while to sink in because she'd expected it to be empty. It seems she'd barely drunk any of the gin that night, after all, whatever story her fragmented memories appear to tell. She didn't understand. She tipped the bottle end to end. Gin sloshed and gulped, swirling to fill the neck of the bottle and plopping back. She noticed the way the colour of the turquoise intensified where the molten glass had folded and set during the making of the bottle.

She had balanced the axe-head on the shelf above the stopped-up fireplace in her bedroom. Despite all the time since someone first patiently knapped the surface, the flint's edge remains sharp as a blade.

Nora squats to pick up one unusually large shell. To her surprise, the two halves are still hinged together. The shell is deeply ridged and treacle-coloured spikes run along each raised rib, giving the shell the look of a medieval weapon. Webbed lines in shades of sand and stone remind Nora of growth lines on a tree trunk, but she has no idea how to read them to find out the age of the shell. She looks around between the clumps of bladder-wrack at the other, smaller cockle shells, lying open and empty after the oystercatchers have prised them apart and jabbed away the internal flesh.

The cavity of the shell, when she wipes off the mud with her thumb, is bone-white. No remnant of life. Since oystercatchers search out much smaller, thumbnail-sized shells, it's most likely this shell has been washed empty by years of seawater currents and tides. The two halves closed together form a fat heart, with spines jabbing into her palm. It will be a perfect addition to her wind chimes, if she can work out a way to attach it without damage.

When her bucket is half-filled with cockles she puts it in the shade where the garden of Creek House drops down to the shore, and continues to walk along the creek path towards the sea. Birdsong is loud, the sky very blue, but today she will not give in to her desire to scurry back into the house and shut the door on the sounds and sights of early summer; instead, she will walk to the sea, right down to the dunes and back.

Years of musical training have taught Nora to tackle limitations of the human physique with imagination and discipline. For a cellist, the most basic weakness is the unequal length and strength of the fingers. *Begin with confidence that inherent weaknesses can be overcome*, Isaac told students in their first lesson. A weakness of mind, she thinks, might prove less easy to combat.

By the time she draws close to the sea, an east wind is stirring. Clouds gather, the sky pinned low over the stretch of salt marsh where the creek widens as it reaches East Head. Anchoring clumps of marram grass provide footholds for her to clamber up and over The Hinge, a narrow strip of dune which joins the sand dunes to the mainland. A few years ago The Hinge was completely destroyed by autumn gales turning the shifting sand dunes of East Head into an island, cut off from the mainland. Without the barrier of The Hinge there was much fear in the village that the sea would encroach further inland, putting homes under threat of regular flooding. In an attempt to stop this, The Hinge has been bolstered by a rock berm; gradually the narrow strip of dune is reforming. Last New Year, people dragged their Christmas trees to the beach and heaped them in a line to form a barrier which might help to encourage the build-up of sand.

In today's wind, the sand is whisked up into scoops and ripples which glisten like sugar. The flying grains will be painful so Nora turns away from the dunes, along the top of the shingle bank towards the line of painted beach huts. The sound of an engine straining draws her attention to the car park below, where a black 4×4 is attempting to reverse, wheels churning the mud, while, behind the car, a man in a hat gesticulates, shouting instructions into the wind. His coat billows behind him, the lining flashing red. The wide brim of his hat – a gaucho, the hat Isaac favoured – hides the man's face until he glances up to where Nora stands high above him on the shingle bank. Her heart pinches. His hair, blown wild by the wind, is longer than when she last saw him, but it is Isaac, she's almost certain.

Her pace slows. He has turned away. Fighting the wind, he hauls open the passenger door and leans in to speak to the driver, a young woman. One hand holding down his hat, he throws out an arm, gesticulating at the mud, before launching himself into the seat. The hat dips with each jerk as the car jolts over the rutted field.

Nora is at a standstill. Below her, the 4×4 swings around in the car park, carving an arc of mud into the grass. The man in the passenger seat turns to pull the seatbelt across and as he does so he glances up at her again.

She was sure; now she is unsure. How can it be Isaac, because why would he be here? The man's height was wrong – though she was too far away to see him properly so it's hard to tell – but the hat, something about the windmill movements of his arm, his gesticulations at the mud. The flamboyance of the coat's scarlet lining.

Windblown sand is sharp on Nora's lips as she watches the black 4×4 move away, bouncing over the grassland towards the road which runs inland until, with a final puff of exhaust, it heads north on the tarmac.

He was with a younger woman.

Somewhere on the beach a child cries out, a high-pitched call of panic. A shadow passes overhead and Nora realises it was not a child calling, but a gull, the wind flinging its cry. She remains motionless for a few minutes, for once allowing the surge of music to rise in her mind, the melodic phrases of Granados's Intermezzo from *Goyescas*. The bow control required steadies her so that she can walk on, heading east along the shingle bank with the wind at her back.

BENEATH THE FLOOR of the boathouse is the creek. To see between the nail-pocked boards requires an adjustment of vision but since she first glimpsed the water's ripple under her feet, Nora can't rid herself of the disorienting sense of its continuous passing below. She makes a conscious effort to notice other things, such as the smell of wet emulsion and freshly sawn pine.

High up a ladder where a web of watery light wavers, Eve is spreading the last of a roller full of pale grey paint on the vaulted ceiling. Her three-year-old son, Zach, pushes a gingerbread man along a line of Smarties in the dip between two railway sleepers joined together to form a low table. He peers sideways at Nora through his blond fringe. She smiles at him but he turns away, chanting, naming colours in a sing-song voice. She tries not to mind. Children, like dogs, sense human unease; she cannot relax around Zach. One minute he'll suck his thumb and lean his head on Eve's breast, the next he'll grit his teeth and kick out at her ankles with his miniature trainers. Zach has the face of an angel combined with a predilection for making guns with anything from Lego to a teaspoon. His moods travel across his face, an expression of concentration forecasting the smash of his plate on the flagstone floor of the Anchor Bleu, something he does whenever Eve takes him in there. He savours the noise, the drama of being at the centre of adult attention. Nora would much rather see Eve without Zach and, through some sixth sense of childhood he's aware of this, she's certain.

'Ignore him. He's in a mood. Can you see any bits I've missed? It's hard to tell from here. Should I have chosen a more interesting colour, do you think? I thought about blue. There's a mix called Barbados. I was this close.' Eve pinches her thumb and finger together and heaves a theatrical sigh. The ladder wobbles. 'Does it look all right, do you think? How's your mum?'

Eve climbs down, pausing halfway to tug at her T-shirt, which has ridden up over her stomach. Wrapping her paint-roller in clingfilm, she slings the straps of her paint-splattered dungarees back up over her shoulders before coming over to kiss the top of Zach's head.

'He wanted to go out with Stavros, not stay here with me.' Eve moves round the room, picking up the sheets of newspaper covering the floor, and begins a story about the other day at the supermarket check-out, when Zach asked if Stavros was his New Daddy.

Zach tips Smarties in and out of the tube and rattles them, his face rapt. Eve describes the supermarket scenario in detail – the contents of their trolley; the cashier's chipped black nail varnish – the memory of which temporarily sidetracks Eve into an elaboration of the term 'Croydon facelift'. She puts her hands

34

flat against the side of her head, pulling her skin back to illustrate the effect.

The last time Nora babysat for Eve, Zach woke and wailed for his mother. When Nora knelt down beside his bed, his cries rose in pitch. He slid away, twisted himself down into his duvet like an animal burrowing to escape. She offered him a drink, his spouty beaker with warmed blackcurrant juice as Eve had suggested, but he flinched at the touch of her hand on his shoulder and twitched out of reach. His cries grew belligerent in tone and didn't calm until Nora left the room. She stood on the landing to listen at his door. His cries soon became quieter and rhythmic, almost humming, a four-note phrase repeating and repeating like a refrain until the sound died away altogether.

Eve has switched conversation again, back to paint and the way a certain colour becomes popular at one particular time, how the popularity spreads, from window-frames and doors, to crockery and soft furnishings.

'Suddenly everyone wants the same colour, everywhere in their life,' she says, and Nora makes an effort to concentrate, to stop her mind dropping to the slide of water beneath the floorboards, back to Isaac and everything she's tried so hard to forget.

Yesterday she saw him again, at the bus stop on the main road when she was driving home from school. Of course she surely must have been mistaken – the road was busy, it was rush hour – but as she'd slowed to signal a man lifted his hat to a woman with a buggy, and the dip of his head, a hand doffing a hat, the charm and courtesy of that gesture, made her sure it was Isaac. She braked, foot flat on the floor. The Wolseley stalled in protest, slewing into the curb. A car hooted and swerved round her, the driver leaning out to give her the finger as the bus into Chichester came labouring up the road behind her, signalling to pass. She struggled with her seatbelt, which had jammed, and managed to release herself just as the bus pulled away in a chuff of exhaust. There was no longer anyone at the bus stop.

Eve is still talking. '. . . and I thought I was being original. How does that happen with colours? Like some sort of plague. The cups too, even they are sea-green. I just went mad.' She sticks out her tongue, cross-eyed, to prove her insanity. It's a relief to laugh with her.

Nora decides not to mention Isaac, to enjoy instead the easy chatter, Eve's effervescence, the way one topic fizzes into another, from intimacy to generalities and back again. She kicks off her sandals and tucks her feet up. 'So, what did you say to him?'

'The man mixing paint?'

'You were talking about Zach and his daddy.'

'Oh yeah.' Eve wipes her forearm across her forehead. 'I was tempted to say "yes" for simplicity, but – don't look all superior – I didn't.'

'Why would it have been simpler?'

Eve treads on the lid of the tin of emulsion paint to close it properly. 'What?'

'Why simpler, when something else is true?'

'Oh come on.' Eve rolls her eyes, a mannerism she's caught from Stavros. 'Is Daddy the man who cooks your tea and reads you stories every night? Or is Daddy the guy whose genes are the same as half of yours but is not around?'

Nora thinks of her own father and says nothing.

Eve carries the paintbrushes into the narrow kitchen and Nora hears the running tap. Eve emerges with a cloth. 'I waffled on about how lucky he is to have two daddies, talked about other people, y'know, countless others who don't fit into your average 2.4 family.'

'2.4 children.'

'Whatever.' Eve picks at a splodge of paint on the back of her hand. She frowns. 'I for one wouldn't want point 4 of a child, would you? Tea?' She laughs as she disappears back into the kitchen.

Nora leans in the doorway. The boathouse kitchen is a corridor of a room with an ivy-covered skylight through which green light filters on to half-fitted kitchen cabinets and piles of plaster-dusted boxes. Eve recites the recipe for the blueberry muffins she baked yesterday. She never wants to eat another blueberry muffin as long as she lives, she says. There's some left. She wonders if Nora would like one; two. Take some home for Ada. Today there are gingerbread men too. Another recipe she's trying out, preparing for when the boathouse opens as a café.

'I met her in the post office the other day; your mum.'

The gingerbread men are cooling on a wire rack. Eve is halfway through icing them with sugary eyes and mouths. 'Have one,' she says.

Nora chooses a gingerbread man without a face. 'She didn't mention it.'

Eve is looking past Nora in the doorway to Zach, who stands on an old leather sofa gazing out of the tall window, the hair at the back of his head mussed from rolling on the floor, his legless gingerbread man abandoned on the arm of the sofa. Eve shakes her head. 'Look at him, permanently in a world of his own.'

She darts past and pounces on Zach, scooping him up in both arms, blowing raspberries into his neck as he giggles and shrieks, a bundle of thrashing arms and legs, until he wriggles away and trots at speed to the other side of the room. He flings himself on another sofa, burying his biscuit-smeared face in the cushions, rubbing to and fro.

'It was lunchtime, I saw her. Has she seen the doctor?'

'Not as far as I know. Why?' Nora is surprised Ada has said nothing about meeting Eve. Usually she recounts the minutiae of her adventures in the village, will repeat any conversation word for word, however mundane, but since a bout of flu a few weeks ago she has been a little vague about how she spends her days when Nora is out teaching.

Zach shrieks with laughter. He is opening and closing his hand around a fistful of Smarties and, each time his palm opens, his eyes widen at the sight of the shiny, multicoloured sweets as if their continued presence is a complete surprise.

'His consolation prize from Stavros. He won't eat them.'

Stavros is great with Zach, adores him, but has always made it clear he is keen to have his own. *Soon, many children*, he says, and holds up all ten fingers with a wink. *Is Greek way.*

Nora pushes the thought from her mind. 'Why do you ask if Mum had seen the doctor?'

'She looked a bit flushed. And she said she was going home to have a nap. I just wondered if she is properly over the flu.'

'She seems OK.' Though it's true Ada has taken up napping in the afternoons and is often in bed when Nora gets home just after four.

They have taken their tea to floor cushions in front of the wall of glass which faces the water. Eve sits cross-legged with a hand on her stomach. She moves her hand, round and round, sliding over her belly in idle circles.

'We came to a decision, me and Stavro: Café Jetsam. Like it?'

The name is perfect. Eve and Stavros are furnishing the boat-house with second-hand bits and pieces from charity shops and skips. *Recycling*, Stavros says, *one hundred percent friendly to environment.*

They debated over Flotsam versus Jetsam, Eve explains. Not knowing what either word meant, Stavros checked Wikipedia, his usual source of information. 'Jetsam' refers to what people 'jettison', or voluntarily throw out, whereas flotsam is things which are lost.

'Got me thinking,' she says. 'In the retirement homes, a lot of them are like jetsam, aren't they, those people who are somebody's parents. Sure, some are too ill to be cared for at home, but it's as if most have served their purpose and their kids don't want them around any more.'

Eve's parents are both dead. Nora thinks Eve's views might be different if they were still alive and complicating her life with the worry of their increasing infirmity.

'So, I'm going to run Memory Lane sessions,' Eve continues. 'Here, an afternoon every now and again. Ada might come and play the piano.'

Nora can't imagine Ada being a part of any such thing, but she says nothing. She's aware of Eve's scrutiny, of the gaze of Eve's startling blue eyes with their striated irises, the pupils surrounded by a starry line of white. Eve sees things others don't, like auras. Though Nora is not sure whether or not she herself believes in the existence of auras, in the face of Eve's absolute conviction she's forced to think about the possibility and, sometimes, this makes her uneasy.

The first time they met, for example, on the creek path travelling in opposite directions, Eve had looked her in the eye and said, 'You have an old soul.' No introduction or greeting, no comment on the weather. Eve and Zach and Benjie were a tangle of linked hands and dog leads blocking the path. Nora's belly plunged at the sight of Zach as he splashed in a puddle, his blond cap of hair lifting and falling.

Eve had come close. Goose pimples rose on Nora's cheeks, the skin tightening across her chest and up her forearms as, like an airport security guard, Eve ran her hands under Nora's breasts, patted her shoulders and torso.

'You are an artist; your aura is indigo and vibrating, here, out of your body.' Eve's child-sized hands had hovered over Nora's solar plexus, shaping the air as if she felt something tangible and solid where there was nothing.

'Maybe she could do some talks about the history of the village.' Eve is still talking about Ada. 'She's lived here all her life. She'll have a ton of stories.'

The starry line of white edging the blue of Eve's irises reminds Nora of forget-me-knots, of Harry grunting as he dug up brambles and ground elder in the garden, his shirt off, the hair on his chest curled like bracken.

'Which reminds me,' Eve taps the piercing in her nose, a turquoise eternity symbol. 'I've got a story I need to report which I heard from Geraldine when I did her head-massage a couple of weeks ago. Meant to tell you before. She was beside herself.'

'Why?'

'They're going to make a film about the tomb.'

'A film?'

'I wonder if it will be like one of those forensic programmes on TV. Do I mean "forensic"? Is that the right word? I just love those programmes. Y'know, with pathologists and dead bodies, but—' Eve pauses. 'They won't randomly dig up the graves, will they?'

'Of course not, they only do that when there are crimes to solve. Which tomb?'

Zach has poured his tube of Smarties on to the floor and Eve is watching him, distracted again. 'I'm sure she only mentioned the one.'

'Eve, if you're talking about Bosham church, there's a whole graveyard. The place is riddled with bones.'

'No, no! Inside the church, your one, King Canute's daughter, they want to make a documentary all about it.'

'Who's they?'

'They?'

'Who's going to make a film?'

'Oh,' Eve shrugs. 'Not sure.' She tucks her feet up again and, with a half-smile, looks down to her hand resting on her stomach. Clearly her attention has shifted to something else.

'I shouldn't really be telling anyone this yet.' She smiles up at Nora. 'I've only just found out myself.' She grasps Nora's wrist and, in the face of her intensity Nora feels a desire to shrink back. 'I'm pregnant! Had you guessed? Could swear I've felt the baby move already, though it's way, way too early and I didn't feel anything at all until about twenty weeks with Zach. *Had* you guessed? I bet you suspected something, didn't you?'

Nora's head is shaking, No, from side to side, No, she hadn't guessed. She mouths the words – *that's amazing, marvellous* – leaning forward to hug Eve, but her feet crash into one of the mugs of tea and she's up, searching for something to mop the spillage, her foot wet and burning.

'That's wonderful,' she calls from the kitchen. 'Congratulations. I'm so pleased.' She wrings the dishcloth with both hands, wrenching the cloth, her knuckles whitened. How easy it is for Eve to say the words, *I'm pregnant*. How pleased everyone will be.

Nora twists again, tighter, the dishcloth burning her palms like rope. She looks up and sees herself in the mirror above the sink, standing still. She has the familiar sense of being behind glass, flattened into a reflection.

THE VIBRATION BEHIND Nora's ribcage travels down into her body's core, the music pinning her to the wooden pew. Judging by the rustling during breaks between performances, others, like Nora, only notice their discomfort once the music has stopped, and shift position too. The acoustics of the cathedral add clarity to the sound and she's glad she saw the notice as she passed and slipped into the lunchtime recital on a whim.

The sousaphone player, with his eyes closed, is enfolded in the instrument's gleaming coils. After a while, Nora realises she has been watching only him for several minutes, watching with a kind of voyeurism which now opens up within her a vast emptiness. To hold back the tears, she looks up at the arches of the vaulted ceiling high above but the stone emphasises the emptiness and chill of the cathedral. Her loss comes down sharp as a pain.

Her own sense of being carried by music, of vanishing into the layers of a chord shift, the fall of an arpeggio, has been dulled for a long time, replaced by the mechanics and techniques she teaches. She finds no joy in it.

In an interval between performances, Nora slips out of the cathedral to the lavatories in House of Fraser opposite, where she sits on the closed lid with her eyes shut. When she gets to the school summer break, she will put the cello in the attic and find something else to do with her life. Unable to go back and listen to the rest of the recital, she joins the queue in Costa's. She ate breakfast very early, before running, and has eaten nothing since, so she chooses a slice of almond and raspberry Bakewell tart for energy and climbs the stairs to a seat by the window.

From upstairs, there's a good view of the road below, where, straight away, she sees a broad-brimmed hat, a flash of red coat-lining in the sunshine. The spin of her blood. The man, now in the long shadow of the cathedral spire, crosses West Street. He has Isaac's loping walk. The coat slung over his shoulder swings from a finger.

The sun through the glass is hot; Nora moves back a little, still watching as the man stops suddenly on the pavement edge. A woman with a shopping trolley bumps into him. Though he shakes his head and waves a hand in apology, he continues the conversation on his mobile. Head down, he swivels on a heel and slides the phone into his shirt pocket. When he glances up at the window of Costa's, Nora jerks back into the shadows behind the curtain but not before she sees him tip his hat. He must have seen her watching. She studies her fingers wrapped around the unwieldy mug of latte; her strong cello-playing hands which Isaac had loved. He used to hold them on his lap, between his own, much smaller ones, and tell her, *with these hands, you were born for the cello*. Useless to think about that now.

They are shaking, her hands. She needs to concentrate on putting the mug down so as not to spill any coffee. On the white plate, the almond and raspberry Bakewell slice glistens. It's moist and will taste delicious, but she is no longer hungry. She straightens her back. The muscles tear a tiny bit, she has learned, each time she runs, but the process of repair is what makes them grow stronger. To speed up repair, to make the muscle-strengthening process even more effective, serious runners have a list of foods they should eat. She is not yet that committed but, determined not to be ridiculous, she makes herself bite into the Bakewell slice.

Miss Macleod removes her cycle clips and rucksack in the hallway, having cycled to Creek House with her hired cello strapped into a bicycle trailer acquired from her nephew and intended for a surfboard. She is wearing black Nike boots with a white swoosh.

'How've you been getting along with "Scarborough Fair" this week, Miss Macleod?'

'Please call me Elsa, dear.'

Nora can't quite manage this, even though Miss Macleod has been her pupil for more than a year, since she took up learning the cello for the first time in her seventies. She rides her bike in all weathers, even the eight miles in and out of Chichester, and it's this lean stamina combined with the Miss-Jean-Brodie accent which reminds Nora of her school PE mistress. Today, Miss Macleod struggles through 'Scarborough Fair', her bowing heavy with determination. She lost the love of her life in the Korean

War, so the story goes. Once the village beauty, her hair went white overnight. Nora can't quite work out the maths but as it was about fifty years ago, she must have been extraordinarily young to have white hair.

'Did you know?' Miss Macleod taps the music stand with her bow and disturbs Nora's reverie. She has pushed up her reading glasses to peer at the sheet music as if it is an interesting but highly debatable article in a journal. 'These are the ingredients of a traditional herbal contraceptive douche: parsley, sage, rosemary and thyme.'

Miss Macleod has forgotten all about the bow in her hands and sits back, glasses now dangling from a string of coloured glass beads around her neck.

'Could you try to remember to always hold the bow by the frog, do you think? The oil on your fingers …'

'Extracts of these herbs were also used for abortion, administered by midwives, sometimes with fatal effects not only on the foetus, but also the mother. And yet here it is, repeated again and again, as a refrain, a song to a lover. Don't you find that fascinating?'

Nora nods, it is fascinating. A few weeks ago she and Eve planted parsley, rosemary and thyme outside the boathouse in old cattle troughs from Ted's farm.

'Are you familiar with this ballad, my dear?' Miss Macleod leans towards Nora with the air of someone just about to impart a secret. 'There are, of course, many versions.' Her fingers run up and down the bead string of her glasses, her eyes are dreamy. 'The speaker demands impossible tasks of his former lover.'

The lesson is, as usual, about to veer wildly off course. Miss Macleod is passionate about history. She likes to talk and, although it means the lesson will almost always spill over the allocated half-hour, Nora likes to listen, to slip into the role of student. Today, however, she has resolved not to get distracted by Miss Macleod's enthusiasm, but to keep a focus on the bow's sweep and explain the necessity to think of the down and up strokes in terms of musical expression.

'The piece is really coming on. Well done.' Nora lifts her cello, prepared to demonstrate one or two points of technique, but Miss Macleod has her head on one side, waiting for a response. There's no ignoring her expectancy. 'Actually, do you know, I only remember the refrain.'

The refrain dominates the song, a spell of repetition.

'You should look up the lyrics in their entirety, my dear. Most interesting, you'll find.'

'I will, I will. Now, shall we look at the opening bars one more time? Keep checking that you are not pressing down. Allow the cello to support the weight of the bow.'

Later, they stand in the hallway where Miss Macleod has spread A4 photographs of sections of the Bayeux Tapestry out on the table.

'For years, the Tapestry was thought simply to be a piece of Norman propaganda,' she tells Nora, 'but we're learning more and more about its complex and subversive nature. We're now certain it was designed by an English artist, within a decade of the Battle of Hastings.'

The Battle of Hastings, the battle everyone who has ever been a schoolchild in England has heard about, and the detail they all remember is Harold killed by the arrow in his eye. Nora has begun to appreciate, from listening to Miss Macleod, how much the past is multilayered and shifting. She has learned the passage of time and the surfacing of untold stories will reveal new histories, changing what was previously thought to be 'true'. The arrow in the eye was the equivalent of a cover-up story, the image a later alteration to the embroidery; Harold II met a death far more barbaric.

Academics began to unravel the secrets of the Tapestry decades ago. Nora imagines pale, long-nosed men donning gloves to pore over Anglo-Saxon documents, turning vellum pages headed with gilded letters and kept in high-ceilinged rooms shadowy as churches to prevent damage from the light, their discoveries written up, but buried in obscure journals. The rest of the world left in ignorance.

From the hall table Elsa picks up the photograph which shows Harold praying at Bosham church. She translates the Latin for Nora's benefit: '*Where Harold, Duke of the English, and his soldiers ride to Bosham. And look, here it says, The church—*'

Miss Macleod will never leave Bosham. Here, she can stand where Harold stood. She can step from her cottage into the churchyard next door and reach out to touch the walls of a building pictured in a work of art which is a thousand years old.

'*Here Harold sailed across the sea.*' She points to a longboat with oars, bobbing on the wiggle of woollen waves. 'What we really need to unravel, my dear, because it will help us solve at least part of the mystery, is Harold's reason for this fated journey to France. There are several possiblilties.'

Little woollen figures wade out, bare-legged, into the sea at Bosham. Real people, alive ten centuries ago, stitched into the fabric, captured busy with their lives, rowing, riding, carrying hounds and hawks on to the longboats.

'An artistic portrayal of events, of course,' Elsa says. 'One has to take this into account. It's a matter of interpretation. But here, my dear, in the anti-Norman subtext, are so many hidden histories. Most people have no idea.'

For photograph after photograph, scene after scene, Elsa points and names characters, the events and stories which surround them until eventually Nora begins to lose track. Distracted by the fantastic creatures whose heads decorate the prows of the English longboats, she can't interrupt to ask what they are without revealing she's not been paying full attention.

'Most exhilarating, my dear. I'll let you know how I get on.' Miss Macleod tightens the strap of her cycle helmet under her chin.

'Good!' Nora says, unsure whether she refers to cello practice, or a particular line of enquiry in her ongoing historical research.

Once Miss Macleod has left, Nora thinks again of the little woollen figures feasting in an upper room before tucking their tunics at their hips to paddle into the water as if they are on holiday. In contrast, later scenes are dominated by horses, disproportionately large and stitched in terracotta or forest-green, their riders weighed down with chain mail, helmets and battle-axes. In the margins of the battle scenes, fantastic-looking birds and beasts give way to semi-naked figures lying horizontally, some without heads. The dead stripped of their armour.

In the dust on the hall table are smudged outlines of the photographs Miss Macleod collected up and slipped into a plastic wallet as she left. Nora wipes a hand across the surface and blows the dust from her skin.

HOW SHE DOES enjoy a drink with Giovanni in the Anchor Bleu of an evening. Charming man, with those dark eyes and his marvellous Italian accent, though he leaves early, as always, says his wife will have cooked for him, there are the children to put to bed.

Brian had been putting the girls to bed, she told Giovanni, while she had a snifter on the terrace, and afterwards there was just something of a disagreement. They didn't row. Brian was a quiet man. Giovanni nodded, but must have thought her quite doolally because she remembered, too late, that he and Brian had never met and everything was too far in the past for him to know who or what she was talking about.

Giovanni is young. Let him go back to his wife and his two little girls.

'Like me, you, two daughters.' What was she doing, holding up her fingers – *Two* – like a nincompoop? Giovanni's understanding of English is perfectly adequate. Her mind is becoming soft.

Giovanni has never met Flick either. He thought there was only Nora. If Nora hadn't come back from London he might have supposed Ada to be a spinster. The very thought! So she told Giovanni about her last visit to Spain to see Flick and her granddaughters, the olive trees with their silvery leaves and almond blossom in February. It's possible she sounded a touch maudlin because Giovanni patted her shoulder when he got up to leave, told her she should fly out to Spain again, soon, for the sunshine. Heat the bones, he said. Warm the heart.

Why come and sell ice cream in the godforsaken damp of this country, this village? How Giovanni must miss the sunshine! Even with the fire lit this evening, it's impossible to drive out the chill trapped within the ancient walls. Even in the height of summer, the windows are too minute to allow any heat from the sun to find its way through to the gloomy interior. And Jason continues to labour under the misconception that an open door suggests a welcome to passers-by.

Ada rubs her palms together, rubs her upper arms. Giovanni and all the talk of Spain has made her long for the heat. How she adored those hot climates! Though in the latter years, she believes working long days in the heat affected Brian's mind. Unlike him to be whimsical – he was a man who measured and recorded with meticulous detail – but what he had described to her was most strange. After he left she'd been unable to shake off his words. They clung like a premonition. When he was excavating a tomb or a burial mound, he said, he'd feel the sweat on his back or neck cooled, as if by a shadow. Then he knew by a drop in temperature he was in the presence of the dead. Concentrating on the point of his trowel, his tools, the digging, while the shadows of their presence breathed at his shoulder, crowding him as they spurred him on to dig faster and for longer.

Their whispers drive me. Those were his words.

The night they rowed, Brian started on again, about telling Nora. He brought the matter up every time he was home. Sod's law, the things you want to forget are the things which haunt you.

She will understand, he said, *she's old enough. She's mature for her age.*

It's not all about Nora, she'd told him.

No, it's about honesty. That's what he said.

And what might that imply? Her indignation rises even now.

Brian packed his canvas holdall for the trip and left the house that night. A minor disagreement. When the project was over, he surely would have come back, if it hadn't been for the accident. The thought makes her quite tearful, imagining their reunion, the generosity of her forgiveness, in the old house which Brian did love so much but she has always hated, ever since she was a girl. None the less, here she remains, paddling in this backwater. But she must pull herself together.

At the bar, Jason pushes a bowl of peanuts towards her. 'Tapas,' he says with a wink, 'like in Spain.'

Impossible to have a private conversation anywhere in this place.

Eric shuffles in with his shoulder bag of second-hand books and takes his usual place, the stool in the dark corner near the door where he can sit and nurse his pint. Customers walk straight past him. Just as well since his coat carries the back-of-the-throat fumes of a mouldy flannel.

Always a strange one, Eric – another who could never be provoked to anger. He'd just stand with his big, piano-player hands dangling, staring at his tormentors, the boys from the council estate. At the village school he was bullied so much, his parents, who had money, paid a woman to teach him at home. Ada used to play in the millstream with him as a girl, when she was home from boarding school. 'Lift me up to the bank, Eric,' she'd say. She raised her arms to feel those strong fingers hot around her ribs.

His face is so ancient now, eyebrows shaggy as draught excluders, and he has a habit of staring at the flagstones even when she's talking to him. He smiles to himself, never looking anyone in the eye. Loves the pianos he looks after better than any person – owns a house full of them – and he's the best piano tuner for miles around. In demand by those in the know.

Ada puts a hand on Eric's arm to call his attention, lifts it to his cheek, where the bristles are silvery-sharp as metal shavings. He has always responded to her touch. Tonight she asks him about the swans, to get him talking, to get his eyes to lift to hers.

Rain, wind or shine, he tells her, every day on my bike.

He takes three dog-eared paperbacks from his bag and heaps them on the bar before removing the top book and laying it on the beer towel, to reorder his pile. When he goes home, the books will still be there, left in whatever order he finally decides is best. They are his gift. Eric travels into Chichester every morning on the early morning bus with the schoolchildren, as he has done every morning for thirty years. He stares at his own feet – great plates of meat – as he shuffles down the aisle and hands out free second-hand books. The mystery is, all the young people love him.

'Know them all.' He nods, rearranging his books, lining up the battered spines. 'Every one of this year's.'

The cygnets are half-grown now, almost adults in size if not in plumage. When Eric tells her this, Ada thinks again of Flick, living the high life in Spain; the granddaughters she hardly ever sees. Every day, Eric sees his swans, his babies.

Making her way back to a seat near the fire, Ada would have tripped on the uneven edge of a flagstone, if Harry hadn't come in at that moment and caught her arm at the elbow, steadying her. Solid as a rock, that man.

Jason has let the fire die down and Ada's feet, in her new kitten-heeled sandals, are cold. Not June yet. *Ne'er cast a clout.*

Brian teased her. Said she misunderstood. Told her 'May' refers to hawthorn blossom, not the month. *There is some debate*, he said in that earnest way of his. A 'clout' is a slab of mud, earth turned over by a plough. He'd witter on about alternative meanings of words until she was utterly bemused.

The saccharin in tonic water always leaves such a bad taste in one's mouth.

Whatever the month, an invitation from Flick to visit them all in Spain would not go amiss. Ada needs to get away from the chill which seeps up through the thin soles of her sandals.

Harry brings her a fresh gin and tonic but the glass is too cold to touch. She rubs her palms together again and holds them towards the smouldering logs, hoping Harry might take her hands in his to stop her shivers.

The ice cracks and settles downwards; bubbles fizz round the lemon slice. Mint. Robert. She gives a little shake of her head to free herself from that particular circle of thought. The air is too sharp for gin.

Harry is drinking his usual. She's not seen him drink it in the pub before.

'I didn't think Jason had the right ingredients.' A little of his drink spills when she points.

'All OK, Ada?'

'I forget, what is it called?'

'*Sol y sombra.*'

'I had an idea it was Spanish, am I right?'

Harry nods. 'A drink they have with coffee sometimes to start the day. Sun and shade. They say the name comes from the seats at a bullring.'

'Ghastly!'

Once, when Ada visited Flick in Spain she'd eaten an entire meal seated beneath the stuffed head of a bull. A black one. Nostrils flared over her hair. She'd thought of nothing all evening but the stickiness of blood, the frightful stab and thrust of violence.

Harry is talking about bullfights, about the most expensive seats having some sun and some shade. 'As in life, a balance.' He swirls the drink in his glass, mixing the clear anis and brandy together.

'Absolutely.' She has not quite followed his gist. Clearly he's not still talking about the weather, but the mention of shade has carried Brian back into her thoughts again, Brian surrounded by his whispers from the past.

No point crying over spilled milk.

Nora came home at Christmas. A mother can tell these things and Nora spoke, when pressed, of a man with a Jewish-sounding name, an older man who spent a lot of time abroad, travelling. Ada kept her thoughts to herself. Nora went back to London as usual and Ada waited in vain for news until, out of the blue – Ada throws her hands up in exasperation, and notices she is perhaps speaking her thoughts aloud. 'Out of the blue she comes home again. Spring, it would've been this time. She is far too thin and she drinks, shut away in her room, when she would never drink before because of the music, and she is a wreck. My first thought was an attack of nerves, but Nora? She's a flibberty-gibbet, but much too strong for all that nonsense. Well equipped to look after number one, that girl.'

Ada is about to go on, but something stops her. She has not mentioned her thoughts on this to anyone. A family matter is, after all, best kept behind closed doors. The gin has loosened her tongue. But – her thoughts move and settle like the melting cubes of ice – she surely has only got as far as telling Harry about the love affair. Harry, bless him, who gazes into his drink as if it will tell his fortune, does not engage in tittle-tattle. He, however, is not Family.

Ada sips her gin and decides to sidestep the issue. 'Nora has simply allowed guilt to destroy her life.' She sighs. 'My guess is, she discovered not only was he Jewish, he was also married.'

Harry gives her a look she cannot for the life of her fathom. He says nothing, which gives her the feeling she may have spoken out of turn.

'He was a powerful man.' She stops. She has forgotten of whom she was speaking – someone important. She brushes white flakes of plaster from her sleeve. In places, the walls are stained brown from sea water which has washed in and out of the pub over the years, one landlord after another marking the height of the floodwater on the wall by the bar. Plaster peels in flakes which drift to the floor. A year or two back the water was very high. Jason added his mark to the wall, to record the level, the highest yet. Of course: *Cnut*. Cnut was a powerful man. His daughter, the little princess buried in the church. Brian was of the opinion, since there are no records anywhere of this daughter, Cnut may have had a love affair.

'The child was probably illegitimate,' she says to Harry.

'Not a problem,' says Harry. 'There's no stigma.'

Time to leave, once she has finished her gin. She lifts the glass to her lips but the gin has gone. The pub is almost in darkness, only one lamp still alight; Jason is wiping down the bar. She turns her empty glass round and round on the cardboard mat. Where has every one disappeared to? She finds she has tears in her eyes. 'Have you a hankie, Harry darling?'

Harry goes to the bar and comes back with a pocket-sized pack of tissues. She wipes her eyes and turns to him. 'Harry? My daughter tells me nothing!'

They are walking past the church – not the quickest route back to Creek House but with the melancholy turn of her thoughts all evening, Ada has a feeling she may have insisted on coming this way. Brian has a theory about the little girl's grave, a theory he keeps to himself. 'First, I need to do more detective work,' he says. She turns to ask him if it was one of his shades who pressed this story upon him and finds it is Harry's arm on which she is leaning.

Harry puts his other hand over hers. 'Did you want to go in?' Ada nods.

The church is skeletal, beams like the ribs of some colossal beast arching high above. Each movement, even a breath, creates a disturbance, an echo which shifts the dust. How close she is, here, where the words on gravestones laid in the aisle have been blurred by the passing of feet, to the dead. Ada leans towards Harry. His body radiates heat, but he crouches down to look closely at the memorial slab.

'Couldn't even get that right, could they?' Ada flicks a hand. 'The grave is under the centre of the chancel arch, not here.'

'They had their reasons,' Harry says. 'Don't know what they were, that's all.'

She could tell Harry. With Harry, the story would be safe.

JUNE

THE LANE RUNS so straight because it was once a Roman road, or so they say. Nora's feet take steady, regular steps; her sandals flash in and out from below the hem of her dress. Some stitching is unravelling and the thread tickles her calf. Between Nora's shoulder blades, beneath the cello case, her dress sticks to her skin. She takes longer strides so that the walk won't swallow so much time; she's already late because of the staff meeting, and she should cook something for Ada before Miss Macleod's lesson – the last of the day.

From the creek comes the ching-ching-ching of halyards against masts and a sudden briny gust tells her the tide is on the turn, sea water pushing into Salthill Creek, frilling over silt and weed to float the leaning boats. She's almost there. She lifts her head to the breeze, worrying about Rachel, her star pupil, whose playing today was accurate, as always, but lacked pungency, as if Rachel herself was not listening acutely enough to the music she was playing.

Ahead, some youths are crouched in a huddle by the ditch. Nora hitches her cello case upwards, lifting the straps from her collarbone. As she approaches, two of the youths straighten, jaws chewing, to give her a sullen stare over their shoulders. Jeans swag low across their buttocks and the tongues of their trainers are swollen. They're not from the village, nor does she know them from any of the schools where she teaches. A sheet from the Neighbourhood Watch through the door yesterday warned of a recent spate of lawnmower thefts and garage break-ins, LOCK UP! USE YOUR CHAIN! scrawled in capitals across the bottom. She'd screwed up the note and chucked it in the bin.

A third youth hooks and jabs at something in the ditch with what looks like a carving-knife. Nora shoves her hands into her pockets and strides towards the boy. In her head runs the forceful opening of the *Appassionato*, Saint-Saëns, over and over, her fingers pressing into her thigh the music's insistent march of rhythm. The group breaks, crossing the lane and loping away, hands in pockets, faces hidden. They're no more than schoolboys: pale and skinny-wristed. *As if they've crawled out from under a stone*, her mother would say.

Bluebells lie trampled in the ditch, milky stems oozing; a screwed-up cigarette box beside a scrap of dusty black plastic. The breeze sways white saucers of cow parsley, causing her eyes to adjust. The curl of claws, a beak; a head twisted sideways, an odd angle, on the grassy slope of the ditch. Not black plastic, but a baby bird, dead. The wing stretches out, a fan of feathers and fluff. Nora glances up at the sky and down again. The bird's beak, open a little, shows a glimpse of red inside. She has a fondness for baby birds. When she was a child, her father brought duck eggs home, along with an incubator and some story about the mother duck being savaged by a dog. Nora saw the ducklings hatch, watched them emerge bedraggled and exhausted. The baby birds responded to the girls as they would to a mother duck, following them around the garden, peeping in protest when they were left. Nora got up early to hold each duckling before school. She remembers the weightlessness of each golden ball of fluff in her hands, the cool of a webbed foot on her palm. She'd sit cross-legged while each duckling flapped and fidgeted on her lap before a sudden collapse into limp-bodied sleep.

Sliding the cello off her back, Nora clambers into the ditch. She skids downwards on the long grass and swears. The slit of eye opens, beady and shining and blue: the poor thing is half-alive. If it's badly injured in some way, she should just kill it quickly, but she can't face doing that with her bare hands.

She climbs out of the ditch. The boys have disappeared. With the cello knocking at her calf, she runs along the last stretch of lane and up the drive to the house. Blood hums through her eardrums. She knows what Ada will say, if asked. The runt of a pet rabbit's litter born with spindly, bent hind-legs; the TV programme about a baby born with two heads: *kindest thing would be to break its neck.*

In the hallway Nora leans her cello against the wall. The house is quiet. Ada must be napping so she has some time. Hoping the bird is merely stunned and she might be able to save it, she flits down the hallway, through the kitchen and out of the back door into the garden to the shed, where she regards the jumble of gardening tools and household remnants: a tea-chest, a budgerigar's bath and a sixties bulky television set with no innards. Must have been one her father used for spare parts, years ago. Out here bent over his workbench, spectacles held together with Elastoplast, repairing things. Her father would not have abandoned the baby bird.

Nora's palms itch from the dust. She can't see the incubator; perhaps it was borrowed and returned. She tips the straw-like remnants of a bird's nest from a Startrite shoe-box. It will do for now. As an afterthought, she grabs the coal shovel, in case she has to kill the bird.

She's halfway down the drive when she hears laughter. The same three youths drift past the gate, two passing a can between them, downing something. The third, a black hood hiding all but the jut of his jaw, has a fag clenched in his mouth. The hoodie is several sizes too big, shoulder seams halfway down his arms, baggy sleeves mostly hiding his hands, but as he flicks his wrist in a repetitive gesture she glimpses a knife, definitely a knife this time, the blade shooting out from the handle each time he flicks. They head back towards the bird in the ditch.

Nora has an idea, and sprints back to the house. Her father's old bee-keeping veil hangs beside his raincoat. She grabs the veil, draws it over her head and reaches for the protective gloves on the hat shelf above the coats. Out on the lane again, clutching the shovel, she bears down on the three boys crouched by the ditch. The mesh of the veil is sticky with dust.

The youths look round. One, gawping at her, belches and clutches his stomach.

'Careful! It's highly contagious.' She makes her voice a gruff bark. 'Bird flu!'

Two of the boys step back, but the one with the black hood grinds his fag end under his trainer before slipping the hood from his forehead. The gleam above his upper lip is not a boil, but a lip piercing. His smile is slick with confidence.

'Gonna get rid of it?' He jerks his head towards the jumble of black feathers.

Nora nods, pointing in the direction of a red van parked a little way up the lane: Harry's van.

'Sick!' The boy kicks the kerb with the toe of his trainer before he struts off, the ragged hems of his jeans scuffing. His two mates scuttle along behind, one glancing back over his shoulder. Nora suppresses the laughter threatening to bubble up inside her. She'll refashion the whole story later for her mother: young hooligans prowling and armed with knives, an injured bird; herself coming to the rescue, festooned in a veil.

The bird opens one visible eye as she bends over it but, although the spread wing has been gathered in to the bird's breast, it doesn't stir. She puts the shovel down. Her father's gloves are too stiff with age and disuse to handle something light and fragile as a bauble, she might crush the bird's ribcage. As the finger of her glove brushes the feathers, the beak opens wider, tongue lifting like a latch, but the bird doesn't peck or claw. She lifts the veil from her face and removes the gloves. Taking a breath, she flexes her fingers and, with a fingertip, strokes the back of the bird's head. The feathers there are smooth, iridescent green and purple.

She'd better get a move on, because Ada will want tea when she wakes from her nap. As her fingers close around spines like plastic drinking-straws amongst the feathers the bird jolts sideways, a heave of body and wing which catches Nora by surprise. She lurches back.

Harry is wandering down the lane whistling, feet slopping in a pair of purple plastic crocs. His buckets hang, clanking, from his wooden ladder balanced over a shoulder, and his Hawaiian shirt, fastened with only one remaining button, gapes over his broad chest. He's holding a brown paper bag.

He stops and contemplates Nora's legs as she stands in the ditch, the hem of her dress clutched up at her hips away from the sappy bluebells. She drops her dress and tugs the bee-veil from her head.

'All OK?' His voice is a rumble.

'Yes.' Nora nods, smiling. 'Yes, yes, absolutely.' He's studying her face, waiting for her to say more. She must look mad standing like this in a ditch. 'There's a bird.' She points.

Harry puts his brown paper bag, the buckets and cloths, the ladder and his bundle of car keys in a heap on the tarmac and hunkers down.

She waits for the deep slow sound of his voice. She has grown to like its vibration, the slur of words as if he can't be bothered to separate sounds. In the few months since he parked his caravan up on Geoff Strickland's old airstrip, he's become a familiar sight around the village. His forehead is furrowed by a long scar which makes it difficult to guess his age but he seems older than her; perhaps forty. More scars, pencil-thin and silvery, web across the backs of his hands, now splayed on each thigh. He has no small talk, leaving sentences to float, incomplete, as he stares into the middle distance over a cup of tea. Now, however, he says nothing. He kneels by the bird, broad shoulders blocking her view. Curls clump at the nape of his neck, as if he's been out in wind on water all day. A gust blows the floral cotton of her dress against her thighs.

She jumps when Harry gets to his feet and steps up from the ditch, the bird's body cradled in one large-knuckled hand, against the fuzz of his chest. His other hand rests over the folded wings. The hair on Harry's forearm spreads over his watchstrap. Nora moves closer; the bird blinks at the fall of her shadow. Against her ribs, her heartbeat skitters as she and Harry gaze down at the bird with its elastic smile of a beak.

'Will it survive, do you think?'

Harry shrugs. 'These birds, man, they are something else.'

In the kitchen, Harry stands with the bird cupped in his hands, his fingers encircling the wings. Part of a black-banded leg and a foot slip out to dangle and thrust at air before withdrawing. When the foot slips out again, Nora reaches out with her forefinger; the bird's toenails – delicate, translucent – graze her skin and pause, mid-air.

Harry sends her to fetch a bundle of old cloths from his van to put down near the boiler as bedding. He arranges a hollow in the cloth and eases the bird from his hand. The black head bobs and jerks.

'Can it fly yet?'

Harry doesn't seem to hear. 'He needs . . .' he murmurs to himself. The furrows in his forehead deepen the scar. He looks up at her. 'Body warmth.'

Of course, body warmth. With the ducklings they'd used a lamp to keep them warm once they were out of the incubator. She fetches the old Anglepoise from upstairs, her father's, the cream paint scratched and chipped. The base, a chunk of metal, crashes to the ground as she rushes back down the stairs and Nora freezes, halfway down, but there's no sound from the bedroom at the back of the house; Ada's nap has not been disturbed.

Harry positions the lamp carefully, raising and lowering the metal shade, moving his palm between the bird and the bulb to test the temperature.

'It gets really hot,' Nora says. During long nights spent on the computer when she can't sleep, her forehead often films with sweat and she has to turn away the lamp's glare.

Harry nods, and stands to usher her from the room. At this sudden movement the bird's neck strains, beak flipping wide to show the scarlet inside, but it makes no sound.

'Perhaps it's in shock,' Nora says, pacing up and down between the French doors and the sofa where Harry is sprawled, hands linked behind his head. 'Won't it be hungry? Or thirsty? What do we give it to eat? Was it the boys who hurt it? Perhaps we should phone the RSPCA?'

She stops in front of Harry, who is gazing into the sooty throat of the fireplace, a half-smile on his face. 'Harry, how do you know it's a "he"?'

Harry nods slowly, deep in thought. Nora folds her arms tight across her ribs to prevent her hands passing over and over each other. *Soaping up a lather,* her mother used to say when Nora was a girl, and she'd put out a hand to still Nora's restlessness. A creak of the floorboards overhead; Ada must have woken.

'There's Mum. She'll want tea. I'll just …' Upstairs, a door opens and closes. 'Help yourself to a drink.' Nora waves her fingers towards the kitchen, unsure why they have left the bird in there behind a closed door and alone.

Upstairs, the bedroom air is misty with eau de Cologne. Ada, hair sleek in a chignon, is seated at her dressing table, leaning close to the mirror, rolling her lips and squeezing them together to distribute her freshly applied lipstick. Nora catches sight of her own reflection, her hair a mass of frayed kinks like old rope. She steps sideways, out of the mirror's range. She should get her hair cut.

'Are you feeling OK?'

Ada doesn't answer. She picks up the silver-backed hairbrush, her movements deft. 'I knew that was a man's voice I heard.' She smiles coquettishly at her own reflection before bending to caress the leather of a pair of knee-length boots leaning against the dressing-table leg. No slopping around in slippers today, then.

'Mum, it's only Harry.'

Ada zips the boots and stands to admire the close fit of the leather around her slim calves. Whatever Eve says, Ada's definitely back to her old self.

Downstairs, the kitchen door is still closed but the front door is wide open. Outside, the poplar leaves rustle. Below the other birds' racket Nora hears the low creak of a rook. Harry steps back into the house clutching his brown paper package. She'd forgotten his heap of buckets and keys outside in the lane.

'Drink?' he asks, with a nod at the paper package.

'No, I meant,' Nora begins, 'I'll put the kettle on.' But Ada clasps her hands together. 'What are we celebrating?' She raises an eyebrow, her hand on Harry's furry forearm. The paper package clinks.

SHE WILL CALL him Rook. Light on her arm, the old willow basket swings as Nora follows Harry along the narrow footpath. She has covered the basket with an old hand towel, beneath which the baby rook sleeps, a bundle of feathers and skin pulsing with each beat of its heart.

'Birds learn the layout of the stars,' Harry announces. 'All of them, the first summer of their lives.' Tucked into the back pocket of his jeans is a paperback he quotes from constantly, a book written by a woman who has lived for years with a pet rook called Chicken, his favourite of the armfuls of books he's brought to Creek House from the library since they found the bird.

Perhaps, Nora thinks, birds sense the presence and position of stars with something other than sight, a kind of vibration or magnetic pull, such as the moon exerts on the tides.

'They use some sort of infrasound.' Harry seems to have read her mind.

The path they have been following ends in the graveyard of an abandoned church, out in the middle of farmland, the building surrounded by overgrown hedges. The long grass is brittle and yellow as hay, but the high arching brambles loaded with thorns are vigorous, their stems, thick and muscular, stretching over and between the gravestones. Harry stops walking and pulls the book from his back pocket. He turns the pages. Feeling the weight and heat of the air in this enclosed, secret place, Nora moves to stand in the shade of an oak. At her feet, roots lift the ground at the base of a gravestone which leans so far it looks about to topple. No one visits these graves, or tends them, words engraved on stone no longer legible.

'Here it is,' Harry says. 'What she reckons birds can hear: *hushed sighs and whispers of hurricanes in far continents, cracks and moans of tremors beneath the earth, the ripping of the fabric of the universe.*' His finger moves along the words, cuticle lined with mud. She has slept with her windows flung wide during the heat wave of the last few days, and the blade of his turf cutter slicing into earth has woken her in the cool of early mornings. Harry has lifted an area of grass, peeling back a large rectangle of the lower lawn, the turf stacked in rolls in the shade. She must ask Ada again what plans she has for the garden.

'*The sounds of sea and wind, of oceans and volcanoes, the explosion of meteors.*' Harry closes the book. 'Man, that's some poetry!' As he gazes towards the trees in the distance, Nora notices flecks of brown in his grey-green irises. Laughter lines spray at the corners of his eyes. He shakes his head. 'Like they can hear the future coming.'

'Will our bird learn the stars?'

The baby rook spends his nights in the kitchen by the ancient Aga, sleeping in his basket covered with the black towel. Not a glimpse of the stars.

'Who knows? We don't even know if he'll be able to fly, he's too unfeathered right now. And,' Harry looks at her, 'we have a problem if he becomes too tame, if he gets imprinted and thinks of you as his mother, no chance then of returning him to the wild.'

They leave the churchyard to cross a field of late-sown maize where rooks fly low, the movement of their wings slow and deep as they lift and settle again to walk the planted rows with their stiff-hipped swagger.

'Eating the bugs,' Harry says, tapping the book in his pocket.

From a distant barn or outhouse comes the sudden echoing bark of enclosed dogs. Nora pushes the hair from her forehead, her skin claggy in the heat. She has a headache coming and wonders whether it's because the hot, dry spell is about to break, if there will be thunder. When Harry described the place where rooks come in their hundreds at dusk to roost – a stand of trees on a slope of land in a remote spot on the Downs – Nora asked him to show her, with Rook. Now she regrets her suggestion. Judging by the barbed fence through which they have just clambered, this is private land. Farmers almost always own guns.

Harry has disappeared through a gap in the hedge skirting the maize field. Nora follows. Standing with her back pressed close to the hedge, she watches him jog, crouched low out of sight, across an open strip of grass towards a ditch which separates them from the wood. The ditch is too wide to step over and filled with stagnant water. She wants to go back.

'C'mon,' Harry says, in an undertone, beckoning her over. 'Cross here.'

They are a long way from Harry's van; she mustn't lose track of time. She has a lesson later and they left the kitchen table at Creek House littered with various chopped foodstuffs and droppers containing milk and water. Harry wouldn't let her stop to clear up the mess before they left, because Rook goes without food only for a short time, before waking, frantic with hunger, his head wavering on a scrawny neck barely able to hold up the weight of his gaping beak. At first it was impossible to get the bird to swallow even a morsel of food. 'It's going to die,' Nora said. 'We're going to kill it.' In the end, Harry balanced chopped egg on the end of his finger and pushed deep into the red throat. Nora held her breath. The bird seemed to choke, swallowing several times with a sound like a strangulated gargle, but then its beak flipped open again, ready for more.

A plank, split and rotten, bridges the ditch. Harry takes swift strides over to the other side. 'It's fine,' he says.

In the wood, the ground is sodden. Some trees are leafless. They lean at an angle, propped on others, half-dying, bark smothered with lichen and trailing moss. Low-slung branches catch at Nora's hair and water seeps through the stitching in her boots. Nora glances again over her shoulder towards the distant farm buildings, squat on the horizon, but the snarls and barking have stopped.

'I don't like this place, Harry.'

'Humans don't come here. That's why the birds like it, in winter. Now, they're at the rookeries. See this?'

At their feet, and close to the fissured trunk of the tree, the ground is covered with bird excrement. Nora looks up. All she can see are fragments of blue sky beyond leaves backlit by the sun. No birds. The oppressive sense of absence, she realises, comes from the lack of birdsong.

'So,' Harry scratches his chin, 'from what I can make out, they leave here in spring and return in autumn.'

Nora's socks are wet. She doesn't like the dying atmosphere of this place but she doesn't want to be left behind, alone, so when Harry strolls further into the wood, hands deep in his pockets, she follows. His voice rolls on in that way he has, a low mumble as if he's talking to himself. 'Best to come now ... occupied elsewhere with their nests ... not to disturb them at night.'

Nora imagines the branches of these trees in winter crowded with rooks, the wood filled with the dry rustle of feathers as the birds shuffle for position. During the day, she carries Rook around with her wherever she can, in the willow basket, but at night he is alone in the kitchen, only the click of cooling pipes for company.

'Can we come back here, in winter?' she says. 'And watch?'

Harry nods. He places a hand on her shoulder, his thumb resting on the nub of her collar-bone, and seems about to say more but when he stands in silence, looking up at the canopy of leaves, Nora's awkwardness rises like a barrier. She bends to brush something imaginary from her ankle and Harry's hand drops to his side.

'We must allow the bird to be wild,' he says. 'Help him return to life among his own kind.'

Nora nods, although a part of her resists the idea. Harry makes it sound as though it's just a matter of giving permission. What if, after the plummet from a high nest and the suffocating rush of air, Rook can't be wild? His beak flips open readily enough for food but so far he has not let out any sound louder than a wheeze or putter. Perhaps the baby bird fell from his nest and squawked or cried or peeped for his parents until the muscles of his parched tongue and the throb of his scarlet throat were strained beyond the ability to produce any more sound. A silent rook would not survive.

They make their way back and are crossing the maize field towards the abandoned church when over by the farm outbuildings a Land Rover fires up and rumbles towards them, accelerating fast, the driver's door swinging open. The farmer is half-in, half-out. Heat rushes to Nora's head. They shouldn't be here. She takes longer strides, to cover the gap between hedge and churchyard as quickly as she can, staring down at her feet and trying for nonchalance by pretending to be unaware of the Land Rover which continues to head straight for them. Harry dawdles as usual, still some way behind her, hands in his pockets. He's whistling something she half-recognises from one of her mother's old Frank Sinatra LPs.

Nora is a few yards from the churchyard boundary and the gap in the hedge, when the Land Rover skids to a halt beside her, raising a cloud of dust. The farmer leaps out of the cab. He is wiry, whipped taut with fury.

'This land is private, very private.'

'I'm so sorry. I didn't—'

'If you've come here for the rooks, you'll only disturb them.'

'No, I didn't know. I'm sorry . . .' Nora's words drain away under the white heat of his glare.

The farmer spits in the dust.

'Wrong time of year, though.' Harry's deep voice is close behind her. He snaps a grass stem, twiddles and pops it into his mouth. The weight of his hand rests again, companionably on Nora's shoulder. 'Got lost, didn't we, mate? Too many beers, lunchtime, sunny day: know what I'm saying?' With a roll of his tongue, he passes the stem of grass from one side of his mouth to the other and winks at the farmer.

Beside Harry's slow calm, the viciousness of the farmer's pent-up fury dwindles. He swings up on to the Land Rover's mounting step to stand high above them in the open doorway. A gun lies across the passenger seat. Harry slips a hand around Nora's waist and with an almost imperceptible nudge, encourages her to start walking away.

By the time they have reached the evergreen seclusion of the ramshackle churchyard, the Land Rover has disappeared.

'He was so angry.'

Harry removes the grass stem from between his lips. 'Jealous,' he says. He peels the broad green leaf from the stem. 'Probably thought we'd been shagging.' Harry chucks the grass stem high into the air. 'Like we'd want to roll around in all that bird shit.'

They look at each other and start laughing.

Through Nora's open bedroom window, sometime in the night, comes a metallic scrape from the flagstones below, and a faint humming: a favourite dance tune of her mother's. Nora dips her head under the sash. In the moonlight Ada is posed like a fifties film star on the garden bench below, slender legs crossed at the ankle and tucked to one side, her right arm raised from the elbow, hand poised in the air holding something balanced there, between her fingers, the way she'd hold a cigarette.

Tonight there's a sheen about her, hair falling silvery over the crimson-and-black silk of her kimono. Ada lifts her hand to her mouth and a cigarette holder catches the light from the moon. She hasn't smoked for years yet Nora watches her shoulders rise as she inhales, holds the breath and savours it, before tapping the holder on the arm of the bench. The smoke is acrid. The cigarettes will be French, skinny and brown, the ones she smoked when Nora was a child. Flick use to steal them to play at dressing-up, posing in front of Ada's full-length mirror, wearing her shoes and hats.

Outside, Nora lifts the lapels of her towelling dressing gown close round her neck and face against the cool air. 'Mum, your coat.' Holding the coat by the shoulders, she offers it, with a shake of the heavy fabric, inviting Ada to slip her arms into the sleeves, but with a second brisk tap of the cigarette holder against the bench, Ada looks away, turning the fine swoop of her jawbone towards her daughter.

Nora says nothing. No point starting another argument in the middle of the night. No point mentioning the cigarette. She swings the coat invitingly. 'Come on, Mum.'

How often Ada must have held coats out like this when she and Flick were small; it's something mothers do, a gesture of waiting. She has seen Flick's impatience with her two daughters, flapping their coats at them, their little bodies jerking as she tugs coat edges to button them, or yanks zips up to their chins. Now Nora waits for her mother.

The shrubs cast moon shadows across the grass and at the bottom of the garden by the water's edge the trees stir in the dark. A smell of algae and mud wafts up from the creek.

Isaac held her coat out for her that first night, after her Wigmore debut. He kissed the back of her neck, just below the ear and she swung around in shock. Afterwards, he told her he'd thought she was going to slap him across the cheek.

She is not going to think about Isaac, she is far from that other life.

Ada raises her arms backwards a fraction to indicate her readiness to be helped into the coat sleeves. Hair falls either side of her face on to her collar as she watches Nora button up her coat.

'Why not, I thought.' Her voice is barely audible. 'Why not treat myself? Make some changes?'

'Come inside now.' Nora takes her mother's hand, aware of the lightness of bone.

Ada sighs and straightens her shoulders. 'After all, no one else is going to.' She looks away towards the sloping lawn where dew is caught on the tips of the grass blades. 'The garden has grown so wild.'

'It's always been wild, Mum.'

Ada draws in a wavering breath. 'Well, we have plans, Harry and I, big plans. So I've told him he can park his caravan here, at Creek House, down near the water.'

On the lawn, footprints in the dew blur across the grass towards the old orchard. Nora wants everything to stay as it is, as it was in her childhood, with the seclusion created by overgrown laurels, hebes and tamarisks which shield the garden from the view of passing boats, or walkers on the creek path. She likes Harry well enough, but is not keen on the idea of his constant presence around Creek House. She knows better than to make a fuss. Besides, it's likely Ada's 'plans' will come to nothing. By next week she will have cooked up some other impulsive scheme and they'll be buying grass seed to reseed the bare patch of lawn.

'Come on inside now, Mum.' Nora stoops to embrace her mother's tiny frame, her cheek against the prominent line of collarbone where Ada's skin is thin and browned as an autumn leaf.

Later, Nora lies awake. An owl hoots; another answers. Rook is downstairs, alone in the kitchen. Nora turns over on to her side.

She will go and see Eve, tomorrow. She's put it off far too long. *I'm pregnant, I expect you guessed*. She is a lousy friend. She should tell Eve how bad she feels and explain what has stopped her calling by, the way, when things she needs to forget get stirred about in her head, her mind shuts down, she can't think straight, and her priorities get disordered so that she doesn't recognise herself.

She rolls on to her back, straightens out her legs, points her toes to stretch out her calf muscles. She should get up, go for a run, but her body is reluctant. She won't sleep, though, because her thoughts will continue to leapfrog. It's why she can't play properly any more, this inability to either concentrate or relax, a constant spiccato, percussive, bouncing in her head, repeated and repeated. Her hands lie empty and useless on the bed. She rubs her face.

To confront Ada and ask directly about her plans for the garden will only make her more secretive. Nora learned, years ago, the necessity of avoiding confrontation with her mother. She remembers her discomfort when a pre-teen growth spurt left her awkward with her body, taller than both Ada and Flick, who was by then nineteen. Reedy and pale, all elbows and knees, Nora looked nothing like her mother or sister. Only her white-blonde hair was substantial, waist-length, fanning out in waves. *My Saxon princess*, her father called her, and from the age of about four she'd fought with Ada to keep her hair long, running away and hiding from her mother and her hairdressing scissors. If caught and lifted on to the kitchen counter for a haircut, she'd bite at Ada's wrists. How she'd hated her teenage body, its angles and bones, until, that is, she was sent to Marlene, the dressmaker's.

In Marlene's mirrors, the indigo of the gown for which Nora was being fitted anchored her against the white puff and gauze backdrop of racked bridal gowns behind. She was about to take up the Senior Scholarship at the Academy, and Ada wanted a perform-ance gown specially made. Once a week over the summer Nora went to be draped with silk and taffeta, measured and fitted, seams taken in and hems lowered. In the wall of mirrors, Nora stared at herself in a full-length gown. *Lanky Legs*, Flick called her.

Marlene, the French seamstress, spoke through lips clamped around pins. A tiny tattoo of a butterfly fluttered at the pulse on her wrist as she prodded and turned Nora this way and that. The silky material brushed, cool, against Nora's thigh and she longed to rip off the cloth-tackiness of an Elastoplast she had on one knee. Marlene leaned close to lift Nora's hair in both hands as she heaped it high to fasten it in place with hair-pins. Exposed to the air, the hairs on Nora's neck lifted.

Pins in her teeth, Marlene gave Nora's hips a pinch and muttered, 'Good for clotheses.' She stood back, studying Nora in the mirror.

'The collar-bones,' her voice was scratchy as sawdust, as if she needed to clear her throat, 'so perfect.'

The smell of cigarettes thickened Marlene's breath and stale smoke coiled into her French pleat, the aroma carrying a complicated sense of dalliances in dimly lit bars. Of romantic, black and white films where the heroines wore scarlet lipstick and Hermes suits cinched at the waist. When Marlene moved away across the room, her pore-deep perfume, animal and earthy, remained behind, at the back of Nora's throat.

Marlene pinched and measured tucks and necklines, the fit and fall across the shoulders, the hips. Nora chewed on a finger as she watched the deft movements of Marlene's painted nails until Marlene slapped at her hand. '*Saperlipopette!*'

Marlene stubbed her cigarettes on a silver-plated bon-bon plate on the floor, pushed with her stockinged foot out of the way. By the end of an afternoon, ash and dog-ends overflowed on to the carpet. On those nights, when Nora lay in bed and thought ahead to the autumn and leaving home for London, Marlene's smoke and perfume, exotic and alien, hovered close, embedded in the mass of Nora's own hair spread on the pillow.

The London in her mind's eye was composed of vertical lines – a squeezed sky jammed between streets lined with shop windows – and thin, crowded spaces; people milling in the endless choice of tearooms, bars and restaurants. She'd fallen in love with the gracious and pale-stoned frontage of the Royal Academy; the graceful plane trees – straight and tall, not deformed by salt winds – casting a flutter of shadows over the broad pavement; the glitter of the looped crystal chandeliers in the Duke's Hall with its high painted ceiling.

London for Nora was also the incense and candle wax in the air of the chapel where she played her entrance piece to Isaac Brennen, who got up from a distant pew and came closer, standing in the aisle under the fall of light from a stained-glass window, hands in his trouser pockets. She drew the final bow across and held herself still to allow the last inner vibrations to fade from her body before she tossed her hair from her face and looked up. She had no doubt she had played exceptionally well.

'Well, your music teachers seem to think very highly of you.' His accent clipped the words. Looking down at his notes, he continued, his voice low and quick, to criticise the naivety of her playing, the lack of emotional control over her body language. Nora gripped her bow. She stared at the gleam of his black hair, the sharp cut of his goatee beard. When he glanced up from his notes, frowning, her breath caught. She would not cry.

'This will cease,' he announced without smiling. 'Perhaps to start,' Brennen waved a dismissive hand in the direction of her kicked-off shoes, 'to start, you should play with the shoes on.' He nodded curtly, tucked a battered leather music case under his arm and left her to his colleagues' further questioning. He was shorter than she expected and walked with a slight limp. Her mind strained to follow the echo of his uneven footfall down the long aisle and she dropped her bow when the chapel door banged behind him.

She turned to the others. The answers she gave them were automatic, easy.

When the autumn came and she sat in the tiered ranks of the lecture hall, she refused to titter or gasp with the other students at the rapid fire of sexual innuendo of Isaac's jokes. She didn't whisper behind her hand about the outlandish coloured socks he wore and which showed only when he sat to demonstrate a technique on the cello. She didn't comment on the flamboyance of his collection of hats. He sometimes twirled a metal-tipped stick when walking stiff-legged through the college courtyards. Rumour had it he fell from a horse as a child.

Isaac was a magnetic performer, and he needed an audience. Nora dreamed of catching him unaware, but she also waited for and wanted the fiercer side of his onstage persona to explode through the repartee, the moment when he would begin to pace the lecture platform, eyes glittering. Something within her responded to the fury he showed towards those less passionate than himself about music.

'Discipline, not emotion,' he'd bark. 'The discipline of the structure, its architectural strength, is what you must look for and understand.' He glared down from the podium. 'Learn control!'

He talked about music with a forcefulness she wanted for herself, for at times the music overwhelmed her. As the term progressed, he glanced her way when she passed him in the canteen or library, or on the grand curve of the stairways, his look private in those public places. Her skin pricked. One day she came across him in the library. He stood with a manuscript in his hands, filling the narrow gap between two shelves where she needed to search. She'd hesitated, held her breath, walked quickly on by. She wasn't brave enough. The leap of tempo in her blood told her he'd seen her pass.

Sometimes, leaving the Academy library, she drifted past his study window and strained to hear him playing. She never did. It was said he practised only in the privacy of his home, or shut away in one of the many cloistered and anonymous practice rooms, rows of identical, soundproofed rooms below ground level, cramped and uniform spaces like cells in a honeycomb. Early in the mornings and every evening, when she pulled, then pushed, through the intimate suck and release of the door-seal, she imagined she'd find him there, in the dark, seated at the piano, awaiting her arrival.

In the end it was a far more prosaic beginning. After a seminar in her final year, a cluster of students were casually included in an invitation to a bar with three or four of the music tutors who often drank together at lunchtimes and early evenings. It was pouring with rain. When Nora arrived at the pub soaked through, Isaac was shaking out an umbrella in the doorway. In the Ladies, she stood in front of the splotched mirror and scrunched clumps of her wet hair to dry it a little, calling up the vision of herself in Marlene's wall of mirrors. She was no longer a too-tall, too-thin girl. She tipped her head upside down to shake out the mass of her hair, lifting it from her neck and ears under the hand-drier. When she looked again at her reflection, her hair was wild, waves tensing to curls as they dried.

In the crowded bar, between people holding drinks and bags and damp coats, Nora was shunted down an upholstered bench and seated beside Isaac. Up close, he seemed smaller. She had a sudden wish to be underground at the Academy, pushing through the double doors into the sealed silence of a practice room to find him there, alone.

Someone, another tutor, was buying a round of drinks and she hesitated, unsure.

'G and T, ice and lemon,' Isaac said. He was so close she could see the wet of his bottom lip, glimpse the twist of his tongue when he spoke. 'Times two?'

She nodded.

The group played drinking games, composers' names and dates and biographical details shouted across the tables, Nora and Isaac hemmed in until the crowd thinned, much later. Long tendrils of her hair curled as they dried, and clung to the sleeve of his wool jacket. She didn't move from her seat, even when desperate for the loo, but stayed, legs crossed tight, squashed up against his shoulder. She saw for the first time that his eyes, usually shadowed, were a brown close to gold, like syrup capturing the light. His oiled hair gleamed under the wall lamp, his face under the prominent brow cast by the spill of light into lines and hollows. An emptiness like hunger prowled through her. She couldn't move away. When he leaned forward or stretched across the table, she smelled the end-of-the-day scent of his skin, and she knew what would happen, later in the evening, when he took her back to his room to find some sheet music she asked him about, when he took her on to his lap and his nose buried into the hollow of her neck, her hair, those darting, expert hands of his exploring, across and low and firm down her belly.

She wore an Indian cotton skirt, wrapped and tied around her waist, falling open from her thighs as he pulled her up and back on to his lap, hard and close to his body, his beard pricking her neck, his fingers on her. The gin she'd drunk was oily and aromatic on her lips.

'I KEEP SEEING someone. I think he may be dead.' Nora brushes the hair back from her face. Her hands carry the smell of the ivy she and Eve have been pulling all morning from the roof and walls of the boathouse.

Eve straightens, her arms filled with trailing ivy clumps. 'I knew something was up.'

Nora tugs on an ivy runner. The roots lift stringy and white from the soil, a metre or more creeping along the bottom of the boathouse wall to join a dense mass of ivy growing like a small tree attached to the bricks, with shaggy appendages embedded in the mortar.

'Go on.' Eve drops the ivy and dusts off her hands.

'I meant to tell you before.' Nora stops. Even though she's rehearsed this conversation, she's unsure how to continue. She might say too much. Never stop.

Eve comes closer. 'It's good for you,' her voice soothes, 'to let go.' She lays a hand across Nora's ribs, just below her breasts, and

89

closes her eyes. 'Right here,' she begins, but her voice trails off and she opens her eyes, frowning. The heel of her hand presses against Nora's ribs. An expression Nora can't fathom, of doubt or puzzlement, flutters across her face. 'You know he's dead?'

'I had a dream. No. Well. Thing is, first I had this dream and then I saw him, here, in the village. I was sure it was him, at first sight, or half-sure, but then, when I consider the likelihood, after all, it's been more than a year, that he would be . . .' Nora shrugs.

'An ex-lover? You shouldn't give him too much attention.'

Nora's not sure what this means. She picks up the bow-saw to tackle the mass of ivy branches and roots, compacted hard as concrete.

'Sometimes, when our present is a little too empty, our past moves in to fill the gaps. We have no room for our future to take root. This guy, he's dead to you, or not?'

Nora hesitates, not sure she can trust her voice. 'I don't know.'

'Was the sex good? Is it that you remember?'

'Yes, it was good.' She works the bow-saw to and fro.

Isaac turned her on with a raised eyebrow, a sidelong glance; that spark remained between them, even when they'd been seeing each other several years, though the time they had alone together was only ever brief and snatched, so perhaps the urgency grew from a necessity for speed rather than intensity of desire. Nora can no longer tell. The teeth of the saw blade gnaw through the bark of the thick ivy. As she saws, she describes the man she's seen, his halting stride so like Isaac's, his dark, shaggy mane – but Isaac is now in his sixties, and when she last saw him, his hair was already edged with white over his ears, along the nape of his neck, a line of white arching up away from his forehead to his crown.

As she picks away at the ivy, Nora dips in and out of the story of Isaac, working to keep the tone of a joke in her voice when she alludes to the many years of their 'romance'. She rummages in her bag to show Eve the photo-booth picture, taken the first weekend they had away together. She was eighteen; Isaac was fifty.

Eve doesn't pull a face or roll her eyes at the age difference. 'So now he's what, mid sixties?'

Nora nods. Isaac's lapels are wide and his tie has a fat knot, his fashion sense arrested in an earlier decade. The photograph has faded to sepia, burnishing his skin. Showing the photo to Eve, Nora sees that even then Isaac looked a man past his prime.

'It's a bad photo. He wasn't that dark-skinned.'

Though, with his eyes shadowed by prominent eyebrows – each strand thick as sewing thread – and the sleek gleam of his hair, Isaac did possess a quality of darkness. His profile, the line of his forehead running straight and firm to the tip of his nose, was powerful. Only when he played the cello, or during sex, did the strong lines between his nose and the downward turn of his mouth, soften; only when his eyes were closed was the brush-line of his thick eyelashes noticeable.

'Hmm.' Eve hands the photo back. 'You always carry that around?'

'Along with all this other junk, old till receipts, general rubbish, see?' Nora pulls a few crinkled bits of paper out from the ink-stained depths of her denim bag. 'Am I seeing him because he is dead?' The photograph slides easily back into the little pocket in Nora's wallet. 'I know that does happen. I mean, to people who've lost someone.'

'No, not necessarily, but there'll be a reason.' Eve idly rubs her belly in a circular motion. She picks up the bundles of ivy once more, chucks them over the high sides of the almost-full skip and brushes off her hands. 'How about I make you some smudge sticks? Some herbs to cleanse and move the soul will help.'

Eve explains about smudge sticks, describes the woman who taught her how to roll the dried herbs, mentions white sage and mugwort.

'Do you want him to be dead?' she asks, abruptly.

'For a long time – months – I wanted him to come and find me. I was sure he would. Crazy, isn't it?' Nora laughs to cover the crack in her voice.

'But he didn't.' Once again, Eve's tone is one of statement, not question, and her certainty stabs at Nora, deflating her attempt at flippancy.

Eve puts her hand on Nora's forearm. 'This is how it works. Smoke from a smudge stick attaches itself to negative energy. As the smoke clears, the negative energy goes with it, to be released into another space where it will be regenerated into positive energy – with me?'

Nora nods.

'So, we might use a combination that embraces air, water, fire and earth – something like pine resin and sage. It's not complicated. I'll make you up a few sticks and you can do it yourself if you like. You might prefer that. All you need is a feather or fan to waft the smoke over you. Start at the top and work down.'

As usual, she speaks with such authority that Nora's doubts seem born of ignorance. 'No time like the present,' Eve says. 'I'll drop round tomorrow. Let's do it!'

She drags another solid chunk of stems and branches towards the skip. One side is flat, marked with the pattern of the bricks it has grown against for years. Eve pauses, bent over, hands on her thighs. 'God, I feel like throwing up. It's this smell.' She sighs and pushes up her sleeves. 'Any smell, to be honest. I can't even clean my teeth.'

Nora picks up the bow-saw once more. She has almost sawn through the ivy trunk; after that she'll tackle the roots.

AFTER THE BRIGHTNESS of the summer garden, the hallway is dark. Ada pauses to light a cigarette, shakes out the match and savours the first inhalation. She takes a step forward, and stops. What has brought her into the house with some urgency she now cannot recall. Patting her head, she finds her reading glasses are not balanced there, so she perhaps was about to fetch them. She moves purposefully down the hallway but when she arrives at the telephone table she knows for certain her glasses are not the reason she came marching into the house.

The telephone is reassuringly solid. Bakelite, provided by the GPO when she and Brian were first married and Creek House became their marital home. Ada chose ivory over the more common black. *A very nice example of the Ivory 332L with drawer,* a dealer once told her. Not long ago. A dapper little man with a peppery moustache; made her upper lip tickle to watch him speak.

She reaches for the telephone. Across her forearm falls blue and green light from the half-moon of coloured glass in the front door and she clicks her tongue, pulling down the sleeve of her dress to cover her mottled skin. The Bakelite drawer of the telephone is stuck. What they kept in a drawer barely the size of a single receipt, heaven knows.

How she'd love to escape from this draughty cavern of a place. Make a fresh start. A little town house in Chichester, right in the centre of things, would suit her down to the ground. The hallway at Creek House, despite Nora's recent spring clear-out, remains the same chilly corridor, with its black and white floor tiles and family belongings heaped in layers on the coat rack.

Very likely the dealer with the moustache called the same time last year, when Nora donned her Marigolds in order to rush about like a simple-minded skivvy to dust off pieces of furniture and sort boxes of junk.

'Mum?' Nora's forehead is crinkled as seersucker. One of her large hands holds down the cardboard flap of a cardboard box she's lugged in from the garage.

Ada makes a show of consulting her wristwatch. 'I'm expecting a call from Felicity at any moment.'

Even that doesn't slow Nora down. She elbows by and climbs the stairs two at a time, arms and neck straining as she heaves the box of ancient paper upstairs. Always hiding something, that girl. Perfectly obvious what's in the box, since it carries the must of old paper and glue: ancient sheet music which Nora never quite manages to throw out, moving reams of the stuff around from one room to another instead.

Ada picks up the telephone receiver and weighs it in her hand. She listens to the hum. Children can be most inconsiderate, at times, not to say inconvenient. She puts the receiver down again.

He telephoned from London the other day, the young man, the one who has called at the house twice, perhaps three times, she can't be sure. Voice like treacle and well-turned vowels; privately educated at one of the better schools, without a doubt. Has her thinking of Robert with his voice and his gangling boyishness, the way he pushes at his flop of hair. Different colouring, but no doubt of his interest, asking questions, a hand on her elbow to guide her down the garden steps where the paving stones are loose. Though, in a man young enough to be her son, there's something disconcerting about the practised widening of those brown eyes when he smiles. A ladies' man if ever there was!

Ada slips off one of her pearl earrings and picks up the telephone receiver once more. She holds it to her ear, glancing upwards, a hand over the mouth of the receiver. Nora is thudding about upstairs. Lifting the telephone cradle, Ada walks with it away from the open stairwell. The flex is just long enough to reach into the dining room, where she leans against the far side of the door.

'Oh, Nora's having one of her fits of temper. Up and down like a barometer. Don't know where we are with her, as I explained yesterday to dear Badger when he was here to talk about the garden –'

'–'

'No, it's just my pet name for him.'

'–'

'Of course your father spoiled her rotten when she was a child.' Ada shakes her head at the memory of Brian and tiny Nora with her thistle-head of hair, the two of them affected by that curious intensity of concentration which excluded all else. Inseparable, until she told him. Put the cat amongst the pigeons.

Ada takes another drag on her cigarette and exhales with a sigh, watching the drift and curl of smoke.

'Temperamental is not the word for it, darling. I don't know what gets into her at times, chewing on her cuffs, twiddling at her hair. I'd like to slap at her hands, tell her to get dolled up and go out for a night on the town with that pretty blonde friend of hers, but she will fly off the handle at the slightest provocation.'

'_'

'She's embarked on her annual clear-out, stampeding about the place like a herd of elephants.'

'_'

The one-sided conversation is not very true to life because Felicity would be vociferous in her response to this last statement. Ada takes another pull on her cigarette, fingering the telephone flex. A kink uncurls and coils back.

'Kind of you to ask. I'd like to take a nap.'

'_'

'Not so well. I was up all night with the storm.'

Last night, the lightning woke her, thunder grumbling in the distance. She went to close the sash, the air in the bedroom dense with the weight of rain to come. Another zigzag of lightning and she was certain she saw Nora outside, down by the old apple tree, lit by the flash of light, Nora with all that hair fanning at her waist. Ada waited by the window but when the lightning flared again she could see no one and rain had begun to fall in noisy sheets, a downpour.

Ada sighs into the telephone receiver, which is no longer humming. The line is dead.

'So, darling, when do you think you might?'

'—'

'Simply delightful, and of course to see the girls. Au revoir for now then, darling.' She depresses and releases the T-bar with her forefinger just as Nora comes banging downstairs and strides along the hallway back to the garden. Always been in a hurry, since the day she burst into the world. Smoke wreathes around Ada's head as she meanders after her daughter, finishing her cigarette. Oh, to make it all disappear in a puff of smoke, the tiresomeness of life.

Out in the garden with the sun warm on the back of her neck, an image comes to her of Nora's wild pale hair, ghostly in the dark last night. She flutters her fingers over her chignon, strokes the tight roll of her own hair.

The upper lawn is greatly improved. Only last week it resembled a field, with buttercups and thistles, grass in tufts and clumps, until Harry serviced the mower and made a start on it.

She walks towards the garage where Nora is galumphing about, shifting boxes from one place to another, flinging racquets and flippers, beach balls and plastic spades out on to the lawn. This sudden compulsion to put the house in order is out of character. Not enough to do, that's Nora's problem these days, but what can she be thinking of, to put the tennis comeback in the pile for the rubbish? Ada lifts the lid from the box and the sides collapse immediately into flatness, allowing the poles to spill out.

Wimbledon on the television when the girls were tiny: sighs, a spatter of clapping and the occasional grunt. Black and white. And the player with all that dark hair, the temper tantrums, who was it, sultry as a thunderstorm? Powerful square knees. She has always been petite and there's something about a big man that makes one feel . . . She lifts her shoulders and shrugs.

The length of elastic attached to the balding tennis ball twists and curls back on itself like an overstretched rubber band, disintegrating when Ada picks with a fingernail at the tangles.

The print on the box is very small and the words pompous. *Assemble tubes as per the illustration. Please try to avoid leaving the set erected in bright sunlight for any length of time as this is inclined to perish the elastic.*

Layers of cardboard separate where the corners of the box are split despite one of Brian's repair attempts. The aged Sellotape flakes off. The repair brings Brian and his near-sighted stoop over a desk or table to mind, the edges and corners of his books and papers aligned with precision. Cogs, wheels and springs from the inside of clocks arranged in lines. A meticulous man – Ada brushes ash from the silk scarf draped at her neck – tidy and careful in both mind and manner, a characteristic which she put down to his middle-class upbringing, a difference between them. His mother was an insufferable snob, yet she hung nets at her windows and referred to napkins as serviettes.

Ada takes out two sections of metal tubing and fits them together. She wants them back, those summer afternoons: the thwack of the ball, the girls shrieking and fighting over the tennis comeback. The fiery tennis player with his antics on the tennis court – Ilie Nastase, he's the one. A passionate man – oh, what she would have given! Tied herself down far too young, thinking

Brian would provide her escape from the confines of village life, imagined herself accompanying him abroad, a damsel dressed in white muslin to protect her skin from the heat: the Archaeologist's Wife. She had been naive – although they did travel together, at first, even for a few years after Felicity was born. How she loved the heat, the filmy mesh of mosquito nets, whirring fans; the chink of ice stirred in a drink. When Nora arrived everything changed. Brian began to talk about giving their two girls stability, a 'settled' home.

The elastic is specially extruded from high quality latex rubber but by the nature of the game will, of course, only have a limited life.

Ada clicks her tongue and tries to replace the lid as best she can. The guy-rope, net and other sections of tube are a tangled mass, but still perfectly good. Perhaps Harry could fix the comeback. Felicity will have a thing or two to say about this, for certain, since all the items Nora has boxed for charity and stuffed into bin bags are also a part of Felicity's childhood.

From the creek comes the clap of canvas filling with wind as the boom swings across and the sail catches the wind's force. The sailing boat going about gives Ada an idea for a diversion. Nora is a perfectly adequate rower; she can take them both in the skiff down to Itchenor Hard. A trip. Ridiculous to pay for one of the scheduled boats with one of their own pulled up on the shore at the bottom of the garden.

Ada steps closer to the garage to suggest this afternoon for their trip when she sees, set down amongst the damp grass cuttings by the path's edge, the picnic case. The cherry-red of the case's covering has faded to pink. Inside, leather straps once fastened the gay floral plates and saucers to the underside of the lid; two tartan Thermos flasks nestled beside a screw-top glass jar filled with jam, the salt and pepper. Ada cannot bear to open the case and find it empty. She takes hold of the handle and carries the case inside.

AT FIRST, WHEN she sees the flash of blue lights, Nora thinks there must have been an accident. A fire engine has parked at an angle, blocking the narrow lane. A black 4×4 at the tail end of the queue of cars swerves off the road and the door is flung open. A man uncurls his long frame from the driver's seat and braces his shoulders, rotating each as if limbering up, resting a hand on the joint to test the roll of muscle and bone. Nora follows his gaze down towards the water and notices Giovanni's ice-cream van parked a long way from his favoured position on the foreshore, right up near the craft centre. He only parks there if the tide is higher than usual.

Wind roars through the trees. Nora gathers up her hair, fixing it in a loose knot with a pencil from her pocket. With this fierce south westerly, if it is a spring tide, the village is at risk of serious flooding. She hopes either Eve or Stavros is at home, because their house, perched on the sea wall, is vulnerable.

The man climbs back into his car and now reverses, fast, two wheels on the pavement, towards her. It's then Nora sees, on the back window-shelf, a coat folded with the red lining outermost and a broad-brimmed hat. She stops in her tracks.

He slams the car door, throws his keys in the air and catches them. It is not Isaac, she sees instantly, though he waves as if they know each other and strides towards her with a slight catch to his step. Wind blows his loose white shirt against his body. He is taller than Nora, much taller than Isaac, with the slight lean to the neck and shoulders of a man accustomed to standing a head or so higher than those around him.

He straightens, pushing dark hair from his eyes in a gesture of impatience. 'Jonny,' he says, and clasps her hand in both of his. 'What's going on?'

His voice is what Ada would describe as 'rich brown'. So too are his eyes, which search her face. Heat rolls upward through her body. She steps back, slipping her hand out of his to take hold of the straps of her cello case, lifting them to ease the rubbed place on her collar-bone. This, then, is the man she's seen around and mistaken for Isaac, yet his build is different, as is the buoyancy in his easy smile. The similarity is in the way he moves, a languid assurance combined with the impression of suppressed energy, something like a big cat, caged. She is probably smiling too much.

'I was afraid I'd missed you again.'

'Missed me?' She has forgotten some meeting, with a parent of a pupil. Someone at school has neglected to pass on a message. Please let it be something else.

He turns to the queue of cars. His black hair, long over his collar, has the same sheen as Isaac's but he is years younger, younger even than Isaac when she first met him.

'It's vanished, the entire road.' He finds the unexpected turn of events exciting, which tells her he isn't local. She must find her tongue and reply properly.

'A spring tide,' she begins.

'My camera.' He dives into the car and flings various items around, hunting for something on the back seat. 'I'm here because of your father,' she thinks he says, but his voice is muffled from inside the car.

She freezes. She can't have heard him right. He turns and holds up a camera bag. 'Perfect, I can't tell you, just perfect.'

'Why did you say you are here?'

'I'll fill you in. Shall we walk and talk?'

Jonny runs a small film company which makes television documentaries. Nora is captivated by the way his arms beat the air for emphasis as he talks, the energetic gestures of his hands like a conductor's, and only half-listens when he lists a variety of programmes he's made, quotes audience-viewing figures. She doesn't watch much television.

'You'll watch this one,' he turns to her, 'because I'm here about Canute, to uncover the story of his drowned daughter.' His face is suddenly serious. 'Nora, your bone structure, it's startlingly photo-genic, you know.' She looks at her feet.

They head down towards the water. Jonny walks fast; she doesn't have to slow her pace for him. He sees her notice the slight hesitation in his stride.

'Knee job,' he says, and rubs at his hair with both hands. He looks rueful. 'Too bloody old for rugby!'

The water is choppy. They step back as scum and froth creep centimetre by centimetre up the tarmac. Jonny seems to know nothing about the sea or tides and asks a lot of questions. Spring tides, Nora tells him, occur just after every full and new moon when the sun, moon and earth are in alignment. She has to shout above the noise of the fire-engine pump as it starts up again.

At low tide, the clutch of buildings which makes up Old Bosham – a terrace of fisherman's cottages with painted front doors, the quaint old pub, the church with its Saxon bell tower – as well as the larger houses on the other side of the inlet at Bosham Hoe, look out over salt marsh and mudflats. With each high tide, incoming sea water raises the water level so significantly that Shore Road, which curves around the inlet, is completely under water. This flooding of the road excites the tourists, who leave their cars parked on the foreshore and, despite the warning signs, go off to the pub or to visit the ancient church or for a wander along the creek path, and return hours later to find a car half-filled with sea water. Villagers, who have lived with flooding for centuries, have prepared for extreme high tides by building low flood walls across paths, gateways and doorways in an attempt to protect their homes. Supplies of sandbags are kept in sheds and garages, beside log piles.

Jonny is exuberant as a child. He takes a lot of photographs: firemen with their hoses, a pair of mallards swimming up the middle of the road, Eric the Swan-man wading in his thigh-high rubbers, seaweed accumulating on the tarmac at the water's edge. Most of the front doors of the houses on both sides of the road are open, already barricaded high with sandbags. Inside, people are busy rolling up rugs, moving books, piling belongings up on to tables. Nora is relieved to see Eve stacking sandbags on to the top of her concrete flood wall to keep out sea water which has turned the lane past her house into a river.

At the far side of the flooded part of the lane people have emerged from the Anchor Bleu with their trousers rolled up. Two small boys paddle in the water. More arrive, congregating behind Jonny and Nora, people from parts of the village further inland, ready to help if necessary. When Ted pulls up with his Land Rover trailer loaded with extra sandbags, Nora rolls up her jeans to help and Jonny follows suit.

THE TIDE IS retreating at last. Nora pushes through the heavy bulk-head door at the back of the bar at the Anchor Bleu and climbs the steps to the high terrace overlooking the inlet towards Bosham Hoe. Waves slap against the brick and flint of the sea wall, the road below still under water. In the summer the tiny terrace is often jammed with people and tables and chairs but today they have it to themselves. Sun appears briefly between fast-moving clouds. Nora puts her feet up on the wall and leans back, lifting her face to search for the sun's warmth.

They borrowed wellies from Mariner's, who keep a supply for customers at the café to borrow on such occasions. With sandbags piled on both shoulders, Jonny sang sea shanties. People joined in. Once it was clear no houses were going to be flooded and the emergency was over, the crowds began to disperse. Jonny, with a hand jammed in his hair to keep it from blowing over his face in the wind, offered to buy her lunch. Nora tries not to think about

Rook and Ada, who will both have been expecting her home a long time ago. Another half an hour won't hurt.

'Amazing! Like being at the prow of a boat!' Jonny pulls up a chair. He grins and takes a swig of his Guinness, lifting his eyebrows at her over the rim of his glass. She can't help smiling back.

'Total serendipity, this happening today. Know why, Nora?' He leans forward, close to her, forearms on his thighs. His voice is low. 'Ten centuries after Canute, and still we fail to turn back the waves. Only wish I'd had the film crew with me!'

Nora hesitates, twisting the stem of her wine glass between her fingers. 'Canute didn't *fail*, though, did he?'

'No?'

'He knew he couldn't turn back the waves. That was the point.'

'It was?' Jonny pulls a notebook from the back pocket of his jeans and flips it open. 'I'd better prove to you I've done *some* research, hadn't I? OK, the bit about Canute sitting on a "chair" comes from the Saxon word for dyke which was *char*. In all probability a dyke or *char* was built across here somewhere.' He waves over the inlet, the choppy brown water. 'That right? And, according to my sources, there's still a place actually called "Mud Wall". Can you show me where?'

She's about to answer when his phone rings, a loud blare of music. Jonny checks the screen of his mobile, stands and steps away from the table, his back to her, phone pressed to his ear.

Nora's mind is racing. If her father was here he'd whisk Jonny away to his study immediately, reach down the appropriate files and documents from a high shelf and confide one or two of his theories. She rolls down one leg of her jeans but it's still wet and there's a chill in the wind, so she rolls it up again.

Synchronicity Media, it says on the cover of Jonny's notebook. She takes another sip of her wine, but she's halfway through the glass and still Jonny stands with his back to her, listening to whoever has phoned him. He stares across to the other side of the water where a light flashes, the glint of sun on a closing car door in the drive of one of the big houses across the water at Bosham Hoe. She must go back soon to relieve Harry from rook-feeding duties. She wills Jonny to get off the phone. It occurs to her it might be a recorded message. Why else would someone talk for so long to him without any response?

'No,' he says eventually, without expression. 'Not at the moment.' He thumbs a few keys, maybe to send a text, before sliding the phone back into its leather pouch and tapping it down into his breast pocket. Slivers of sunlight bounce on ripples blown sideways by the breeze.

Jonny slips on his sunglasses and rakes his hands through his hair. 'Sorry. Where were we at?'

Condensation has gathered on the bowl of Nora's wine glass, making her fingers wet. She wants to make herself clear, to make sure Jonny has understood her point about the King Cnut story.

'It's one of my things.' The words trip over each other; she forces herself to slow down. 'Nearly everywhere you come across Cnut's story these days, online, in newspapers, magazines, or people just talking, the story's told as if he was trying to turn back the waves, when of course he wasn't; just the opposite.'

She tries to read Jonny's face, unsure of his angle. He gives an easy smile. 'Go on.'

'Cnut wanted to prove he was *not* God. To show, powerful though he was, even he could not turn back the tide.'

Jonny riffles through the pages of his notebook, pen at an angle behind his ear. 'People hear what they want to hear, Nora, in my experience. The first version heard is the one they stick with. Bloody hard to turn them around.'

'Then you need to go back to the first version of the story for your programme, back to the first half of the twelfth century.'

'But you agree a battle with the sea is one the village can't win.'

'We *are* winning, though. We now have a water bailiff and thanks to him and his team, Bosham's off the high flood risk register.' She explains about the voluntary flood team appointed to oversee the maintenance of the surface water drainage system, how successful their work has been.

Her glass is empty. They have not yet ordered food. A little light-headed, she returns to the subject of King Cnut. 'His motive is crucial,' she repeats. 'Motive tells us so much more about character than actions. If we tell his story wrong, we misrepresent him.'

Jonny downs the remains of his pint and studies her thoughtfully. 'This project, Nora,' he taps a page with his pen, 'is very exciting. I've a list of contacts. All sorts of people round here to see. Consult. Persuade. And when I read about your father's work on the grave of the Saxon princess, I knew you'd be top of the list.'

They turn at the noise of water in turmoil. White feathers and water droplets snare the light as a swan heaves its weight out of the water. With the power and swell of a strongman's shoulders, its wings spread and smack the water again and again while, in the white-water commotion, mallards flee, quacking and flapping over the surface. When finally the swan concertinas down, wings folding with a settling shake, it glides past them on the terrace, neck looped in elegance, one dark-rimmed eye turned towards Nora.

The swans in the margins of the Bayeux Tapestry, Miss Macleod has told her, appear whenever Harold is pictured hunting or flying his falcons; she believes they refer to Edyth Swan-neck, Harold's 'hand-fast' wife.

The waitress brings olives. Several times she glances surreptitiously at Jonny, pen poised over her notepad as they choose their food. She tucks hair behind one ear before reading the order back to check it's correct, standing with her feet in schoolgirl pumps turned on to their sides. Barely glancing in Nora's direction, she gives Jonny a dimpled smile as she leaves.

While he eats the glistening, black olives, rolling the stones around in his mouth before slipping them from between his lips to collect in the ashtray, Nora tells him about Edyth Swan-neck, with whom Harold lived for almost twenty years before he was crowned king and required to make a more strategic marriage. They had many children. Edyth had stepped aside to allow another woman to become Harold's queen, though it was she who continued to follow him to battle, to cook and care for him in the camps. His new and pregnant queen was sent elsewhere, for safety.

The words 'hand-fast' carry a sense of loyalty and permanence for Nora. 'In the end,' she says, 'it was Edyth who identified Harold's mutilated body on the battlefield at Hastings.'

Jonny slides an olive stone from his mouth. 'Hang on a minute, this Harold, the one with the swan-like mistress, he's 1066 King Harold?'

'Yes. His name was Harold Godwinson. The Godwins had a big estate near here, it's where he grew up.' Nora remembers something. 'It might not be relevant to your programme, but my father had this idea about Harold's mother, Gytha. He thought she might have had a love affair with King Cnut.'

Jonny has stopped eating the olives. His lips are shiny with oil. 'Canute and Harold are the same era?'

'Yes.' Nora is surprised at his ignorance. 'Cnut was Harold's parents' generation. He came to England in 1014 when he was twenty, with his father, Svein Forkbeard.'

'What a name!' Jonny underlines something in his notebook.

'Dad had so many theories. Cnut and Gytha were cousins but he thought they had at least one child together: Swegn, Gytha's eldest son. He was by all accounts a bit wild, and different from the younger brothers. He himself even claimed Cnut was his father, not Earl Godwin. Dad thought the daughter buried in the church may have been a child they had together, illegitimate, hence the unmarked coffin.'

Jonny's head is bent as he writes this down. She can't see his face. He lives in London, he has told her, and comes down by train or drives if he's bringing equipment. He wears a silver ring on his right hand, but nothing on his left.

She wonders who the young woman was, the one driving the 4×4 the first time she saw him on the beach.

He looks up. 'So, tell me more.'

'Cnut granted Earl Godwin, Gytha's husband, many favours, favours which in part accounted for the rise of the Godwins to such a position of power in England. Dad thought this was because he was Gytha's lover.'

'Guilty conscience?' Jonny closes his notebook and props his pen back behind his ear. 'Or perhaps he wanted to keep his mistress moving in the same circles as him. The plot thickens!' He leans back on his chair legs and stares out over the water. 'The illegitimate offspring of a passionate love affair, aged eight and the daughter of a king, falls into the millstream behind the church and is drowned. Can you imagine?' He tips his chair forward, suddenly, leaning over the table close to her again. His eyes are so brown she can barely distinguish the black of the pupils. 'Can you imagine what it was like? To find it was actually *true* – this story bandied around Bosham for the last few hundred years?'

Nora nods. She has imagined, many times.

'What wouldn't I give to have been one of those masons chipping away at the church floor. The old vicar says, "Hey guys, why don't we check out this 'ere long-held village myth?" and, hey presto!' Jonny drum-rolls the table with his forefingers, 'in the very place, right under the centre of the chancel arch, they find a tomb, a child-sized tomb. You couldn't make it up! And the poignancy – they lift the covering slab and find the remains of a child, buried for nine hundred years. What a discovery!'

Jonny's notebook lies open at a list of names, the handwriting copperplate and so miniscule it's impossible to read. Some names are crossed out: others have ticks beside them. Nora wonders if Elsa Macleod's name is on the list.

'Imagine,' Jonny says, 'a child's skeleton outlined in dust. Just imagine.'

HER BEDROOM DOOR is closed, a chair wedged underneath the handle. One by one, with the flick of Nora's wrist, photographs skim across the room. The waste-paper basket is full. The photographs are coloured and glossy, most of them expensive studio portraits. In them, she too is expensive, dressed formally in a variety of gowns, hair up or down, brushed or coiled, an earring to catch the light, the cello between her thighs, sometimes held away from her body. In them all, her arms and neck are exposed. She has posed for either the camera or the photographer; it amounts to the same thing: these photographs are a lie.

At one photograph, she stops. The photographer was Italian, or she was in Italy; one of those high-ceilinged rooms with shutters on tall windows. No, he was not a photographer, and he didn't flirt with her; he was a cello restorer, in love with her Goffriller. He'd scrawled his name and number on the back of the photograph when he gave it to her a few days later. The Goffriller is the centrepiece of the shot, her hand merely an artful extra on the cello's neck, the pale skin of her bow arm contrasted against the curdled-red varnish of its body. 'Godzilla' her first boyfriend, Mark, had called her beautiful four-hundred-year-old instrument – *an old lump of wood she wrapped her legs around*. Mark complained at her habit of stroking the cello body, caressing its curves. If he and the cello were both in the room, he needed to be the one getting her attention. He felt the cello was male, aggressive and possessive, his sexual rival.

In some ways he was right. She could never properly explain her fundamental connection with the Goffriller, an intimacy of mind and body and soul. Mark was too immature to contemplate how inert maple and strings might come alive under her fingers, in her arms, to understand the way the lithe and muscular action of the music erased her separateness from the instrument and its voice.

She had given the cello away, her beautiful Goffriller, her soulmate, when she felt she no longer had the right to have care of such a precious instrument. Before she left London, she took it to one of her old teachers at the Academy and asked them to lend it out to the most promising pupil of the year.

This photograph she can't throw away. Not yet.

For the heated aftermath of many concerts over the years, Isaac, already semi-retired from performing, often managed to be present; the two of them with the Goffriller in the back of a taxi, winding through city streets between concert hall and hotel room. Is it Paris, she remembers? Holding hands, their bodies swayed by the stops and starts of the taxi, the gear shifts and tight corner turns barely registering as they touched each other's fingertips, dipped and slid fingers between fingers, where hidden skin is smoothest. All of Paris at night, car headlights, the blare and toot of horns, people yelling out farewells, everything melted into the background by the current which passed between them.

She had thought what they shared was enough, and for years, it was. She rarely considered his wife or his grown-up children. She had never met them, so it was easy to feel no guilt. His family life was something with which she did not connect. She didn't want what they had. She liked living alone, desired the hours of solitude for practice. Isaac understood – without the need for her to explain – the aftermath of exhilaration, the physical exhaustion, the mental tension after a performance. She was always starving, emptied out by the music, and Isaac would be there to steer her away from the press photographers and the crowds to a restaurant of his choice, a table reserved for them, tucked in a corner or alcove where she could sit and eat and observe, or relive her performance if she needed to, analyse, go over and over the weaker points, deciding which sections had to be worked on before the next performance. Afterwards, they would go to her hotel room.

They gave each other something they both needed and took nothing, so she felt, from his family, but their relationship was dishonest. She had thought of their relationship as a secret, when it was a lie which ran a snagged thread through both their lives.

Her striped dressing gown hangs on the back of the door. Her childhood bedroom at Creek House, a room in which she has been alone many times before but never thought she'd return to for good. What comes back to her is a day two years ago. Almost two years ago. Her period was due. She'd been in the practice rooms of a music conservatoire in Moscow all morning, dashing across the courtyard every half an hour to the toilets to see if she was bleeding. The air was freezing, painful on her skin. Something was wrong with the heating. Ice patterns branched and fanned across the inside of the toilet window; her breath huffed white. She was so very regular, even down to the time of day. Isaac used to joke that the rigorous strength of her bodily rhythms gave the particular sensitivity to musical rhythm and timing for which she was known. She had not quite dared to believe, each time she sat on the cold toilet seat, in the non-appearance of the blood. She considered the effect of the freezing temperatures, pre-concert nerves. If she was pregnant, her relationship with Isaac could grow into something more. It need only mean a few months' break from the concert circuit and the more she thought about a break, the more she wanted a reason to provide the chance of escape. After scurrying across the frosted courtyard half a dozen times, she sat once again on the toilet, knickers at her ankles and knew her period was not coming. Isaac's child! Delight skipped through her. As she rinsed her hands in the icy water, she examined her face in the washbasin mirror and was convinced either the sparkle in her eyes or the flush on her cheeks would announce to everyone her body's cataclysmic changes.

'GO INSTEAD OF me and make sure that woman doesn't act First Lady,' Ada said. Nora has left her mother in her element, entertaining Dr Robertson with the brocade curtains drawn against the low evening sun. Dr Robertson is in his nineties but always elegant, in a three-piece suit with a starched hand-kerchief in the pocket. He was a young doctor in the village when Ada was a child, and carried out his visiting rounds on horseback. He is the only person in the village who still calls her mother 'Adie'.

Daphne Johnson's husband Jerry has been the chairman of the parish council for more than a decade and Daphne loves to hold parish council meetings at their house, everyone seated around her long, polished table. 'Ideas above her station, that one, don't you think, Robbie?' Ada had added, lifting her chin.

Rook, just fed, is in his basket, puttering with his beak at strands of willow on the handle. All Nora will have to do is find somewhere out of the way to put his basket and remember to sneak out of the meeting in time to give him his next feed.

At the tumbling roar of an aeroplane, Nora stops to look up. A white line is visible between the smudges of cloud and as the aeroplane swoops down, she sees a shape forming, half of a love-heart. The engine noise changes, the aeroplane pumping out puffs of white as it labours upward, and the half becomes whole, a heart shape feathering across the blue. The plane banks, cuts away to one side, and the line of an arrow-shaft appears, piercing the heart.

A love-struck heart in the sky is the kind of flamboyant gesture Stavros might make, typical of his impulsive displays of love. Like the star he bought and named after Eve one birthday; the patchwork coat he sewed from fabric scraps, taking a year to stitch together, in secret, with a multitude of names and signs and symbols significant to them and their life together. Eve might be wrapped in her patchwork coat right now, standing on the deck of the boathouse with Zach on one hip, pointing to the love-heart in the sky.

With a burst of crescendo the aeroplane drops once more, hurtling downwards, a flume of white streaming from its tail. Nora's stomach tips, until she sees the pilot is simply redrawing the outline to emphasise the heart's shape.

One Valentine's Day, early in their relationship, she sent Isaac the King of Hearts from a pack of playing cards. She didn't entrust the card to the post, but pushed the pale pink envelope into the middle of a pile of internal mail in his pigeon-hole at the Academy. The remainder of the pack of cards, kept for a long time, was another of the mementoes thrown into a maximum-strength dustbin liner and put out with the rubbish when she left her London flat.

Before she rings the Johnsons' door bell, Nora, hot from running, scrubs at her forehead with Rook's black towel, which carries his sandpapery smell.

'A *rook*?' Daphne lemon-sucks the word and twists the stud of one of her gold half-hoop earrings.

'A young one. He can't fly.' Daphne's probably worried about her hair. 'He's asleep now.' Nora nods down at the towel-draped basket on her arm. 'He won't be a nuisance, I promise.'

Tessa, the Johnsons' overweight black Labrador, nudges past Jerry's calves as he comes out of the kitchen with a wide tray loaded with cups and saucers, and clatters down the hallway barking wildly. The dog skids to a halt by Nora's legs. Just in time, before Tessa leaps and slobbers, claws scraping, Nora swoops Rook's basket high and out of reach. She gives the dog a hard shove with her knee, muttering, '*Get!*' under her breath.

'Tessa! You *are* a naughty girl,' coos Daphne, bending to ruffle the dog's ears.

Nora takes her chance and slips down the hallway to catch Jerry as he makes his way with the tray into the dining room.

'Shall I just pop this in your shed?' She raises the covered basket into Jerry's range of vision, hoping he is too preoccupied to wonder what it is.

'Sure, sweetheart. Thanks. Go ahead. You know where 'tis.' He shoulders the dining-room door open and calls back: 'How's your mother?'

Around the polished table are people she has known since child-hood. Miss Macleod is there, head down, reading something. Ted, who, now his son has taken over the day-to-day running of Manor

Farm, has time on his hands so sits on many committees and is governor of the village primary school. George gives her a nod, jowls wobbling like wattles. Patricia, Ted's wife and locally famous for her bridge suppers, flutters her fingers in a wave. Steve, the vicar, gives her a wink, and points to the empty chair beside him. A single father of three small children, Steve is not what most people expect in a vicar. He doesn't wear a dog-collar and today's T-shirt has 'You Are the Weakest Link' in cracked, plastic-coated capitals across the front. Strung on a leather thong around his neck is a lump of sea-glass Nora would like to wear herself. She squeezes past the backs of the other chairs to slip in beside him and he passes her a copy of the minutes, his square hands rough and red around the knuckles as though he's been too long scrubbing at sheets in very hot water.

The group is already deep in discussion about flooding. Steve hands Nora a photograph taken from Bosham Hoe looking across the inlet towards the village during one very high spring tide a few years back. The relentless churn of the water dominates the fore-ground of the photograph while, on the far side of the grey expanse, houses huddle around the church steeple, marooned. Waves foam against first-floor window sills, the only glimpse of colour the red flag which flies from the sailing-club flagpole. In the harbour, the boats themselves have sunk, masts leaning at odd angles. The village looks abandoned.

Nora had been abroad at the time, but she'd heard from Ada about the severity of the flooding. Residents had been shocked into coming up with more proactive ways to protect their homes, and appointed Will Holden as water bailiff. However, Nora's heard a rumour that Will, who sits opposite with a ring file, a pile of photographs and three pens lined up on the table in front of him, is about to resign. She tries to catch his eye, but his head is bowed.

'... and then the manhole covers burst off, my Lord!' Patricia is saying, 'Water pressure, the firemen said. In the Craft Café we thought the electricity was sure to blow.'

Nora is thirsty after running and the coffee Daphne pours from her cafetière into exquisite bone-china cups amounts to a mere thimbleful or two. Its strength makes her mouth and cheeks hot.

Jerry, the chairman, hands over to Will Holden, who opens his file. His report covers the precise order of events on the day of the spring tide. Long and detailed, it includes a list of possible causes, problems encountered and how they were dealt with, suggestions for precautions to be taken in the future. He clears his throat several times and reads directly from his notes without looking up.

His obvious tension makes others around the table fidgety. Nora remembers her confident conversation with Jonny about the flood team, before she'd heard of the rumours circulating about Will's resignation. She wonders when Jonny will next be down from London. She's heard nothing from him, not that she was expecting to, exactly. One of her male colleagues at school asked her out for dinner last week and when she turned him down she found herself wishing the invitation had come instead from Jonny. And then she bumped into Steve as she left the church one evening after lighting a votive candle, and he told her two men from the television had been to see him, asking to look at the Reverend's notebooks from the 1865 excavation of the Saxon princess's tomb.

Discussion has now shifted on to side issues: a request to replace the noticeboard in the church porch, which Steve will have to pass on to the parochial church council. Ted delivers a tirade about litter and fly-tipping. Nora reaches for a piece of Daphne's home-made shortbread and bites into it, scattering sugary crumbs all over the sheen of the table's veneer. Sometime later, glancing up from doodling in her notepad, she realises the drop in noise levels is because they are all looking at her.

'Do you know how much damage they do, my dear, scavenging in my maize fields for seed?' Ted's gnarled hands tremble as he lifts, for a refill, the delicate coffee cup still balanced on its saucer. He smiles benignly down the table at Nora. Her knee knocks the table as she uncrosses her legs.

George swallows a mouthful of shortbread. 'My father bought that strip of land down by the manor specifically because there was a rookery in the copse.'

'He bought a rookery?' Nora's surprised and pleased, eager to talk about rooks.

George nods. 'Held regular rook shoots in spring to thin out the branchers. Had rook pie more than once.'

'Really?' Patricia pulls a long face. '*Four-and-twenty black birds,*' she warbles.

'Damn difficult to shoot in the field, rooks.' Ted addresses George, ignoring his wife. 'Not like pigeons.'

Patricia looks at her lap. A flush creeps up her throat.

'Terrible trouble on the peas last year.' Ted nods sagely at George.

'I'm surprised your mother gives the thing house room. They're *evil*.' Daphne shudders. 'A bad omen too. I'd get rid of the thing.'

Ralph puts down his coffee cup. 'Old Herbert Caper used to tell stories about the rooks in Hundredsteddle Copse, where they've been for centuries.'

'Doesn't make them suitable pets,' barks George. He snaps another shortbread biscuit in half. 'Vermin,' he says, with his mouth full.

'No. My point was that in fact the rookeries are said to bring a household good fortune. Apparently one year they shot down too many at Hundredsteddle and the rooks didn't return the following spring. That was the year four members of the family died. Flu epidemic, I believe.'

'Pure folklore and ignorance.'

'Actually, George—'

'Ted, you're whistling.' Patricia points to her ear. Ted scowls and fumbles with his hearing aid.

'Starvelings like yours would be killed by the parents. Nature always knows best.' George leans back in his chair, arms folded across his belly as if that's an end to it.

At the end of the meeting, Miss Macleod puts a hand on Nora's arm. 'A quick word, my dear?' She slides a slim booklet from her canvas rucksack and holds it up for Nora to admire, her hand smoothing the cover. Pictured on the front is a reproduction of a section of the Bayeux Tapestry. 'Professor Frank Barlow read my manuscript,' she says. 'We had several most interesting conversations.'

The cover shows stylised horses, soldiers in helmets and chain mail; axes, swords, shields and arrows, with the words HAROLD: REX: INTERFECTUS: EST sewn above the battle scene where a soldier with a moustache looks up at the letter O as he pulls at an arrow from the nose-shield of his helmet. This must be Harold. Underneath the picture, typed in large bold capitals, is the question: IS KING HAROLD II BURIED IN BOSHAM CHURCH?

'This copy is for you, my dear, a present. Your father would have been interested.' She offers the pamphlet to Nora and for a moment they hold it between them. 'The only King of England since the Dark Ages whose burial place remains a mystery and I am this close,' she releases her grip on the pamphlet to raise both hands to a position of prayer, a centimetre or so apart, squinting at Nora through the gap, 'to being certain we have him right here, in Bosham.'

Nora holds the pamphlet against her chest. This is something Jonny would want to know about. Deciding it's too early for bed, she heads for the church, striding along the lane in the dark with Rook in his basket.

To Nora, Creek Lane has always led towards the sky, until the dip in the road by the kissing gate in the hedge where their father used to stand when he was back, hidden in the hedge, waiting to spring out on his girls as they walked home from school, waiting to kiss them, lift them high in the air and swing as they giggled and shrieked. She remembers the tilt of the flat wheat fields as he spun her, the roughness of his bristles on her neck. She'd told Isaac this once, stroking his fierce black beard that left her neck enflamed. 'Girls and their daddies,' he said, closing his eyes.

At the millstream, she sits on the bench. The bird rustles in his basket and she pulls back the towel. Rook is awake and alert, tipping his head to look up at her. He hasn't yet managed to get out of the basket by himself but, at home, if she lifts him out, he fluffs his feathers to bulk himself up before he waddles and jumps around the kitchen, exploring under tables and chairs, pecking at the patch of cracking plaster in a damp corner by the fireplace. She's constantly worried about treading on him.

'Look at the stars, Rook,' she whispers. She scoops the shaky bundle of feathers on to her lap. 'Tell me what you know.'

Through her cotton dress, Rook's toenails dig lightly into her thigh.

The Milky Way unfurls like a veil across the black, layer upon layer of stars. When they were children, she and Flick had a book called *The Observer Book of Stars*. It must be somewhere. She will have to search in the attic.

The winking light of an aeroplane makes steady progress across the night, reminding Nora of the plane she saw earlier, chugging out its love-heart. Humans read so much significance into the arrangement of stars and planets, signs and symbols in the sky. Like Halley's Comet, the fiery star which appeared early in 1066 and is stitched into the upper margin near the start of the Bayeux Tapestry: a portent of doom.

Not far away, water crashes from the old millwheel. The wheel's dripping wooden jaws – with their slow, relentless turning – terrified her as a child, reminding her of a picture she'd seen in one of her father's books: the Lady of Shallot with her wet weed hair. She'd calm her fears by straining to hear instead the pianissimo sounds she listens for now: the sluggish trickle of the millstream as water licks the bank at her feet.

My Saxon princess, her father called her, a hand on her hair, and she basked in the glow of his attention. Her hair was almost white-blonde, while Felicity and Ada both had black hair which swung heavy around their faces. Nora would rest her elbows on the breakfast table, peep sideways at her sister's plump forearms and push her own arm close to the waft of hairs which lay against Flick's olive skin. Nora's own skin stretched tight and translucent over knobbles of bone at her shoulder, wrist and elbow, veins showing blue beneath the marshmallow-white. She was the ugly duckling.

Her father often told them the story of the Saxon princess. Crouching forward on his thighs in a circle of lamplight between their twin beds, he removed his spectacles, squared his shoulders and ran his hands through his hair until it stood in crests and he was the fierce Viking – wild-haired, moustachioed King Cnut – who lived near their home a thousand years ago.

'One whole *thousand*?' Nora asked, voice muffled by her pillow. She slept on her tummy, sometimes with her head under the pillow, because feathers had magical properties which floated into the texture of her dreams.

'Yes, a whole thousand. And fierce King Cnut had a pretty daughter.'

It was Nora's birthday and she'd made a special request for the princess story. She was sucking her thumb, her curled hand cupping the burnt-sugar smell of condensed milk fudge she'd made with Ada as a special treat.

'The princess—' he continued.

'What was her name?'

'Her name was—,' Dad rubbed his nose, 'a secret.'

Nora sat bolt upright, hair fuzzy from the pillow. 'If he was her Daddy it wouldn't be secret from him!'

'Well, sweetheart, fact is, nobody knows what her name was. That's the truth.' Dad leaned in to kiss Nora's head. 'King Cnut's daughter had blue eyes and long golden hair.'

'Like mine?'

'Like yours. And her favourite game in all the world was to make boats and float them down the millstream.'

Dad said always this; floating leaf-and-stick boats in the millstream was what Nora and Flick liked to do.

Nora slid her thumb from her mouth. 'Did she go crabbing too?'

'She went crabbing too.'

'And cockling?'

'And cockling.'

'And did she make drip people in the mud?'

At this, Flick thumped her bed with both feet, her face pinched with the furious effort of screwing her eyes shut. Nora slipped her thumb back into her mouth. She asked questions because questions delayed the story's ending, when the pretty Saxon princess with the long blonde hair drowned in the millstream and proud King Cnut drummed his chest and wailed in grief. She asked questions because when the end of the story came, their father would kiss them goodnight and leave.

Nora takes the long way home through the graveyard. Inside the church, the rough stone walls hold the briny smell of a cave awaiting the return of the tide.

Near the chancel arch she stops at the memorial tile for Cnut's daughter. She has seen this image countless times over the years but tonight she stares down at the etching, hit by a disorienting sense of a displacement of time. A charge runs through her like a current. The bird, drawn with oversized beak and claws, is so like Rook the shock of resemblance raises the hairs up her forearms in ripples.

NORA PUSHES HER little finger loaded with chopped cheese and cherries mixed with egg deep into Rook's throat, where the muscles clutch and squeeze, forcing the parcel of the food downwards. Between mouthfuls, Rook wilts, his beak dropping fast, head tilted, with one eye shining and focused on Nora's face. His eyes have changed colour, blue darkening to black.

She dreamed last night about holding Eve's baby. All day the dream's sensations have haunted her, the weight of the baby in her arms, its wriggle and kick, a thrust of rounded limbs against her belly. They'd been to the cash and carry that evening, Nora lifting the boxes of café supplies for Eve.

'I'm not chucking up any more,' Eve had said. The top she wore was close-fitting and stretchy with horizontal stripes which emphasised the swell of her breasts and the curve of her growing belly. Her eyes shone as she bit into an apple. 'I'm even back on sex.' She giggled and rolled her eyes.

Rook makes a noise like a sneeze, head ducking and his body twitching violently, as if the food has travelled along the wrong passageway. Nora pauses to give him time to recover before offering the next morsel. Some people react to him with fear or repulsion, yet Rook is still small enough to cup in her hands, a lightweight and unsteady bundle with a wobbling neck and an elastic-sided beak which widens like a clown's smile the moment he sees her. She recalls her own instinctive unease when she first saw him lying in the ditch. Not everyone would have felt the same, but she couldn't have lived with herself if she'd left him there to die.

The superstitions surrounding corvids and the association with death, Harry says, are down to two simple things: the colour black, and the fact that corvids feed on carrion, the flesh of dead animals.

'The human mind has a weird thing going on with colour,' he'd said. Nora hoped she wasn't blushing. One day when he was out, she'd seen one of his paintings through the open door of his caravan, on an easel, unfinished, and half-covered with sheeting. Most of the canvas was taken up with the back of a woman's head and shoulders, her pale hair falling in waves down her back to her waist, strands here and there painted in brown, ochre, black and gold, like the colours found in grains of sand. In places, skeins of hair were twisted and three thin plaits were woven with white feathers. The woman pressed one hand against the fissured bark of the trunk of a silver birch, her fingers disproportionately long, the skin on the back of her hand and her forearm very white. Above her head, light filtered through a canopy of green oak leaves.

The colours of the painting disturbed Nora, or rather the bleached-out absence of colour. The bark was silver, and the sky beyond the leaf canopy was white. So too was the sun, or moon; it could have been either. The woman's skin was a rosy-tinted white, and so were the feathers in her hair. The only colours apart from these shades of white were the green of the leaves, and the pale sand of the woman's hair. The effect was ghostly. Nora had not mentioned seeing the painting, to Harry or anyone else.

She strokes the top of Rook's head. His feathers, a lustrous black, are no longer patchy. His head, weighed down by the heavy beak, begins to wilt again as his appetite is sated. She wouldn't like to see crows scavenging on dead human flesh, as they did during the Black Death. Witnessing a dead person, maybe someone you knew or loved, pecked at by the black birds would be horrifying, an image you'd never forget but, as Harry pointed out, ugly as it might have been to witness, their scavenging helped to prevent the spread of the disease.

Because rooks have lived closely with humans for centuries, stories about the birds' habits have sprung up, embellished through repetition. Passed down over generations, legends and folklore entwine with omens and superstitions, taking root in the human mind. But not all are negative. North American legends, Harry told Nora, describe rooks accompanying the souls of the righteous to heaven.

Rook's eyes are closed. 'Go to sleep, little one.' Nora strokes the top of his head again, where the feathers are silky.

As a child, she collected feathers, from her pillow, from cushions, any she found lying on the ground, and hid them in her ballerina jewellery box. Not a safe hiding place. Flick would lift the lid of the jewellery box to watch the plastic ballerina turn round and round while the music played, then she'd jump up and run off, leaving the lid open when the ballerina had stopped dancing. Once, Nora came across Flick standing on one foot in the doorway of their bedroom swooshing the door to and fro to make fat puffs of air. The ballerina box was open and Flick watched Nora's feathers float up and away on the breeze.

Nora covers Rook's basket with the black towel and opens a window. It's another sultry night, almost midsummer. Eve and Stavros will have reached Stonehenge by now, in time to celebrate the summer solstice. She is glad not to be trapped beside Zach on hot nylon seats in the back of their cramped 2CV.

The smudge sticks Eve made for her lie on the bedside table. About four inches long and made from dried herbs, they are bound together with a wispy, rough thread. Their aromatic smell has wound its way into Nora's dreams, where the sun beats down, hotter and hotter until the heat becomes a stage light, blinding her. Weak with the white heat of panic, she can't find her bow. The audience stirs restlessly as the sea, with nothing to keep them at bay. Her empty hands shake until she hears Isaac's voice: *The bow is where we create most of our expressivity*, and then she's awake in the hot darkness, sweating, rising out of bed to fling open more windows.

Now feels like the right time. She reaches for the box of matches.

The lit end of the bundle crackles and glows, the tip smokes and blackened fragments flake off, so she rests the stick in an upturned scallop shell on the window sill and picks up a pheasant tail-feather, already selected from her collection for this purpose. With her eyes closed, she breathes in the aromatic smoke.

Bonfires, autumn bonfires in the garden with her father; dead leaves and newspapers in the incinerator; his shadow and hers, cast black by the orange leap of flames. Above them, scraps of burnt paper drift and waft, higher and higher, towards the treetops, where bare branches are silhouetted against the sky.

She and Isaac stood between the high racks of music manuscripts in the hushed library of the Academy. In her hand, tightly rolled and hard as a stick, was the money. Her thumb flicked at the red rubber band which held the roll together until it slipped off and the notes began to separate, layer upon layer, peeling away from the centre of the roll like charred wood flakes, releasing a smell of smoke as notes drifted like leaves to her feet. Isaac had already begun to walk away. Scattered twenty-pound notes lay around her feet, their edges curled.

The pheasant tail-feather skims through her fingers like silk. She smells a bonfire: her father is there. She is a child with a stick, poking leaves in the incinerator, her face hot in the flames.

Nora and Flick didn't know their father was gone until weeks after he'd left. In her memory his death is overshadowed by the shock of his leaving. They were used to him being often away on trips and returning with a browned face and arms to tell stories of the treasures he'd found, so Nora at first noticed nothing unusual in the more prolonged absence. She continued to compose letters to him, imagining him in the glare of a foreign sun, head bent as he dug and scraped the bone-hard earth with his triangular trowel. At weekends, home from boarding school, she folded the inky pages in half, taped the puffy, over-full envelopes to seal them and handed them to her mother to post.

Then it was Whitsun, a fortnight at home. She moped down by the creek or practised particularly demanding phrases from the Martinů sonata over and over again until her mother slammed doors to indicate her protest at the repetition. She checked the post for letters from her father. Flick returned from university with a beribboned perm, fingerless gloves and outfits composed of lycra and ripped net. Sitting on Flick's bed watching her unpack joss sticks and light one, Nora heard about the parties Flick had been to, the boys she'd slept with. Flick showed her the green foil packets of contraceptive pills she took, one every day.

One sultry afternoon Ada caught Flick in the bomb shelter at the bottom of the garden messing around with one of the younger Tanner boys from the village. There was a fight. Ada dragged Flick from the door of the shelter; the boy cringed, his shoulder blades prominent as wings, pressed up to a tree trunk. He had a cowlick of hair on his forehead. Flick, hands fisted, screeched at her mother until Ada stood straight, swung back one shoulder and slapped Flick hard on the cheek. *And don't think you can run to your father!* Ada drew her lips tight against her teeth and sucked a breath, *because he won't be back.* She lifted her hand high and slapped again, so hard Flick stumbled backwards, holding her jaw. The sound of the blow made Nora flinch. She clambered higher into the macrocarpa tree where she had been hiding to spy on Flick and the boy, up to where the branches were thinner but greener, and fallen, brown needles and pine cones clumped together in shaggy platforms screening the ground from sight.

Nora rested her cheek on the bark, the resin so strong a smell it was a taste in her throat. Her mother called into the dusk, *Time to come down now, Nora,* and then, later, *You're far too big to be climbing trees and hiding,* followed by the rattle of the glass in the window as the kitchen door slammed.

At dusk, caws and chooks filled the air with jubilance as rooks and jackdaws gathered above the stand of trees. Darkness fell and the bird noise quieted to muttering and, finally, silence. Nora clambered down, limbs stiff, not belonging to her, only the scrape of the bark real against her palms.

In the unlit house, corners and closed doors were unfamiliar. No one was about. Ada must have been out; she often was, on a Saturday night. Nora trailed through the house, feathery hunger combining with a fiercer hollowness, her fingers shaky as she felt her way in the dark along walls and ledges to the hallway, where her father's raincoat hung, his trilby still jaunty on the hook above. The cool linings of his coat pockets parted as her fingertips delved deep, down to the seams: nothing. Not even the jab of one of his wooden toothpicks. Upstairs in his study, his spare reading spectacles were balanced over the crook of the Anglepoise lamp on his desk, a book open face down, spine bent back.

One day not long afterwards, the house still electric with tension, Ada tripped over their father's gardening shoes by the back door. Snatching one up, her back rigid, she flung the shoe on to the lawn. Hurling the other in the same direction she yelled, *You bastard!* stamping and swearing out into the empty garden. *Bastard! Bastard!* Next door, the paws of Arthur's Great Dane clawed the fence as he leaped up in a barking frenzy.

In the night, Nora retrieved the abandoned shoes from the lawn. They were caked with mud, the leather so moulded to the curve of his toe joints they might have been fashioned from clay. Nora stuffed balls of newspaper into the toes as she had seen her father do with wet shoes. She swaddled them in layers of newspaper and hid them in the junk at the bottom of her wardrobe, along with other things she didn't want anyone to discover.

A gust of wind rattles the glass in the window frame and Nora comes to. Her father is a presence in the room, close enough for her to see the dent in his hair at the side of his head where the arm of his glasses has pressed. Mesmerised by the smoke which un-scrolls from the smudge stick, she lies down, exhausted, to sleep.

She must have slept deeply because it seems only moments later that birdsong – a blackbird or thrush, the repetitive purr of wood pigeons – wakes her. She goes quickly to the window. The garden is sponged with early-morning mist. It's dawn. She hears a burst of *chook, chock, chook*: the jackdaws' calls and answers, ecstatic, and below them, the deep croak of the rooks, slow as the creak of an ancient door. The ragged cloud, a jumble of black birds, passes overhead through the milky air, cavorting. Nora hurries downstairs to find her cello where she left it, propped in the hall.

So as not to disturb Ada at this early hour, she goes down to the cellar. The concrete steps are narrow. To negotiate the twists of the stairwell, she holds the cello close, fingers flat on the wood, the flecks and ripples of varnish, the intimate flaws in the gleam of the cello's surface, the strength of its body's curve and filigree against her hip and breasts. The cello carries the scent of the eau de cologne she uses for cleaning the strings and, just detectable, the fibrous undertone of rosin.

At the bottom of the stair way she pauses in the gloomy half-light. The cellar has three rooms. The smallest room with the ancient and rusty chest freezer she doesn't consider. In the biggest room the oil-fed boiler roars in its cage and from the ceiling hang the clothes airers they hardly use these days. She steps into the third room. Long unused flower vases and Kilner jars are kept here, cobwebbed in rows on shelves. There is a stool used to reach the highest shelves, where she sits without thinking further and, with the urgency of long deprivation, begins to play the Martinů Cello Concerto no.1; the first movement – *Allegro poco moderato.*

When she's finished, her arms are shaking and she's breathing hard. Heart racing, she leans her head against the cold of the cellar wall. Gradually, her pulse slows. She can hear breathing. Someone is sitting on the stairs. From where she sits purple crocs and muscular calves are all that is visible through the doorway: Harry.

Hastily, she pushes the cello away from her body, pulling her knees together. She wipes her face with a hand. Unable to think what to say into the silence, she closes her eyes, hoping they can both pretend this has never happened. He might go away.

'Nora.' No sound of him moving, just the rolling boulder of his voice. 'Is this where you always come,' there's a pause, 'when you play like this?'

Fuck off, she wants to say. Go away and leave me alone. None of this is any of your business. Her cheeks are wet. She scrubs at them with the hem of her T-shirt.

'Because,' a change of pitch in his voice, a rough edge, 'this is something else and it's like . . .' She opens her eyes, sees the fuzz of hair on Harry's calves. She has nothing to say. Harry exhales, a long sigh of breath, '. . . an *excavation*.'

He moves – a sound of cloth. She can't see his face, but the change in angle of the lower part of his knees tells her he must be standing. The blood rushes in her ears as if she's drowning. Harry gives another sigh, which ends in a whistle of breath. 'And that's good.'

His crocs scuff the concrete step. She waits to hear his breath again, expects at any moment to feel his presence beside her in the unlit space stacked with empty jars, but when she opens her eyes again, she's alone.

ADA COMES DOWN the stairs carrying a pair of court shoes with heels.

'Ready,' she sings out, twirling to show off her outfit, a cream wool coat with a fur collar that swings from the shoulders, a cream hat with a wisp of veil across the crown.

'Mum, it's June, and we're going out in the skiff, not to Goodwood! You can't possibly wear those shoes.'

'I'm past the age when anyone can tell me what I can and can't wear. Do I criticise your shabby appearance day and night?'

Eventually, Ada is persuaded out of the cream coat and hat, but she insists on the heels and dons a mink stole to replace the fur collar. She complains about a wakeful night which has left her chilled to the bone and, shaky in the heels, is not reliably in control of coordinating her slender limbs. The balancing act required to step between bobbing skiff and jetty will be too much. Since he overheard her playing in the cellar Nora has avoided Harry, but unfortunately today she will need his help.

She finds him sitting on a fold-up garden chair in a patch of sun outside his caravan, legs akimbo in his dressing gown, headphones on and eyes closed. Conscious it's Saturday, his day off, and she will be disturbing the solitude of his early-morning coffee, she turns to leave but he seems to sense her presence and slips off his headphones. From them, growls the rich bass of Leonard Cohen. If Harry sang, it occurs to Nora, his voice would sound similar.

When she explains, Harry downs his coffee and tightens the tie of his towelling dressing gown around his waist.

He cradles Ada like a bride, carrying her from the house down to the shoreline, where the skiff is pulled up on to clumps of eel grass, ready.

'Light as a feather, no worries.'

One arm draped across his shoulders, cheek close to the stubble of his jaw, Ada darts her eyes up to his and away again, lowering her lashes like a girl. While Harry and Nora slosh in the shallows to get the boat afloat, she sits serene in the bow of the skiff, eyes closed, hands flitting over her lap. Nora has wrapped her legs in a moth-eaten tartan rug because the sun this morning is weak and watery. It might be chilly out on the water.

Ada tucks a wisp of silvered hair behind her ear and offers her cheek to the sky, displaying the dainty and intimate whorls of her ear as if for a lover's kiss. Her lips move, almost imperceptibly, and she smiles, head inclined further. She appears to be drifting, elsewhere, a place altogether more glamorous than Salthill Creek under a pale English sky.

Nora has handled the clinker-built skiff since childhood. She'd like to tell Harry, breathing noisily beside her, she can manage fine, thank you, now Ada is safely seated in the boat, but she's worried her words will come out wrong and she doesn't want to appear ungrateful. A sudden swell laps water over the tops of her wellingtons.

'Right, in you go.' Harry offers his hand, which Nora pretends not to see. She climbs easily over the side of the skiff and bends to reach the oars just as Harry gives the boat a final, unnecessary, shove. One of her feet lands on a heap of rope spilling out from under the central seat, and she staggers, arms windmilling as she struggles to regain her balance against the lurch of the boat. She lands with a bump on the seat across the stern and has to steady her breathing before reaching for the oars, manoeuvring them into the rowlocks without clouting the wooden sides or knocking her mother sideways. She's done this time without number but as usual having her mother as an audience makes her clumsy as a cart horse. Ada clicks her tongue. *Must come from your father.* Nora waits for her to say the words. *Those big bones.*

Harry stands on the shoreline, hands in his dressing-gown pockets, watching their progress. He hasn't done much in the garden beyond lifting the turf and mowing the upper lawn. Besides the bits and pieces he does in other gardens in the village, Ada has kept him busy creosoting the fence and repointing brickwork. Nora decides to ask him to look at the Wolseley too. With any luck, more lawns to mow and hedges to cut over the summer will mean it'll be autumn and nothing more done.

Ada's face remains beatific. When composed, stationary like this, her mother – with her haughty swan's neck and fine cheekbones – looks poised and graceful as a ballerina. She doesn't slump or shuffle or sit bent in half, nor is she slack-jawed like some of the elderly women in the retirement homes. Though, even there, barely suppressed anger lurks beneath the floral polyester.

Nora winds up her hair, fastening it away from her face. Harry has hung a tin whistle around her neck, ready for when they want to come in. Running a hand over his stubble, he winked and told her it would all be fine, *no problemo*, getting Ada back on shore. He's around all day, he'll just wade out. *Simple.*

Simple: the plop of water from the oars. No wind. Her mother is quiet, perhaps even content. She has brought her opera glasses for looking at the herons and egrets. Nora has also brought the more practical binoculars. Only a few sailing dinghies are out, keeping to the deeper channel. Nora soon settles to the rhythm of rowing, the dragging weight of water against squared blades, feathering the oars to skim the surface. Because she was older by eight years, Ada taught Flick to row first. For years, only Flick was allowed the oars when they went out together in the skiff. Nora's impatience was volcanic, the pressure in her chest keeping her awake at night until she crept out and sat in the skiff pulled up on the shore, to practise rowing through the night air.

Ada taught them both to swim too. To dive off the jetty when the tide was in; if it was out, to lie afloat in the shallows and feel their way, palms and fingertips grazing over bladder-wrack and eel grass clumps, probing for flinty pebbles softened with mud, testing their way out into deeper water.

Ada is humming, swaying her torso to some inner melody and murmuring every now and again.

'Mum, fancy cockles again tonight?'

Her mother opens her eyes and gazes, unseeing, at Nora for a moment. 'Cockles.' She seems to come back to herself and claps her hands. 'Delightful.'

Water ripples against the sides of the skiff. Nora squints to try to make out who is driving the tractor which is spraying on the far side of the creek. The strain of an engine at full throttle distracts her. From behind them a rubber inflatable smacks through the water, prow high and passing too close. The skiff tips and rocks. Ada's hands fly out to grip the sides, her mink stole slipping from her shoulders. As the RIB passes, a boy crouched in the prow whoops as he clings to the bouncing craft, one arm circling in the air as if swirling a lasso. His eyes lock briefly with Nora's before sliding away.

The inflatable gouges a deep 'V' through the water as it travels up the creek. From behind, Nora notices another teenager in charge of the engine. She pretends not to notice the youth in the prow give an exaggerated lasso-wave of his arm, showing off for her benefit.

Ada clutches the sides of the skiff as the boat rocks, tendons standing in her slender wrists. 'Bloody brats!' she hisses.

Bloody parents, busy getting pissed-up in the sailing-club bar.

A few seagulls wheel and cry overhead. Ada, breathing fast, darts a look here and there across the water as if looking for something in the middle distance.

'Relax, Mum. It's fine.'

She's always been fit and healthy, Ada, despite her delicate frame; this shaky breathlessness is new. Nora feels for the whistle Harry gave her and finds the metal is comfortingly warm.

Up the creek towards the sluice gates, the RIB engine cuts to idle, the turmoil of its wake continuing to rock the skiff. The boys' shouts and calls bait her; a shrill wolf-whistle echoes across the water. The engine revs again. On one of the moored sailing boats, a man washing down his deck stops, rag in hand, and turns to look upstream at the RIB. He drops the rag in a bucket to yell through cupped hands, 'HEY!', then stands watching. The boys' laughter skims across the water as they swing the RIB into a wide curve over to the other side of the estuary, going back to wherever they came from.

Ada has worked herself up into a state. She gabbles incoherent snatches of sentences, her voice rising in a crescendo of anger, hands tugging at the stole around her neck, plucking at her coat buttons. Nora rests the oars in the rowlocks and stands ready to step over the middle cross-seat to her mother in the prow, but at the same moment Ada also stands abruptly. Her arms flail and the boat rocks.

'Mum, it's OK.' Nora reaches out to hold her mother's hands in her own. As she does so, the RIB's engine roars out again, deep-throated, the inflatable rears up, engine now a high whine, and heads straight for them across the water. Both boys are crouched, pale faces pinched with concentration.

Nora curses her stupidity. The man on the sailing boat hollers and waves his arms. Between the RIB bearing down on them and their skiff is a line of three, virtually submerged, wooden struts, all that remains of an ancient rotten jetty. The RIB is heading straight for the submerged struts. She'll have to get the skiff out of the way because if the RIB strikes a strut at this speed, it will fly out of control.

'DOWN!' Her hands press down on her mother's shoulders and they both tumble to the boat's floor. Ada mews in protest. Nora scrabbles on to all fours, banging her elbow on the rowlock. Her mother lies on the tangle of rope, arms lifted to Nora for help.

Nora's diaphragm jars with a shock of sound as rubber thwacks on water. The inflatable is mid-air, flying towards them. Keeping low, she grabs an oar and reaches for the other to try to swerve the skiff in time, just a fraction, into shallower water, but now her mother struggles up, brushing her hands on her coat, tottering, one foot raised to the wooden cross-seat, her head dipped to resettle the mink stole across her shoulders. Nora drops both oars and lunges for Ada just as the hull of the RIB punches the side of the skiff, ramming it so that her mother slides sideways. The skiff jolts and tips. Nora fastens her arms around Ada's body, toppling them both, a jumble of limbs, into the freezing hit of water that streams past in gulps of swelling bubbles.

The cold halts her breath; water gargles and belches through her ears. Eyes strained open, all Nora can see as she stretches out her arms, fingers searching, are floating particles of silt until, at last she catches a glimpse of her mother's face, her eyes violet-brown, wide open, coming closer under a looming shadow. Nora stretches out her fingers, touches the textured fabric of her coat-sleeve, and tugs her mother closer.

JULY

ADA SWAYS AT the top of the stairs, ears buzzing with the silence of walls and doors closed on empty rooms. The telephone has stopped ringing. Her foot hovers over the stairs, which cut back beneath her, slanting suddenly more steeply, and a sensation of falling washes over her; for a moment it seems she will step into mid-air. Behind her eyes, colours spray like exploding dahlias. She feels for the banister, heart banging. Far below, the edges of the black and white floor tiles scissor across the hall floor. She would be dead before she hit them.

One foot in front of the other, step by step, she moves back towards her bedroom and, with relief, sits down on the edge of the bed. In one hand she holds a fan of photographs but her mind is blank. She tries to retrace the events of the last few minutes, the telephone's jangle, its shrill echo bouncing around the house as the noise persisted with no one except herself to answer it. Nora has waltzed off somewhere, as usual, without so much as a by-your-leave. Felicity may have been calling from Spain — that is, if anyone has thought to let her know of the boat accident. Always the same with Nora. Once she starts playing that infernal instrument all hours of the day and night, she can think of nothing else and sooner or later she ups sticks and is gone.

The photographs in Ada's hand have scalloped edges. The papery surfaces scuff against each other as she sifts through them, her knuckles, scraped when she fell against the sides of the boat, stiff as rusty hinges. Something has slipped her mind, something for which she was searching, before the ring of the telephone jarred her thoughts. She lies back on the bed and closes her eyes, listening to the reassuring rhythm of Harry splitting logs, down near the creek. Once the garden is tidy, the croquet lawn weeded and rolled, she will telephone Roger and invite him to call round, ask his advice, probe him for his opinion on how much the house is worth, though he is retired now and his son has taken on the family business.

With a start, she remembers. How foolish to let it slip her mind! There is a reason she has pulled out the Louis Vuitton suitcase, a reason good enough to get her out of bed even though she is still a little shaky. Once again it happens, a sense of fading, her surroundings peeling away as her ears grow deaf with the pressure of water, sealing her off from the outside world. The sensation spreads. All she can hear is the sound of her own swallowing, the seep and trickle of something fluid, the edges of her mind softening like sponge as she begins to sink again.

She knows enough to hold her breath, to grip the suitcase. For a moment, underwater murk fills her vision, floating silt as her blood slides slow and she slips further from the light. To prevent herself from falling she concentrates on holding on to the suitcase corners, which dig into her palms.

The doctor says it is the shock, her mind fighting to forget the accident her body remembers. He says they will pass, but she doesn't like these peculiar turns, thought she had grown out of them years ago, after she was sent away to school when her mother died because her father couldn't cope with a little girl. When he abandoned her, there was Brian. Safe, steady Brian, and for a while it was better.

She takes a slow, steadying breath and rubs the dents in her palms. The suitcase . . .

For ease of access to past occasions – tennis and shooting parties, the weight of a silver fork in her hand, bone-handled knives – these days she keeps the Louis Vuitton case under the bed. Ada shuffles letters and postcards, theatre programmes, tickets. Round horn-rimmed spectacles, nubby sports jackets, cars with running boards, the salty smell of their leather seats: she misses these things. A man's white handkerchief, a stiff shirt collar, starched and pressed. She sighs at one photograph. She is wearing furs, leaning forwards for a man to light her cigarette. The line of his jaw is familiar but his name has gone.

What she needs is to feel a little more like her old self. She will send Harry for cigarettes. He will need money.

Photographs are spread all over the floor. From them, Robert smiles up at her. No fool like an old fool, nevertheless . . . She picks Robert up, recalling the other tall young man with the rich brown voice, waving his arms about, talking nineteen-to-the-dozen as he strolled away down Creek Lane with Nora.

He had come about the child's tomb; this is why she has pulled out the suitcase. She knows now what she was looking for and exactly where it is hidden, in the red silky folds of the pouch pocket at the back of the suitcase.

The piece of stone in the pocket of the suitcase is greyish white, small enough to cup in her hand, its texture roughened by tiny ovals of shell closely packed in lines, sharp as barnacles. Perhaps this is why she's thought of it only now, this stone from under the sea. Nora has simply no idea, waltzing off without a by-your-leave. Ada closes her fingers around the piece of stone, the shells embedded there sharp as little teeth.

From the depths of the ocean, she'll explain, before dropping the stone casually into his hand, her fingertips grazing his palm, *but well travelled since then.* Well travelled indeed, through ten centuries, both ocean and time.

He will crave it, as she did, will itch to snatch a piece of history, to possess. She knows this, because the need comes off him like heat. Ah well, nothing new on this earth.

And when the moment is opportune, today, or is it tomorrow, she will produce her treasure. *How on earth did you get hold of it?* he'll let slip, before realising the question is indiscreet.

Ada looks down at the photograph in her hand in which Robert clutches the garden griddle heaped with rubble. The shine on his shoes is dulled with dust from the graves.

'Tertiary limestone from Binstead on the Isle of Wight; a shell bank there.' The cadence of Robert's voice is clear to her ears, as if he was in the room.

'Let me take a snap,' she'd said, because she wanted to capture Robert, to keep him with her. The irony is the camera was

Brian's. She and Robert stood together in the church, bathed in a downward slant of light from the high north window while Brian, somewhere behind them, unfolded his ruler to measure the larger grave of the two and conferred with the man whose job it was to make a drawing of the positioning and size of the coffins. That summer, for weeks, all Brian talked about was the excavation. How a coffined grave meant the burial of someone of great importance. She might just as well not have been there, for all the notice Brian took.

'Quarr stone, first used in the late Anglo-Saxon period,' Robert said. He was no ignoramus but he held the chunks and chips of rock and stone aloft like jewels, with a foolish look on his face.

The puzzle for her was in the missing detail. None of the men would answer this, how the stone coffin had been hewn, and where. The sides were marked, chipped into shape with a tool like a chisel, Brian said. Ada wondered about the drowned girl's body, where she had lain before burial, whether her warrior father carried her in his arms to the open tomb which awaited her, a chill bed with the covers drawn back. The way Harry carried her up from the creek, the warmth of his body a comfort; the taste of silt in her throat.

Ada shifts on the mattress.

A drowned child, buried under the chancel arch in the position reserved for those of high standing, yet the tomb was simple, without decoration. The result of an illegitimate liaison, Brian had said, by way of explanation, in that bored, dismissive way he had. *Don't let your imagination run away with itself, Ada. Don't get carried away.* The lack of decoration might have been due to haste, a need to bury the child quickly. Perhaps she died at this time of year, in the height of summer.

Ada shivers, remembering the smothering weight of the wet cloth which dragged her body down. Harry strode up the slope to the house with her in his arms. Nora peeled off her clothes, wrapped her in a bath towel and rubbed her dry as if she was a child, while Harry fetched wood and laid up the fire in her bedroom. A fire lit upstairs, in June!

The Saxon princess was laid in a coffin hewn from Quarr stone, which has another name – *featherbed* – and this is the name Ada prefers, the name she will give the young man from the television when he returns. As she knows he will.

Strange name for a grown man, Jonny; a diminutive more suited to a child.

No matter what opinion her daughter holds, Ada will not be taken for a fool. She will gain pleasure from mentioning Robert's name when she next speaks with the young man, and advises him to add Robert Flatholm to his list: *Dr Flatholm* – airily – *a geologist I knew quite well at the time.*

She has the facts at her fingertips. Featherbed stone was used in Bosham before the Norman conquest. Ada smiles to herself, gives a shrug of her shoulders, a demure shake of the head. The quarry was worked out by the fourteenth century.

She can speak this language Robert spoke because she taught herself at the time, to be able to converse with him. Robert took pride in his area of expertise, pride in being able to date the different parts of the church through the stone used as building material.

Ada hasn't thought of the piece of featherbed stone in years but here it has been all this time, nestled in one of the silky inner pockets of the suitcase. Jonny's questions about the little princess's grave brought everything back. He'd love to have a look at Brian's photographs, he'd said, and so she invited him to call again. Yet on the appointed day, he hadn't so much as crossed the threshold of Creek House, thanks to Nora's appearance.

Robert's blond head is bent to his diagrams. The renowned chancel arch, built in Quarr stone and stitched on to the Bayeux Tapestry, he coloured purple. How simple to slip a piece from the rubble in the griddle into the pocket of her new cashmere cardigan, to nod and tilt her cheek towards Robert when he pointed with his pencil to the purple and yellow blocks of shading, to nod a second time when he spoke in another language about nodules and limestone, her mind on other things — the blond hair at the base of his throat, the way his Adam's apple moved, prominent as a boy's — as her fingers closed around a piece of featherbed stone from the thousand-year-old tomb of a princess.

Ada is not certain which of Brian's books contains, folded between the pages, Robert's diagram of Bosham church, a book with Robert's signature and the date, April 1954, in the bottom right-hand corner. When she's back on her feet she will go into Brian's study and make sure she can lay her hands on it.

Strictly speaking, opined that white-haired busybody on a bicycle — whose name Ada forgets — the 1954 excavation of the tomb was performed unlawfully; Brian and the others chose to disregard the fact. The Reverend, tubby little man with his white goatee beard and half-moon spectacles, the churchwardens, someone from the Ministry of Works – they all had their own petty rules and observances, the archaeologists, geologists and historians. The Reverend Jones – that's his name – referred constantly to the copious notes of one of his predecessors. He had several notebooks detailing the original excavation of the child's tomb in 1865, plus a dusty tome a previous incumbent had written on the traditions of Bosham.

Since the mother of the little princess who drowned is unknown, Ada feels a sense of responsibility. Though several experts were gathered together to take measurements and notes, no women were invited to visit the opened grave. She was there merely as Brian's wife, her name not mentioned in the newspaper reports of the time. She will be an invaluable asset to Jonny's television programme. She must tell Nora to book an appointment for her at the hairdresser's as a matter of urgency.

Ada neatens a pile of photographs. Fifty years ago, near as damn it. Dust in the back of her throat from the sifted rubble. Her new cardigan was powder-blue cashmere, snug across the bust. Pearl buttons. She can feel them, the way each button rolled hard as an acid drop between her fingers as she fastened them.

A mere trifle, in the grand scheme of things, to smuggle a tiny piece of another life, another time, Cnut's time, a man whose sons were warriors who felt the pulse of daring.

She will appear on Jonny's programme to talk about the various types of stone: the Archaeologist's Wife, widowed for almost two decades. The piece of Quarr stone will captivate him, Jonny, with his practised look. Doubtless some woman has made him her pet, told him he is adorable, some woman made foolish by those puppy-dog eyes, the treacle of his voice; an older woman, most likely, or a girl.

She will call him Jonathan, the young man with an appetite, if she's not mistaken, but – she recalls the disappointment of his handshake – likely to be lacking in staying power.

CREEK HOUSE AT first seems empty. Nora leans her cello against the wall in the hallway and slips off her shoes. She hears her mother's laugh and muted voices from upstairs, followed by a thud and the sound of something moving across floorboards. Rook hasn't come swaggering down the hallway to greet her, so he must be shut in the kitchen.

In her bedroom, Ada kneels by a suitcase, one Nora doesn't recognise, old fashioned and boxy, a pattern tooled in leather around the edges. Beside the suitcase, Jonny's long form is stretched out on the floor, his head propped on one hand. From the stairs, only his back and the rolled-up shirtsleeve of the arm supporting his head is visible, but he must know she's there because, without turning his attention from Ada, he lifts the other arm and beckons her into the room.

Nora hesitates before stepping forward. Though she must be aware of her daughter in the doorway, Ada doesn't look up. Her hair is loose, damp on her forehead. She's flushed. This is the first day, since the accident, she has got up and dressed. Hefty at her neck is an ornate necklace of red glass stones. Although a window is open, the air is stale with cigarette smoke and liberally sprayed perfume.

'Brian was thrilled at the opportunity, of course,' Ada is saying. 'Some regular repair work was being carried out, paving stones being renewed to the west of the chancel steps, I believe, which necessitated the lifting of slabs. They knew the child's coffin existed, of course, that was found in the eighteen hundreds, but the memorial tablet is in completely the wrong place so they were not expecting to uncover it. The second, larger coffin was a complete surprise to all and sundry, despite the fact it had been vandalised on some previous occasion.'

'How could they tell?'

'The skull was missing. Other body parts were absent, if I remember rightly.'

Ada talks on. Jonny pats the floor beside him and puts a finger to his lips. Nora sits cross-legged beside him. The room is hot so she unfolds her legs, stretching them out in front of her on the floor. Jonny glances down, the flick of his eyes tracing the length of her thighs, her calves and ankles. Glittering through her limbs, Nora's blood responds. Ada's chin lifts; she tosses her hair.

'The vicar sent for Brian straight away. It was fortunate he was at home, he was so often away. They called in other experts too – someone from the Ministry of works, Dr Langhorne from the village, and a second archaeologist and a geologist came down from London. One or two of the churchwardens were there too, I believe.'

Ada runs her fingertips over the photographs, fanned in her hand like a pack of cards. She tips her head, glancing at Jonny over the top of them, focused on him in such a way Nora is cut from her field of vision. Nora is left with a sense of not being entirely present. She decides to say something, to take more control of the situation. 'So sorry not to be here when you arrived, Jonny. Mum, has Jonny had something to drink? It's so hot today and he's had a long journey from London.'

'At the time the national press were terribly taken with the little princess and the story of her drowning in the millstream,' Ada continues, as though Nora has not spoken. Clearly, her arrival is an unwelcome disruption.

'The larger coffin was quite magnificent.' Ada selects several more photos and, with a flourish, leans over the open suitcase to hand them to Jonny. 'Horsham stone. See the apsidal head, and the way the stone is tooled? Brian said it must have been someone of great importance not only to be coffined, but to also be buried beside a king's daughter.'

'Any theories?'

Ada kneels over the suitcase. She shakes her head. 'Only some talk at the time it was Earl Godwin.'

Ada's gaze shifts from Jonny to the window above and behind his head, where poplar leaves stipple the sunlight. Her eyes are dreamy. 'One of the London men stayed here with us for a few days, at Creek House.' She glances at Nora and down at the photographs in her hand before passing them over. 'Quite a gathering, as you can see.'

Jonny hands Nora a photograph in which three men in suits bend over the pit of an open coffin. The stone lid has been prised open and leans against the church wall, broken. The coffin is empty. No skeleton, just rubble heaped together in the centre. A few sticks.

In the next photograph two men stand near an opened coffin, one looking on, a splay-bristled garden broom in his hands, while the other stoops astride the pit and holds, between thumb and forefinger as if ready to cast it to one side, a length of bone. The camera's flash has caught the gleam of his shoes. To one side, stands a third man, tall and angular, a mop of fair hair falling forward as he bends over a garden griddle filled with rubble.

'The vandals had left so few bones – a frightful disappointment. The pelvis was there, I held it myself.' Ada shivers. 'All such a shambles, just bits and pieces.'

Nora shivers, looking again at the photograph: not sticks lying in the tomb, but a bundle of bones.

'So, even though it was not a new discovery, the smaller grave made the nationals for obvious reasons.' Jonny runs a hand through his hair, nodding. 'King Canute has mythic status, everyone's heard of him, and the death of a child always draws sympathy.'

Nora pulls in her feet, preparing to stand. She will have lunch and feed Rook.

Though it's late in the day, she might go for a run, and leave these two to it. Before she can get up, Jonny passes her a piece of paper, a charcoal drawing, the edges softened with age, the paper stained with damp. An illegible signature and a date, 1865, beside the sketch of a skeleton, marked out with pencil lines and numbers, measurements. The breadth of the ribcage is eight inches. Nora stretches her fingers wide. The ribcage is little more than the span of one of her large hands.

Sweat slicks behind Nora's knees, but she can't stop herself from lifting the paper closer to examine the drawing, the mess of what looks like horse-hair surrounding the leer of a skull-face. The hand, all bones visible, looks unnaturally elongated. This can't have been what they saw when the child's coffin was first opened, not after eight centuries. Her stomach crawls. The paper falls to the floor.

'For pity's sake, Nora!' Ada has snatched up the drawing. 'This is well over a hundred years old!'

Nothing changes: Nora has to do something wrong before her mother will acknowledge her existence. There is no air in the room. A wave of nausea passes through her, and she puts a hand over her mouth.

Jonny's brown eyes lift to hers and away again towards Ada, who is replacing the lid of a cardboard box, which she then puts back into the suitcase and covers over with other bits and pieces.

Nora steps across the heaps of photographs and papers spread across the floor to open another window, but her muscles have turned to water. Dizzy, she makes for the bathroom instead when, from the bottom of the stairs, comes the clatter of the letter-box. She remembers Rook downstairs, cooped up in the kitchen. He'll be hungry; she needs to get away.

In the kitchen, a jug of water on the draining board holds a bouquet of crimson and purple anemones still wrapped in a cone of brown paper and tied with raffia the same crimson as the flowers. The simplicity of the wrapping accentuates the vivid colour of petals. Jonny has bought flowers. Nora wonders if they are for her, or for her mother.

Rook hops and swaggers across the floor towards her. He pauses a little way from her feet and, with a twitch of his head to one side, eyes her up and down. With an extravagant shimmy of feathers, he shakes out his wings before stretching out his neck to dip his head in greeting, his long-feathered tail fanned as proudly as a peacock's. He is now almost full grown and can feed himself from a bowl of offerings, but occasionally when, as now, he first sees Nora after an absence of a few hours his beak opens wide for food.

'Shall I, or shan't I, Rook?' she says, moving her hand very slowly towards him to stroke his head. 'Mum will not forgive me for stealing her thunder, but Jonny will find out one way or another. Might as well be me who tells him about Harold, don't you think?'

Rook's feathers brush Nora's skin. The man at the bird sanctuary told her rooks are highly intelligent, far more intelligent than most humans, he'd added with a wink. Nora liked the way he rolled up the sleeves of his denim shirt and washed his hands before touching Rook. You hardly ever seen a rook hit by a car, he'd said. 'Pheasants and magpies, yes. Not rooks. If this bird can't fly,' he said, as he held Rook's wing spread out over one forearm, 'he must have something wrong with him.'

The bird sanctuary man examined Rook's wings for deformity. His forearms were tattooed with mermaids and fish, which made Nora imagine a seafaring past. He told her in detail how rooks make use of zebra crossings to crack nuts, dropping a nut on to the black and white stripes and then waiting on a wire or in a nearby tree until the lights change. When the traffic stops, the rook swoops down to pick up the nut, the shell having been cracked open by passing cars. Researchers at Cambridge University have also discovered a rook will make a tool out of wire. 'Wouldn't have believed it unless I'd seen it with my own eyes,' the bird sanctuary man said. 'They put some food in the bottom of a bottle and left the rook with a piece of straight wire. Bloody bird only picks up the bit of wire with its beak and bends the end into a hook, don't he? Uses the neck of the bottle to bend the wire. Takes him a while, dropping the wire and picking it up again, but he does it in the end.'

The bird sanctuary man could find nothing wrong with Rook that might affect flight. Nora, seeing Rook in his hands, one long wing stretched out, fingertipped as if in flight, had felt unaccountably sad. Rook, with his beaten pewter beak, his feathers iridescent as silk in the sunlight, doesn't look remotely deformed or damaged.

'I hope you know what you've taken on,' the sanctuary man said, as Nora left. 'Got that bird for life, you have.'

'And that's just fine,' she says to Rook, 'because you're my beauty, aren't you?'

Rook fluffs himself up and places a foot over her big toe.

ROOK HAS BEEN ripping paper again. He greets Nora at the door
with a strip of paper torn from a magazine and hops sideways
under her feet as she walks down the hall. He may be a silent bird,
but his hearing is not impaired and the sound of paper tearing
seems to give him pleasure. He works with his beak at a page from
a newspaper or magazine until the whole sheet is reduced to strips,
when, given the chance, he'll move on to the next one.

In the sitting room, remnants of a newspaper are shredded all
over the floor. Ada and Harry sit on the sofa, Ada's body set at
a tilt beside Harry's bulk. She's in full spate talking about rooks,
telling Harry the story of old Arthur next door, back when he
was new to the village and driven nearly insane during the breed-
ing season by the endless rowdy calls and chatter of the rookery.
The poplars grew close enough to scrape his eaves and block his
gutters with leaves. The birds' racket woke him at dawn, kept
going until dusk.

'Naughty Harry made tea then talked me into trying his favourite tipple. Have some.' Ada nods absent-mindedly towards the tea-tray where two teacups sit nestled on top of the piled saucers, untouched.

Ada sips from a sherry glass, though it's not sherry she's drinking. It's Harry's usual, sweet anis and brandy. Nora hopes he's not mixed it too strong. The smallest of the nest of coffee tables has been placed within Ada's easy reach and her feet, slim ankles crossed, rest on the leather pouffe. Harry must have rearranged the furniture for her convenience, as well as serving her drink. Ada does love to be fussed by a man.

The tea pours dark and tarry and is completely cold. Nora nurses the cup. Ada continues to regale Harry, putting out a hand every now and again to touch his wrist. The surface of Nora's tea swirls from the stir of the teaspoon, pallid compared to the rich amber glow of Harry's drink. She thinks of the turquoise bottle of Bombay Sapphire in the bottom of her wardrobe, glass the colour of a jewel. Since that night, Nora doesn't often drink alcohol, certainly never gin, the smell of it carrying her straight back to the slip of her foot catching on the too-long hem of her nightie, the jolt as her body smacked against the stairs. Drink affects the body in frightening ways. Tonight, her mother looks as if she has been dismantled and put back together, missing more than one essential component.

Rook lurches his way up Nora's arm to the back of the chair, where he balances and pulls very gently at a strand of hair. She puts up a hand to stop him, but he hasn't hurt her, his beak hasn't even touched her scalp so, gingerly, she lowers her hand. It comes again, the gentle tug on her hair right near the roots, the puttering movement of Rook's beak. He's grooming her with the same meticulous care he grooms his own plumage each morning.

'Arthur's house is as old as this one, and called Rook Cottage. One would suppose he might have guessed what he was in for!' Ada exhales a puff of laughter. 'But, he was a city man, unaccustomed to the country.'

A local farmer shot a rook and strung it fifteen foot above the ground in one of Arthur's trees, telling him it would keep the other rooks away. It didn't. The dead rook swung upside-down from one leg, claws curled, one eye a grey slit.

One dawn, Arthur could tolerate the racket no longer. Nora must have been no more than six or seven, and the story has many times since been told and retold, how her father, woken by the sound of shots and rage of the rooks, went to the window. Arthur, head hunched as rooks swooped and dive-bombed, tried to start up a chain-saw, one he'd borrowed, to trim his hedges, from Nora's father. A shotgun lay abandoned on the grass. As Arthur set the saw's teeth to the trunk of a poplar where six or seven nests clustered high in the bare branches, a rook dived close enough to lift a clump of hair from his scalp. Arthur dropped the saw and floundered backwards. He reached for the gun.

'The rooks have been there hundreds of years, maybe even thousands. My Brian did have a mind for these things, you see, the history of a place. He'd quote Domesday at you and relish the chance. Well, quick as a flash, he ran out in his dressing gown and wrestled poor Arthur to the ground.'

Nora's version of the story is different. A window pane pressed against her nose, glass misting as she stood on tiptoes to squint down at Arthur's garden; the whine of the chain-saw and the rooks' cacophony; a gust and squall of wings. Her father in his paisley dressing gown lifted his palms to the rowdy air. He reasoned with Arthur. The rooks, because they knew her father, with or without his binoculars, kept their distance. And his voice would have been quiet. Her father never shouted. Arthur would have lowered the saw.

Nora leaves the room without saying anything to Harry or Ada. She tips the tea into the kitchen sink, feeds Rook some raisins and banana and carries him upstairs with her. Tonight she needs his company. She lies on her narrow bed with him nestled on her stomach and picks up Elsa's pamphlet. In the photographs from the fifties, the two stone coffins look empty; all that's left of two lives is a handful of bones and some rubble. At the time, a doctor who examined the bones from the larger, newly discovered coffin, could identify only one femur, a fact which delighted Elsa because once Harold was knocked from his horse, according to one blow by blow description, one of his legs was hacked off and 'hurled far away'. Elsa consulted a pathologist and two further medical advisors herself, and showed them the photographs. From their findings she began to put together her argument.

The cover of Elsa's pamphlet shows the scene from the tapestry which depicts Harold's death, a scene littered with arrows, battle-axes and swords. Weapons stitched in wool. An English soldier with a moustache, thought to be Harold, falls to the ground as a Norman soldier on horseback leans forward and down. His sword strikes Harold's left thigh just above the knee.

One surgeon Elsa spoke to about the fifties photographs observed that the femur in the tomb is the left femur, and it has a fracture in the lower third, that is, above the knee. All three medical advisors she consulted agreed this bone fracture shows no evidence of having healed, meaning, if the damage to the bone occurred during life, rather than through any act of vandalism after burial, death must have followed within a week.

Rook is very still, head sunk low into his feathers. The one eye Nora can see is closed, so he could be asleep, though it's hard to tell. Rook has an uncanny ability to be half-asleep, one eye closed while the other eye remains open, alert and looking around. She should take him down to his basket in the kitchen for the night, but the lightness and warmth of his body resting between her hips is comforting.

Her stomach is flat, hips and ribcage prominent, her body shape so different from Eve's, which is rounded and ripe. When the baby moves, Eve's face lights up. 'Quick. Want to feel it?' Not waiting for an answer, she will place Nora's hand on the rise of her pregnant belly for her to feel the slide of something small but insistent moving beneath the skin.

Next week, because Stavros is away on a small business management course, Eve has asked Nora to go with her to the hospital for her twenty-week scan.

'We'll be able to see the baby's organs and skeleton,' Eve said. 'You can have 4-D images too, if you pay.'

The fourth dimension is movement. Eve described a friend's CD of her 4-D scan, the baby's thumb moving in and out of its mouth.

Rook twitches, head rising briefly, eyes open and alert, before sinking again. He often hears things she can't, sound waves the human ear is not equipped to detect. Trying not to disturb him again, Nora reaches sideways for the matches on the bedside table and lights a smudge stick. The peacock tail-feather is just within reach. She closes her eyes. The feather wafts smoke aromatic as the hot scrubby land around Flick's house in Spain. Nora wants to focus on being outside, to stay there on a Spanish hillside, but as Rook shifts on her belly, her mind turns inwards of its own accord, to her own body.

In the waiting room of the clinic Nora was the only one without someone, the only one alone. She sat by the radiator and, although the air was stifling, hunched herself into her oversized fleece, her hands resting in her lap. Close to tears she lowered her chin into the fleece's softness. She had the hard roll of money in her pocket. The schoolgirl opposite wore mocha-coloured tights with white fluffy knee socks over the top. She was with a woman whose eyes were red-rimmed. At the other end of the room sat two blowzy middle-aged women wearing too much gold and with too much blonde hair teased like candy floss from their scalps. One stared at the print of a stag standing atop a rock on Scottish moorland while the other patted her hand.

Nora turned her head to the tropical fish tank where electric blue and red fish darted in cohorts through the plastic ruins of a castle. Outside, lorries and buses thundered down Sawyers Hill and the glass in the window-frame shivered. People who passed bent forwards to slog up the hill, oblivious to whatever knives or potions or suction implements were used behind the opaque curtains. Nora rubbed her eyes.

The shift in gears of a lorry straining up the hill distracted her from the stagnant air in the room and Nora's mind brought to her snatched phrases of the slow cello lyric of Max Bruch's *Kol Nidrei*, which Isaac had dismissed with a slice of his hand as 'a minor romantic work'.

Kol Nidrei – 'All Vows' – a minor romantic work? No, Isaac was wrong.

She stared at the nylon which sheeted the window and listened, paid proper attention to the music in her mind until the vibration slid from her skull to her throat, to her fingers and ribcage, pushing down to her solar plexus, the inner core of her body where a tiny bunch of cells, like bubbles blown through a wand, clustered and multiplied while she sat in this silent room, waiting. She studied her cupped hands. She never was any good at waiting.

After half an hour she stood, walked across the room past the girl's knees in mocha tights and the blonde woman's patting hand, down the corridor and out through the blue door with potted bay trees on either side. The door had no handle on the outside so she pulled it closed by putting her hand into the brass letterbox. She turned left. Pulled up the hood of her fleece and bent her body to haul herself along with the other walkers, up the steep hill and past the rows of windows blinded by net curtains. After a few minutes the rain started. She walked faster. The awareness of the strength of her body, the solid muscle and bone, gave her an exhilarating desire to increase her pace, to overtake the other walkers, push harder up the hill.

She caught a train out of London and walked ten miles in the rain from Chichester to Creek House. Ada was shocked by her sudden appearance and by her weight loss. She thought Nora simply needed a good rest between performances and Nora at first had not the courage to tell her all concert performances were cancelled for the foreseeable future. She planned to choose the right time. She was not a child any more, she reasoned: she had made her own decision. She could return to performing, perhaps part-time at first, and Ada could look after the baby. She waited for the right time to talk to Ada, but it didn't come. She'd been home a month before she fully accepted the probability her mother would not want to spend weeks at a time looking after a baby. Instead, Nora considered adoption. You could have a baby adopted at birth, she'd read. Her baby could be given to a couple who desperately wanted a child but were unable to have their own. She'd need only a few more months at home, before life could return to normal.

It was April and the rooks were in pairs everywhere. Nora drew them in charcoal or with blunt pencil on creamy cartridge paper, page after page littering every surface in her childhood bedroom, and the floor. She was compelled to draw them, to capture their beauty. She drew them gathering to mate, to nest and to roost; she drew them in fields, their feathers gleaming like shot silk in the sun as they rooted for leather jackets; she drew them in the trees, in pairs on the leafless branches; in the air, soaring and banking, swooping across the lane with twigs and grass dangling from their beaks. The creak of their caws, the wet-sheet slap of their wings at take-off, these sounds were the familiar background of her thoughts, as was the cledge of mud underfoot by the creek.

At dusk, she took her father's old binoculars to watch and listen as the birds swirled over the rookery. Their nests were repaired and ready for the spring. Watching the rooks gave her a reason to be out of the house, out in the flat fields under the high skies. Unable to sleep in her narrow girl's bed, at dawn she took to walking along the creek path, an old raincoat of her father's to keep off the mist. The hem of her nightie brushed the toes of her wellington boots. High in the poplars, where there had been a rookery for hundreds of years, bobbed the black heads of rooks. The nests themselves, chunky twigs anchored in the spindly heights of trees, had only the appearance of strength. Her father had told her rooks do not line their nests with the mud as other birds do. Consequently, without the mud to act as glue, their nests are vulnerable to every movement of the wind through high branches.

ELSA MACLEOD PUSHES up her sleeves and picks up the rolling pin. 'Well, of course, what we have are *two* fascinating local traditions associated with stone coffins in Bosham church, but it's my opinion,' she fixes Jonny with a severe look, 'you may well be pursuing the tradition with the least historical significance. Excuse me, but I must get on.' She sprinkles flour on the work surface and as she rolls out dough, Nora glimpses the half-smile on her face, hidden from Jonny's view. Elsa's enjoying playing him along.

Jonny sits astride the kitchen chair, his legs and feet folded into a squashed Z. Beneath his long limbs the chair looks child-sized. Nora hasn't told him why she's brought him here. He's accepted Elsa's Earl Grey tea with one of his wide smiles, paid polite compliments on her house and garden, but now the confinement is making him restless. With his forearms resting flat along the top of the chair-back, he moves his chest forwards and back as if performing vertical press-ups; he lifts and jabs an elbow sideways, rotating his shoulder joint, massaging it with one hand, his shirtsleeve tightening over the swell of muscle, the languor in his movements suggesting he luxuriates in the tension and release of muscle.

Jonny had phoned earlier that week, wanting to find out when he could come with his laptop to scan copies of Ada's photographs, since she won't allow them to be taken out of the house. Nora spoke about Elsa, explaining she was an amateur historian.

'Your mother hasn't mentioned the name.'

'She wouldn't. They don't get on.' More to the point, her mother will have said nothing to Jonny about Elsa's local knowledge because his television programme is Ada's chance to be the focus of attention.

Jonny flexes his shoulder joint again, elbow circling in the air, the muscles in his upper arm hardening. All the men she's known have been musicians or academics, slender men like Isaac, whose energy sparked from mental or emotional strength, rather than physical. Sex with Jonny would be different.

'Yeah, yeah, yeah – we're talking about the second, larger coffin, found in the fifties?' Jonny's eyebrows lift, an upside-down V over the bridge of his nose.

'Of course.'

'Vandalised, only fragments of bone remaining.'

'You've read Geoffrey Marwood's pamphlet.'

'Also contemporary newspaper accounts . . .'

'However,' Elsa talks across him, 'the body was mutilated before burial, not vandalised.'

Jonny seems not to have heard. He rubs vigorously at his hair with both hands, leaving it tousled.

'The thing is, forgive me, Elsa, but we're talking television here. A Saxon princess is pretty hard to beat. Everyone has heard of Canute, absolutely everyone. Who, apart from historians such as your knowledgeable self,' he bows his dishevelled head of hair, 'has heard of Earl Godwin? I, for one, had not, until recently.'

'Have you, I wonder, read my own, more recent effort?'

Copies of both pamphlets lie on the kitchen table, with Marwood's on top.

'I do apologise. I've not come across yours.'

'I interpret the significance of the facts presented by Marwood. For example, the larger tomb was "tooled Horsham stone, magnificently finished", from which Marwood correctly deduces a person of some importance is buried there; a person of more importance, if we compare tomb decoration, than the daughter of a king. This piqued my interest. The *Anglo-Saxon Chronicle* records the burials of all the important people associated with Bosham during the eleventh century.'

'Meaning?'

'The number of possible candidates for the larger tomb is actually very limited.'

'I've always wondered,' Nora says, 'how they could tell the man had been powerfully built?'

'From the thigh and pelvic bones, where muscle attaches to bone; the bone thickens as it grows, to support the muscle. A Saxon warrior led an extremely active life.' Elsa's rolling pin rests in her hands. She stares into space as if she sees her Saxon warrior mounted on his horse, straight-backed despite the weight of chain mail, his face obscured and flattened by the helmet's nose-shield. The horse snorts; the bit clanks between its teeth.

Jonny is thumbing through Marwood's pamphlet. 'This guy has some useful stuff on Canute.'

Elsa returns from her reverie and listens to Jonny talk about the Saxon bell tower, the chancel arch and the rubble work. He waves his arms about as he talks. Nora wills him to stop, to look properly at Elsa's pamphlet.

'Of course,' he finishes, closing Marwood's pamphlet, 'Canute was known to be a great builder.'

'Cnut. He was a Viking. Can-newt is an attempt to Anglicise his name.'

'Fair enough.' Jonny straightens his back. 'Elsa, I'll be frank with you. This has to be a project with substance, not mere sentiment or sensation. To be awarded funding for this project, I need sound sources.'

'I can save you some trouble,' Elsa retorts, unfazed by the reprimand in his tone. 'Whoever it is buried in that magnificent stone coffin church, it is *not* the first Earl Godwin. Your "sound sources" tell us he is buried at Winchester, where he died.'

'*Godwin*,' Jonny repeats. He chucks a sugar cube into his mouth and at last picks up Elsa's pamphlet, though he does nothing more than riffle through the pages without giving the content any attention before replacing it on the table. He pats the cover with the flat of his hand, about to say something, before he glances down. He stops moving.

Is King Harold II buried in Bosham Church?

Apart from the knock of the wooden rolling pin on the worktop as Elsa rolls out a second batch of dough, the kitchen is quiet.

The sugar cube crunches in Jonny's mouth. 'Harold?' His thigh begins to jiggle, up and down. Elsa nods.

Jonny swivels around, his eyes meeting Nora's, eyebrows twitching upwards in query or excitement, she can't tell, as he unfolds his body from the chair, and in two strides is across the kitchen, beside Elsa.

'Am I right, Elsa,' he points to the pamphlet's title, as if Elsa might be unfamiliar with something spelled out with her own hand. 'Your title refers to our King Harold, the Harold who grew up here?' Here Jonny looks at Nora and grins. 'And whom the Bayeux Tapestry shows praying at Bosham Church?'

'Nora has filled you in.'

'Arrow in the eye, 1066 Harold?'

'Debatable,' Elsa answers, and selects a pastry cutter. 'The arrow, that is, not 1066.' She holds up a cutter shaped like a shooting star, but rejects it.

'Could—,' Jonny strides to the kitchen door and back. 'Would you mind filling me in?' He fetches his notebook from his laptop bag, sits down only to stand up again and pace the floor. He asks questions and scribbles fast, leaning against the worktop. Elsa waves the rolling pin as she talks, her face flushed with animation. The high voltage of their joint excitement thrums through the room. Sponsorship from a TV company could provide the money Elsa needs for further research; Elsa's theory could transform Jonny's programme into one of enormous historical significance.

Elsa talks of 'clues' and 'evidence', the coincidence of certain dates and details recorded in the *Anglo-Saxon Chronicles*, with an eleventh-century Latin poem entitled 'The Song of the Battle of

Hastings' which describes what happened in 1066 between August and 25 December, when William the Conqueror was consecrated King of England. The poem, discovered in a library in Brussels in the 1800s, was written in 1067 and is the earliest record of events. Elsa refers to it with reverence in her voice as the 'Carmen'. Jonny writes everything down in his notebook.

The Carmen provides a more accurate version of the way Harold died, a version which was hushed up in the years immediately after the Conquest. 'The Norman Court would have considered it bad press. William's close involvement in the precise way Harold was slaughtered on the battlefield would have undermined the God-given legitimacy of his accession, so the true details were suppressed, kept alive only where the influence of the ruling elite could not reach, at the lowest levels of society through songs and oral tradition.'

'The arrow in the eye was a lie, just propaganda?' Jonny whistles through his teeth. 'William had mighty good spin doctors.'

'So good, that by the time of the Domesday survey, in 1086, Harold's name was blackened, his reign wiped from the historical record. The Carmen, however, describes four knights, one of whom was William, surrounding Harold to hack him to pieces. A lance through the heart, disembowelling, one leg hacked off and decapitation.' Elsa sees Nora's grimace. 'On the battlefield, such mutilation was commonplace. The problem for William was that he took part.'

The lower border of the tapestry shows many images of decapitation, of chain mail dragged from the torsos of fallen soldiers. Edyth Swan-neck, Harold's lover, was summoned because only she would have been able to identify what was left of his body.

Nora stares down at the table. Isaac's feet were high arched, with widely spaced toes. In the hollow of his back lay a triangle of hair, just above the shallow slope of his buttocks. He used to smoke after sex, stand naked at a hotel window, inhale sharply as he glanced down to a city pavement below, his mind leaping away from her already. Back at the beginning of their relationship, the contrast between his renowned ferocity and the pale-skinned vulnerability of his narrow-hipped body had fascinated her, the thrilling intimacy of being able to watch him walk around a room, naked.

Elsa, too, has her gaze fixed once more on something outside the kitchen, beyond the dough, the rolling pin and pastry cutter in her hand. Lanterns held by whispering gravediggers. Gytha, Harold's mother, shoulders bowed under the weight of a bear fur, weeping in the dark as she watches another burial, the remains of yet another son. Scenes from the past hold Elsa's attention in a way nothing in the room can.

'With the princess's burial place, local tradition proved astonishingly accurate. Another tradition suggests the coffin made of Horsham stone is Earl Godwin's. This should not be lightly dismissed. However, the presumption has always been that "Earl Godwin" refers to the first Earl Godwin. In consequence, this long-held tradition has been disregarded, forgetting,' Elsa smiles to herself, 'forgetting that, from 1053 to 1066, Harold himself was, in fact, the *second* Earl Godwin.'

'Good God!' Jonny smacks the counter.

'The villagers at the time must have known Harold was buried here, surely?' Nora asks.

'The local gravediggers certainly, though it's probable they were made to swear an oath.' Elsa rubs more flour on to the rolling pin. 'But here's the thing about secrets. A secret is charged with the pressing urge to tell. Sharing a secret bestows a gift – and think, a secret of such magnitude! Thus secrets, information, a little changed or elaborated may pass between loved ones.'

The covering slabs of the two tombs are at more or less the same level. They could have been placed within the same gravediggers' living memory, before the floor was raised in the eleventh century.

'Cnut came to England, we know from records, in 1014,' Elsa continues. 'So, if his little girl died aged eight, as tradition says, her burial could not have been before 1022. Her tomb is under the centre of the chancel arch, in the place of honour which would otherwise have been claimed for the occupant of the more splen-did tomb, which suggests it is the earlier of the two. After the Conquest, according to Domesday, the secular estates in Bosham passed from Harold directly to King William. The fascinating point about this is,' Elsa's voice rises and she waves the rolling pin again, 'of all the estates in Sussex, these were the *only* ones William took into his possession.' She slides the first baking tray with its neat rows of raw biscuits into the oven before turning to Jonny. 'You see, my dear,' she closes the oven door with her foot, 'William wanted to ensure the grave of King Harold II did not become a shrine. Since Bosham was a naval station at the time, secrecy here would have been simple to enforce. Furthermore, the raising of the floor in the church was instigated not long after the Conquest, and successfully sealed King Harold's resting place from sight for 900 years.' Elsa's voice rings with the triumph: she has uncovered one of history's untold stories.

Jonny has turned to a new page in his Synchronicity Media notebook and written THE GODWIN GRAVE PROJECT. He underlines the words twice.

Nora and Rook doze in a deckchair in the sun. When they left Elsa's, Jonny suggested a celebratory drink in the Anchor Bleu. They arrived as Jason was outside with a blackboard and chalk, drawing a cocktail glass filled with bubbles to advertise his new champagne-by-the-glass deal.

'My man!' Jonny slapped Jason on the shoulder and sent him straight inside for some. He insisted on a bottle, though Nora drank little more than a glass. She has brought the half-full bottle home to the fridge while Jonny drives to the supermarket to buy them some bread and cheese for a picnic on the green by the church. Languid after drinking champagne at midday, Nora lies back in the deckchair, enjoying the sun on her skin. Rook is snuggled on her lap, a collapsed fluff of feathers preparing for rest, but at the sound of the side gate rattling open, his head is up, neck straining to look for an intruder.

'Hello?' Jonny calls out.

Instantly, Rook's body-shape transforms into a black origami of angled wings. His neck contorts and his claws scrape Nora's bare thighs, forcing her to stand and shovel him to the ground. Jonny steps on to the terrace – smiling, talking, gesticulating – but Rook hurtles, loose-bowelled, across the paving slabs, to high-step around Jonny's ankles, his beak jabbing forward and back in jousting thrusts.

He leaps up, clinging to Jonny's leg, claws fastened into Jonny's calf as his beak stabs Jonny's shin.

Jonny staggers backwards. 'Christ Almighty!'

Seeing the look on Jonny's face, his smile gone, Nora whips forward. Her hands grapple for Rook, whose feathers dust her skin as she misses, and he flails to the ground, wheeling sideways before straightening to shoot again towards Jonny's legs. When she finally manages to scoop the flurry of wing and claw into her arms, Rook strains to get away. He scrabbles at her arms, his body heaving so much she's frightened she'll be the one to hurt him in the battle to hold captive his writhing strength, the springy resistance in his wings as she holds them clamped against his body. Several times, he escapes her grasp. Nora turns away from Jonny, putting herself between the bird and the man, and makes her way to the kitchen, bending over Rook, clasping him to her with a hand and her forearm as he thrashes, his beak opening and closing.

When she lets him down in the kitchen, Rook hurls himself at the door, which Nora closed only just in time. Legs working furiously, wings spread, he heads for the open window instead.

'Rook, Rook.' Nora tries to soothe him with her voice, attempting to stroke his wing feathers but he won't be calmed. He's become an unfamiliar dervish of beak and claw. In the end she closes the kitchen door and leaves him there, flinging himself in silent fury against table legs and cupboard doors.

Outside, Jonny has taken off his socks and his expensive-looking leather shoes. The stitched and pointed toes are covered with grey-white lumps and splats of guano. His jeans are rolled up and he's hosing down his ankles and bare feet. Steam rises from the sun-baked paving slabs.

'Fuck, fuck, fuck,' he mutters, inspecting his calf.

When he sees Nora, his expression changes to one of astonishment, then hilarity and he starts to roar with laughter, doubling up. She looks down at herself. Her dress is covered with guano – only now she notices the weight and the damp cling against her legs. Before she can move again, water hits her, full force; behind the wide arc of water, she sees Jonny's mouth, his straight teeth as he leans back to laugh, the hose pointed in her direction as he prowls round her. In seconds, she's sluiced from the waist downwards and the temperature of the hose water has dropped from lukewarm to icy. Her dress sucks to her body. Jonny steps closer to squirt water upwards, soaking her breasts, her hair. She yelps at the breathtaking force of it against her face but springs forward, hair swinging and heavy, into the water's spout, tasting its saltiness. Her weight knocks Jonny back against the wall and she wrestles with him, determined to prise his hands from the hosepipe. Her fingers are far stronger than his. She has the hose. She tugs at his shirt and her hip catches on the jab of his belt buckle. He has stopped laughing. The drag of water has soaked them both. When he kisses her, their noses and lips are already wet.

A ROLL OF thunder growls overhead; the waiting room darkens. When Nora phoned, they said someone would come to the house but she's due to meet Eve at the hospital in half an hour so has come straight to the station to report the theft. For something to do, she stacks the polystyrene cups with their dregs of congealed tea. The fluorescent lights flicker. There is no bin.

Eventually, avoiding a chair with chewing gum stuck to the seat, she sits and massages her neck where the tendons are tender. Recently, she's been playing so much more – the Shostakovich, gutsy music, for the first time in a couple of years. Last night she'd tackled properly the opening phrase of the Elgar, its sliding depth, the lingering adagio, a listening pause as the sound fades to vibration – she played the phrase over and over again until it was better. Not right, yet, but better. Good enough to let her play beyond the hollow spaces, to be caught up with the pumping muscle and blood of the sonata. She's not sure how long she'd been playing, down in the quiet of the cellar, when she finally lifted her cheek from the cello's neck, exhausted. When she woke late this morning, Ada had already left the house.

She rubs at a healing patch of eczema on her palm and checks her watch again. Twenty minutes. She's arranged to meet Eve at the entrance to the maternity hospital. The officer behind the glass still has his head down, apparently busy, although the waiting room is empty. She tries to recall any extra details which might be useful.

She had been eating her porridge on her lap in the kitchen, had sprinkled more raisins on top and given some to Rook, who fluffed his feathers at her feet and began to groom. When the door banged, the sound echoed through the house like a shot. She leaped up and her bowl shattered on the floor. Rook stretched his beak wide in protest, wings flapping wildly, as porridge landed in splats around him. Her body too, had reacted with fear and she stood, frozen until the ricochet of panic died away. Rook was absorbed with helping himself to the spilled raisins and hiding them under the doormat.

In the sitting room, the French doors were half-open, the bolt of the lock shot across and banging on the frame as the door swayed in a rising wind. Had someone come in, or had someone just left? Ada was helping at one of Daphne's fundraising coffee mornings and there was no sign of Harry, the terrace and the garden both quiet and deserted. An anvil-headed storm cloud was building on the horizon. She locked the French doors and mopped up porridge splatters. Roy, the milkman, knocked and she went to pay him. Her bag was not hanging on the end of the banister in the hallway where she'd left it, so she searched the coat hooks, her bedside table,

she was a child, the family had many picnics here, her parents spreading the tartan rug in a hollow. Flick, eight years older, would play the big sister and take her hand to lead her off to hide in the dunes. They were allowed to take their sandwiches with them on their explorations. Time stretched with the retreating tide, the sea far off. When she crouched in a dip in between the dunes, the distant, outside-world roar of the wind and waves disappeared, leaving only the sound of her breathing, the bristly whipping of marram grass. She'd hold her breath to listen for the scuff of sand grains as they fell.

Today, sand lifts from the dune tops like spume from sea-swell and builds in drifts against the beach-hut doors. Her back teeth grind on grit. She sees her father, as she almost always does when he first comes to mind, in a trench, a hat shading his head and neck. The 'V' point of the trowel; his fingertips brushing off dirt, the neat half-moons of his nails. The landscape which surrounds him is brown and barren, a desert, somewhere she has never been except in imagination.

She knows very little about how her father died but after years of imagining, this desert place is familiar. Sometimes she dreams about the tunnel, hot and airless, dust in her mouth and nose and eyes. Her mind can conjure up all this, the tunnel's dryness suffocating, but she can't see her father's face. He reads a story to her, his mouth moving; his Adam's apple slides. His reading glasses with the broken frame are propped crooked on the bridge of his nose. Out in the garage, an eyeglass in one eye, a cocktail stick rolling between his teeth as he lined up cogs and wheels from the clocks he enjoyed mending.

Nora would like to ask her father if what drew him to archaeology was his preoccupation with time, and whether it is from him she inherited her own strong and natural sense of rhythm, her body's instinctive feel for time. She'd like to talk to him about the way the passing of time changes what we once believed to be truth or fact into something previously unknown. She minds that she never had these adult conversations with him, but knew him only in the way a child conceives of a parent.

Sometimes Nora tries to gather the details of the accident from what little she knows to create a narrative, but in her mind the story caves in on itself. The earth cracking, a rumble as the tunnel begins to collapse: these elements repeat again and again. She wonders if Ada does the same. She has always been vague. All she has ever said is that they were all killed, the four of them in the underground vault or tunnel or tomb, so there can be no one who really knows what happened or what it was like. No way of knowing, she told Flick and Nora at the time, nothing to know, except they are all dead. *His life is insured. We'll be all right.*

Nora hopes her mother had someone to talk to. There was no funeral, because no bodies were found. Without him, their family began to separate into parts, like the cogs and wheels from her father's broken clocks. A memorial service was held, about which the girls were not told until years later. Flick was at university and Nora stopped coming home from boarding school at weekends. She was never good at phoning or writing. Seeing how much Ada enjoys Flick's weekly phone calls from Spain, she feels guilty about that now.

Ada saw plenty of different men, it seemed, after her father's death, but no one moved in. Her mother has lived without a man for more than twenty years. Like Elsa Macleod.

She should have come out running sooner. Day by day, week by week, her body is becoming stronger. Her feet pound the coarse grass of the Greensward, a steady rhythm.

PARTICLES OF ROSIN float like dust from the bow into the air. Nora's pupil is blonde. A strand of her hair is trapped on the frog and, as she bows, it bounces in the sunlight. She is about eight, Nora thinks, her mind immediately sailing off to Bosham, the millstream and the little stone church by the water. Later, she and Jonny are going to visit the vicar and talk about the Godwin Graves Project.

She has chewed on her pencil, the end splitting into soggy splinters. She can taste the lead. Cross with herself for not concentrating, Nora shoves the pencil into her hair and puts a hand to the child's wrist to stop her playing. She draws her own cello between her legs, slips off her shoes, leans into the neck. A sinewy hum vibrates through her ribcage as she draws the bow across the strings in a long, firm stroke, but she resists the instrument's lure.

'OK. Your left hand is a dancer. Make it strong and flexible. Curve your fingers as if you're holding a tennis ball.' Nora raises her left hand to demonstrate. 'Now, play with the tips.'

The girl flips her blonde plait over her shoulder and bends, breathing noisily, as if she has a cold, to her left hand, which rests, fingers flat, knuckles collapsed. Her expression is fixed, obedient.

'I don't mean all the time. Just give it a try. OK. Good. Five minutes a day?'

Nora takes the child's cello by the neck. Does she really care so little about her pupils that she can't remember their names?

'Now, remember The Squid? Show me, can you?'

At the vicarage, nobody answers the front door bell.

Jonny examines the cast-iron surround, runs his finger over the ceramic button with 'PUSH' inscribed in cursive script. 'Does this thing work?' He presses the button a second time, holding it down. A clang echoes through the house.

The village is suspended in mid-afternoon heat. From the wheat fields beyond the vicarage comes the rumble of a combine harvester. Nora wonders if she can persuade Jonny to make time for a swim, to run into the sea with her and sluice off the tiny thunder-bugs she has been brushing from her arms and neck all day, but in weather like this she knows the queue for the car park at West Wittering will stretch for miles, and he has squeezed in this trip to Bosham before an early evening meeting in London.

She wanders back up the front path to stand under a weeping willow while Jonny paces around the side of the house. He peers in the windows, face pressed to the glass. When he joins her under the tree, he slips his mobile phone in and out of its black leather case several times to check the time.

They're here to talk to Steve about the Godwin Graves Project. Jonny phoned Creek House a few evenings ago to say he'd heard from someone at University College London about the DNA comparison. He spoke fast, in breathy-half sentences and the mobile reception was poor, with chatter and the scrape of chairs in the background, so his words were indistinct. Nora found the detail hard to follow.

'He needs a piece of bone weighing one gram, but he has the techniques, he can do it.'

'Who is he?'

'A pioneer in his field, which is the integration of modern and DNA data with archaeological information, so perfect for our needs. He says it is entirely possible to extract DNA, even from such ancient material, and to compare Y-chromosomes with those from living descendants, as well as from Earl Godwin. You'll have to read his email. It's all there. Bloody exciting.'

'What about the fact they've already been exposed to the air, the bones? And been handled without gloves?'

'It's his area of expertise, human genetic variation – ancestry, population evolution, that kind of thing. Old school mate of mine put me on to him. He can deal with all that side. He's pretty confident we'll discover the truth.'

Jonny made it sound very simple. Mouth swab kits would be supplied for collecting DNA samples, which could be sent and returned by post, and analysed within six to eight weeks. Nora explained about the complications associated with getting permission to exhume the grave, but Jonny didn't seem worried.

'We need to jump through a few hoops – so what? It shouldn't be too much of a problem to get Steve on our side. Churches always need money, don't they?'

Nora had been the go-between. To find a time convenient to both Jonny and Steve had been the first problem, necessitating a number of phone calls back and forth, but she's flattered Jonny is keen for her to come along.

Jonny slips out his phone yet again just as Steve arrives at last, arms stretched with bags of shopping and his daughter Frannie in tow.

'Sorry,' he says, fishing in his leather shoulder bag for the key. 'The childminder's off sick so it's been the supermarket and Mums and Toddlers today, hasn't it, Frannie?'

Frannie's mouth hangs open. She slides in her thumb and hides behind her father's leg, dimpled fingers stretching around his knee. The two men set off down the front path, with Frannie swinging on Steve's arm.

Jonny exclaims about the heat and slips off his jacket, describing his dash from London office to train.

'Train rides are spoiled for me by the air conditioning,' Steve says. 'And mobile phones. So different from when I was a child. I used to love those long train journeys down to the West Country.'

Jonny slings his jacket over one shoulder. His red cufflinks are shaped like scarab beetles and he's dressed very formally compared to Steve, in dark grey trousers, charcoal-grey button-down collared shirt and a silk tie patterned with bright wriggles of red, which make Nora think of tadpoles, or sperm. She should probably go back on the pill.

As Steve unlocks the front door, she hears Jonny ask him about his wife, and where she works. He's drawn the wrong conclusions from Steve's mention of a childminder. Nora had assumed Jonny knew already about the family dynamics at the vicarage.

'Frannie,' Steve says, swinging his daughter between his legs, up and over the front-door step and into the hall, 'shall you and me make a cup of tea for our visitors?'

The child nods and disappears through a doorway into a large front room where the floor is strewn with brightly coloured toys.

'I'll finish unloading the car later. Kitchen's this way,' Steve says, with a jerk of his thumb.

'My wife left,' he adds over his shoulder. Jonny looks back at Nora and mimes zipping his mouth.

'I'm—'

'Don't worry.' Steve holds up a hand to stop him. 'Easily done and I won't bore you with divorce statistics, which is what I used to do. Vicars and their wives are, it seems, refreshingly human. As well as Frannie, I have two sons, five and seven. Just about manageable now that they're both at school.'

Steve fills the kettle and reaches into a cupboard for teabags and three Cath Kidston mugs, which surely must have been bought by the restless vicar's wife before she left. Jonny swings his jacket over the back of a kitchen chair and lounges against a worktop, cracking his knuckles.

When Nora explains why they are here, and the change of plan for the TV project, Steve runs his sea-glass pebble to and fro along the thong around his neck before he answers. 'Well.' His thumb rubs the lump of clouded glass.

He's going to say no. No exhumation, no DNA testing. No project and no more trips down here for Jonny. Nora holds her breath. Jonny leans forward, studying Steve's expression.

Finally Steve looks up. 'It's more complicated than with your first project. *Much* more is involved.'

'Yeah-yeah-yeah.' Jonny nods. 'This is a one-off, Steve. Already created a great deal of interest among specialists in church archaeology, many of whom will want to roll up their sleeves and get involved. It's unique, a programme which will shed light on history and mysteries reaching one thousand years into England's past.'

'All sorts of people will need to have a say on the matter.'

'Rightly so. It will be a substantial historical programme.'

They discover Elsa Macleod talked to Steve about her ideas months ago. He had known of her theory before Nora, and read through a draft of her pamphlet before it was published. He aims to have it on sale in the church.

'Of course, some would say a conclusion that the grave is *not* Harold II's might be almost as valuable,' Steve adds. 'Some parishioners aren't keen on the church as a tourist attraction.'

'The situation and the coffined nature of the burial both indicate high status. Bosham would have been a much more practical place for Harold's burial after the Battle of Hastings than Waltham, which is the only other real contender. Waltham would have been difficult to access.'

Steve holds up his hand. 'I know, I know. You don't need to persuade me of all the probabilities, Jon, Elsa has already spent several evenings convincing me. However, before we so much as lift a trowel in the church, permission must be sought. There will be objections, naturally, to the interruption, the intrusion for regular churchgoers.'

Frannie edges into the kitchen, carrying two plastic teacups on saucers, but when she sees their mugs of tea on the kitchen table, she bites her bottom lip. Steve sweeps her up off the floor and holds her high in the air, throws her up and catches her. Soon she is giggling wildly. He goes to the sink with her on one hip and fills a washing-up bowl with water.

'We need some water for tea, don't we, Frannie?'

He disappears from the room, Frannie still on one hip, and they return with the plastic teapot and two more cups with saucers. 'Enough for one each.' He winks at Nora.

He lifts the washing-up bowl on to the floor, sits down beside it and offers the teapot to Frannie. She plunges the teapot under the water.

'I have an idea,' says Steve.

He tells them a recent five-yearly inspection of the church has shown up some pews with woodworm, and an area of the Victorian floorboards which is rotten, all of which will need to be replaced. Coincidentally, the rotten floorboards are very close to the position of the tomb. It would be possible to argue that the excavation of the tomb will cause very little extra disturbance. The next meeting of the parochial church council is in a week's time. Steve will raise the matter then, and let Jonny know of the outcome as soon as possible.

'Just one question, which I know will be asked of me at the PCC meeting,' Steve says, as they leave. 'The costs, all these experts, the technology . . .'

'Costs will all be met by us, our company, absolutely everything. Please assure everyone of that fact, Steve.'

'Where does the money come from?' Nora asks, once they have left the vicarage and are walking through the village.

'We'll have the funding squared away in no time, don't worry. Once the proposal's written.' Jonny grins and takes hold of her shoulders to kiss her. 'The discovery of the burial place of Harold II, our last Anglo-Saxon king – they'll be falling over themselves to snap up this one, no shadow of a doubt. They can't possibly turn this one down.'

AS HE STEPPED on to the train they had exchanged brief promises to phone each other, but for some reason Nora can't settle once she gets home from dropping Jonny at the station. She walks to the church to light a votive candle and on the way back to Creek House, stops off at the post office for milk. With the milk pressed against her belly, she dawdles along the lane, her hands linked around the carton. She tries to imagine holding Eve's baby in her arms. She might be able to, although at one time she couldn't even look at a baby without seeing her own.

Down by the mossy base of the wall is a purple wide-toothed comb with gaps where the teeth have snapped off: her comb. Her lip salve lies where the tarmac dips to the drain. She pockets both items just as Stavros, shrugging on a cracked leather jacket in the doorway of their cottage, yells, 'Nora! Is yours?' He waves a bundle of frayed denim, her shoulder bag.

'I thought I was losing my marbles. Where was it?'

'It is by bins in car park but,' he points inside the bag and pulls an exaggerated moue, raising his hands, 'is now ninety-nine percent empty, only cheque book.'

Nora peers into the ink-stained bag, her throat tight. Stavros puts an arm across her shoulders. He smells of Eve's patchouli oil and his dark-lashed eyes are full of concern. 'Someone take? You hurt?'

She shakes her head. 'It was the other day. There's nothing else?' Her voice trembles. She'll have to check the ground by the recycling bins.

'Money? Cards? You want me phone people?'

She shakes her head again.

Benjie's whines grow to a crescendo and he yaps once, high and sharp. He glances up at Stavros, down along the lane and back up at Stavros, who tugs once on the leash and looks severe. The dog's tongue flicks over his lips, but he sits quietly, panting.

'The lessons are working?'

'Very fine.' Stavros gives a thumbs-up.

Nora turns the denim bag inside out and shakes. A few hair grips fall to the ground. She unzips each pocket and pulls out the linings, peels open the crinkled, in-folded corners filled with crumbs and dust, but Isaac's photograph has gone.

'At Café Jetsam I have made cheese pies,' Stavros says. 'Good for the hips.' He slaps his own skinny thighs and grins. 'You want some?'

Nora has nothing else planned so she walks with Stavros to the boathouse. Harry has been helping to sand down the double doors ready to paint and he's in the kitchen talking to Eve about the significance of the black bird on the memorial stone in the church.

'Just a white silk banner, plain white.' Harry's fingers make a *scritch scritch* noise on his chin. 'According to the legend the black raven only appeared in times of war. If the Danes were going to win, the raven appeared, beak open.' Harry lifts his arms and spreads them wide in the narrow kitchen. 'Wings flapping, jumping about like crazy.'

Like the bird etched on the memorial tile. And just like Rook whenever Jonny is nearby. Nora has to shut him in the kitchen if she's expecting Jonny to visit.

'If the raven appeared on the banner and didn't move,' Harry adds, 'it meant a Danish defeat.'

The four of them eat the cheese pies out on the wooden balcony of the boathouse. It's very hot. The creek slides below and the skin on Nora's face tightens with sunburn.

Harry plays with Stavros's string of worry beads as he tells them about the Danish god of war, Odin. He had two ravens, Hugin and Munnin – mind and memory – who sat one on each shoulder. It turns out the bird on the memorial for Cnut's daughter is a raven, not a rook, despite the startling similarities to Rook when he was a starveling. A symbol of war seems to Nora an odd choice to mark the tomb of a child, but the tile was placed 900 years after the princess died, by which time no one remembered the little girl herself, only her father, the warrior king who lives on in the stories told centuries after his death.

'If the child's tomb is not, after all, Cnut's daughter,' Harry says, 'will Elsa's theory still stand?'

Nora looks at him in surprise. She had no idea he even knew Elsa. 'Why?'

Harry flicks the string of black beads up. They fall with a click-click-click before he deftly catches them. 'I've been reading about the stone effigy.'

In the north wall of the chancel is a canopied recessed tomb on which lies the damaged stone effigy of a girl with a lion at her feet. At some point in the past her body has been broken in two and repaired. The effigy is unnamed, but believed to have been carved in the late thirteenth century as a memorial to Cnut's daughter. Nora has often stroked her head, the outline of hair in a simple style which frames what remains of the girl's face. Though the arch of an eyebrow and the bridge of her nose are still visible, her mouth and most of her lower face have been worn away by time, or the stroke of hands like Nora's.

'Does it make any difference now we know the effigy was not *made* in the eleventh century?' Nora says, following her own train of thought. 'If that's what you're talking about. It's crazy to use that as an argument against Cnut's daughter being buried in the church, surely?' Nora snatches Harry's plate from where it is balanced on the arm of his seat. 'Have you finished with this plate?'

'Yes.'

'It doesn't mean she wasn't carved as a memorial at a later stage, does it?'

'No.' Harry closes his hand around the worry beads and looks steadily at Nora. 'No, it doesn't.'

'She's been moved around. It's said she originally lay on a tomb which stood on the exact spot where the coffin was discovered, did you read that anywhere, in any of your books or papers?' She carries the plates indoors, glad to be out of the sun's glare.

Later, Harry had made them smoothies. He piled fruit from Eve and Stavros's fridge on to the counter: peaches, blueberries, mango and blood oranges, and began peeling and stoning fruit, his back to Nora, his hands, broad across the knuckles, thorough and slow.

'Here,' he said, throwing her an orange, which she caught. A mango, a peach – her mouth watered at the smell of them. Peaches: her mother's favourite fruit. She used to freeze them, years ago, buying wooden cratefuls heaped with them at the market when peaches were cheap and in season. A scented sweetness filled the house as Ada peeled and cut the peaches into slices, which she covered with home-made syrup before freezing. Nora preferred the taste of defrosted peaches to fresh ones.

Nora cradled the collection of fruits. Each had a different weight, texture, colour, shape. She held them up one by one, testing the weight and substance, then began to juggle, the technique coming back to her. She'd learned as a teenager, taught by a boyfriend. Orange, peach and mango: different shapes and colours flying through the air, between her hands.

The liquidiser's rattle was gritty and loud. Harry poured the smoothie, deep red, into two glasses, adding fresh black cherries on a cocktail umbrella. Nora was thirsty. She gulped down the delicious, icy concoction.

The two of them stood in the narrow space between work counters as Harry refilled her glass, and filled another glass for her to take out to Eve. His hand passed, quickly, down over his own face before brushing hers lightly, lifting her chin to inspect it, running his thumb across the edges of her mouth.

'Juice,' he said, and paused, before kissing her, not on her lips, but either side and below her mouth. The sudden shock of his body against hers made her start, pulling sharply away. She snatched up her drink and the glass for Eve, raised the glass in thanks, without meeting his eyes, and hurried back outside into the sunshine to join the others.

NORA IS WORRIED the cockle-shell heart will break. She puts down the drill. The rotten wood of the wind chimes she has already replaced with freshly collected sticks of driftwood and she's added swan feathers to the assortment of pebbles. The cockle-shell heart would finish the whole thing off perfectly. Nora turns the shell over in her hands, opening and closing the two halves. Rook hops towards her feet and stops. He thinks she has food. He hops again, trying to get her attention, head twitching this way and that, tilted to one side, to examine her face from various angles. Only on the ground do rooks become awkward and jerky; in the air they soar and swoop and glide.

'One day, Rook,' she says to him, 'you will be able to fly.'

The spines of the cockle shell are fierce; the fragility lies in the brittle hinge which joins the two halves. She places the shell on the fireplace beside her axe-head, where it's more likely to remain whole.

Once she's tied the final knot in the string, she holds the mobile up to check the hang is balanced. She will tie it to the same branch, the branch which already has string wrapped round it in various places from previous wind chimes. She's used tarred string this time, so perhaps it will last longer. She knocks one of the pebbles with a finger and watches the mobile spin and bob.

'I had a baby once.'

At her feet, Rook blinks, twitches his head to see her face.

Nora shuts her eyes against an image she doesn't want to remember, her baby's limbs swaddled close to his body. She had kissed his forehead to say goodbye. She sits down on the floor beside Rook.

'I had a baby once,' she tells him again.

The feathers on Rook's head rise and he stretches his neck towards her.

'I called him Noah.'

She called him Noah because, as a child, she loved the story of Noah and his ark, a round boat built against all odds. Her father told her the story of the ark illustrated the triumph of imagination over catastrophic events. She also called him Noah because the name sounded so close to her own. Names do have a certain magic, as Eve says. Noah, with his too-thin limbs, ribs which pressed through his skin. He was so tiny and fragile she couldn't bear to be separated from him, to leave him alone in her room for longer than half an hour at a time. Her breasts were painful and heavy with milk, a constant reminder. She found excuses to go to him, tried not to disturb his miniature fingers, his curled toes and soft nails which peeled like skin. She trembled each time she unwrapped him to marvel at the translucency of his skin. She loved the dark hair stuck flat on his pomegranate-sized head; his old man's neck. She lay with him in the crook of her elbow for hours as she studied his body, his eyelids and the wrinkles of his face. He was going to be safe and loved. Every night, she kept him close beside her on the pillow.

In Mothercare she'd seen mobiles for hanging over a baby's cot; wind-up toys; a music box to attach to the bars. Though she hadn't bought a cot for Noah, on the last night they had together she made him some wind chimes. She swaddled him well and carried him down the garden to hang the chimes on the apple tree where the forget-me-nots which reseeded every year spread a haze of starry blue.

In the hallway, the phone rings. Nora carries the repaired wind chimes downstairs, Rook sitting on her shoulder.

'Who is he then, this man Mum's always talking about?' It's Flick.

'Hello, Flick. I'm well thanks, how are you?' Nora transfers Rook from her shoulder to her hand. His feathers brush skin as he hops on to the floor to run, stiff-legged and tail up, in to the kitchen.

'Too bloody hot! We're thinking of coming over to England to escape.'

'Great. Mum will be pleased.' Nora leans against the wall, cool against her back. 'All of you?'

'There's plenty of room for us all in that great mausoleum of a place. Mum wants to sell up, you know. Move into a bungalow near the shops. I think we should encourage her. This man hanging around, he after her money?'

A knot forms and tightens below Nora's ribs. She slides down the wall until she's sitting on the hall floor. 'It's *her* money.'

'And it's *our* inheritance. We don't want her marrying some man who has flattered his way into her affections.'

'She's not dead yet, Flick. She may leave her money to the Cat and Rabbit Rescue Centre. She wants to move into a bungalow, or you want her to move into a bungalow? I don't think—'

'It's not all about you, Nora, I have enough on my plate without ...' and so the conversation with Flick continues. Whenever Nora tries to say something, Flick snaps, 'Please don't interrupt. Let me finish a sentence.'

By the time the phone call has ended, Nora needs somewhere to lie down. The way she would before a concert, to steady her mind and body, to prepare for the intensity of concentration required in performance. An empty room in an expensive hotel, sealed off from the outside world by triple glazing. A jug of water on the bedside cabinet.

You must be spiritually prepared for each encounter with the Bach Suites, Isaac said. Once he had made a student walk on to the stage seven times before allowing him to play. *You must carry with you the inner sensation that inhabits the music you are about to perform.*

She stands up, takes a breath and walks down the hallway, holding the wind chimes. Oh yes, Isaac had plenty of advice when it came to cello instruction, but absolutely no advice to offer when it came to having his baby. His only answer was money.

The kitchen is hot, airless. A note, from Ada, is stuck under the kettle, on the back of a telephone bill. *Why are there no cigarettes in the house?* it demands. Nora doesn't know how she missed the note this morning. *Pay Harry.* Sweat trickles down her back. She pushes open a window and hears something, a grunt. Harry is down near the old apple tree, smashing a pickaxe into the flinty ground. A spade is propped against the gnarled trunk, his shirt hanging from it. Dropping Ada's note she runs out, shouting his name. The sight of dug earth in that place brings a scorch of pain.

'What on earth are you doing?'

He swings around, breathing hard. Sweat has dampened the hair on his chest into whorls. 'Your mother . . .' He rests the metal head of the pickaxe on the ground. 'Wants a vegetable patch.'

'A *vegetable* patch?' Nora snatches up the spade. Harry's shirt drops to the ground. 'It will be far too much work for her. And here—'

Harry allows the pickaxe handle to fall sideways. He picks up a six-litre plastic milk bottle half-filled with water, and unscrews the lid, a tremor in his hand.

'You're dehydrated. You drink too much. And you shouldn't encourage my mother to drink all the time either.' Mid-sentence Nora realises Harry is the man Flick was talking about on the phone: Harry, after her mother's money. 'My mother is an elderly woman. It's irresponsible.'

If she releases her grip on the spade handle, her own hands will be shaking.

Harry tips back his head to drink. Water spills from his mouth and trickles down his neck as he pours water from the plastic container down his throat.

'She'd been drinking with you the night before the boat accident, hadn't she? She could hardly put one foot in front of the other the next morning.' The words come spewing out. Overwhelmed by the smell of dug earth, the sight of nodules of chalk and flint mixed in with the disturbed soil, she hears what she's saying, accusation in her words, but the anger in her is unleashed. On the ground between them lies the pickaxe. She takes a step towards it.

Harry puts the water bottle down, picks up his shirt from the ground and begins to do up the buttons.

'She could have drowned that day. She was so unsteady. People drink too much and accidents happen.'

Harry has stooped down for the pickaxe. 'Your mother,' he says, as he offers her the wooden handle, 'makes up her own mind.'

She carried the pickaxe and spade back up the garden, put both away in the shed and found herself back in the kitchen. She shut the back door and leaned against it. On the draining board, spread like flotsam, lay her mobile, a jumble of string and sticks, pebbles and feathers.

AUGUST

THE ANCHORING WEIGHT of the book is a comfort to Ada when she wakes to find herself cradled in the deckchair under the green shade of the macrocarpa at the bottom of the garden. She cannot remember how she came to be here, or for how long she has slept. Her tongue is dry and stuck to her throat. The hardback is one of Brian's history tomes, pages like cardboard and most of the sentences just as stiff. Reading Brian's books, she can hear the quiet persistence of his voice, the way he smothered with a blanket of academic language the fire of his enthusiasm, his eyes round like a child's behind the thick glass of his spectacles. Mild as milk, was most people's impression, yet how wrong about him, in the end, even she had been.

She is sleeping very badly. Up in the early hours and wide awake with no one to distract her, she drapes herself in doorways to revisit scenes and conversations, longing for past company in the empty rooms. The dents in the horsehair seat of the sofa, the threadbare tapestry of the carpet in front of the fireplace – these things remind her so vividly of the people who were once here, in Creek House, she sees them again, smoking or clattering cutlery together on a plate or sipping at a glass of sherry. Sometimes Nora is up early too, but she'll have donned those ill-fitting shorts and be tying the laces on her plimsolls ready to go off out running.

From the house comes the slam of kitchen cupboard doors: Nora home from the supermarket, unloading carrier bags and filling cupboards. Ada closes her eyes and leans back under the tasselled deckchair canopy. In her thirst, she imagines peaches in one of Nora's ghastly orange supermarket carriers, the bag bulging with juicy fruit, downy skin slipping from ripeness. Ada rests her cheek on her hand. How heavenly it would be to sit on the terrace sipping a Bellini as the day cools: the delicate taste of peach juice, its sticky remnants of sweetness on her lips.

Harry promised to make her peach Bellinis. Was that today? It could have been one of those nebulous promises certain men habitually make to women, but she doesn't have Harry down as that sort, though he is hard to tie to fixed arrangements, dates and times. He hasn't come to work on her vegetable patch today, or the day before. Where has he got to?

In the kitchen, Nora is banging tins. She's emptied the wall cupboard of its contents and is placing newly bought tins right at the back, turning each so the label faces outwards. As usual, she's humming some baleful cello piece or another. She'd do well to choose a gayer tune, something with more of a trill to lift the spirits but she does have a tendency to hum in this manner, screwing up her face, dropping her head, to reach the low notes. Something she's done since childhood, chin squashed and folded into her neck. Not an attractive habit.

Ada drops Brian's book on to the table with a thud. 'Darling, shall I put on Radio 3? For a little music?'

Nora stops humming. She pauses for a moment in her busyness with the tins to look at Ada and shake her head, but then she continues, arranging each with more precision, a twitch of her wrist to straighten the Heinz Skinned Tomatoes. Ada tweaks open a shopping bag and peers inside.

'Won't bite, Mum. That bag's for the fridge.' Nora glances at her wristwatch. 'I could do with a hand. I've got a lesson in less than half an hour.'

Ada's insides pinch with irritation. She'll be left to her own devices again just when she was looking forward to a prolonged conversation over supper. She closes the bag, smoothing it over corners and edges which poke through the thin plastic; nothing with the succulence of fruit. She sighs. These cartons of egg and milk she doesn't want to touch.

'Surely you don't have to turn out again, when it looks like rain.' Nora lines up tins of kidney beans. 'You poor dear.'

Nora leans across the draining board towards the window. Outside, the sky is blue. She lifts a hand to her forehead in an exaggerated mime of a sailor searching the sky. 'Not a cloud in sight, Mum.' Their eyes meet. 'I'll only be half an hour or so. I'll cook when I get back.'

'Oh, no need to fuss.' Ada's fingers find the nub of her locket, warm from her skin and the sun. She slides it up and down the gold chain. 'So much food, Nora! Do we live in daily expectation the government will again order rationing? Is a strike predicted?'

'Flick's coming next week with the girls, remember?'

Ada had forgotten it was next week. Time stretches and pings back, like one of those tiny rubber balls. 'Of course. Only just now I was thinking we shall need to air the beds.'

'Why Flick can't make up her own bed when she comes to stay, heaven only knows, she's no more of a visitor than I am. One of Dad's books?'

Ada puts her hand on the book which lies on the kitchen table. This is the conversation she wanted to have, a conversation about Brian's book. She sighs again. Nora glances over her shoulder.

'You've been in the sun too much, Mum.'

'Are you referring to the course of my entire lifetime?'

Nora half-smiles but turns away, her head back in the cupboards. Jars: marmalade and honey – the glass clinking. She is no longer humming but her arms fly between bag and shelf. Always has been hectic, that child.

Ada has been reading old Sussex words listed in one of the appendices of Brian's book. Old Sussex words for mud: *cledgy; sleech; slommocky*. She mouths the *sl* and *bl* of them, shaping her tongue and lips around their texture. *Stabble* means to walk thick mud into the house. She likes the squelch and spread of the word, its peaks and smears. A memory surfaces: Nora at about four, squatting by a tin of gloss paint, her hair like thistledown. Nora plunged her arm into the paint tin right up to the elbow, an expression of total absorption – bliss – on her face. Now, Ada's arrival in the kitchen has put an end to her daughter's humming and, chill as sea mist, a mood rolls off Nora, seeping through the sunny kitchen. She wedges the twelve-pack of toilet tissue high up on the top shelf.

Ada clicks her tongue. 'Oh that's impossibly high! Can't they go in the lavatory, the spare rolls, where they always used to be kept?'

'What about here?' Nora says, and pushes the pack into the cupboard under the sink. The door won't close.

'You don't want me tumbling off a stool and doing myself an injury when you're out at work, now do you?' Ada smoothes the hair over her ears.

Nora takes a knife and stabs open the packet of toilet rolls. 'Mum, will you tell me what's going on with the garden?'

'The garden?'

'Harry said . . .'

'An unkempt garden devalues the house.'

Nora stands with a toilet roll in each hand. 'You're having the house valued?'

She has an expression on her face Ada recognises; the expression she wore when she came home that spring, all skin and bone; a tight look. Not quite a frown.

'You're getting too thin again. It's all that running.'

Never did get to the bottom of it, giving away that priceless instrument, coming home to shut herself in her room.

Nora bites her lip. Her face droops as if she will cry. 'You are going to sell Creek House?'

'Who knows?'

Nora says nothing. She turns away to squeeze the toilet rolls into the cupboard. They will be squashed out of shape.

'Creek House is far too big for one person.' She should make reparations. The urge is strong to put out her hand, to get Nora to refrain from her frantic motion, but at that moment the bird comes hop-stopping into the room like one of those clockwork birds one used to buy. At least this one makes no noise. He jumps with a flutter on to Nora's shoulder and then down again to peck at a roll of toilet tissue.

Ada purses her lips. She runs her fingertip along the dry skin. Too much of her body is dry, these days. She puts the thought from her. Upstairs is the new coral lipstick she treated herself to, an expensive brand in a showy gold case. A smooth twist and the moist colour will emerge. She shouldn't have, not really. Money doesn't go far these days. Creek House would raise a tidy sum, without a doubt.

Nora has her head in the cupboard.

'Roger is going to pop round to see what he thinks.'

The bird pulls a length of toilet tissue out across the floor and proceeds to shred the paper into strips.

'Can't you stop it doing that?'

Nora pulls her head out of the cupboard to reply, but both women turn towards the sound of whistling outside. The handle of the back door rattles. It's Harry, rapping a belated *rata-tat-tat* even as he opens the door wide and steps into the room. He beams at them both. A powerfully built man, one who gives full attention to everything a woman has to say, and remembers.

Ada swivels her legs to one side and crosses her ankles, drapes her arm over the back of her chair and smiles back. 'Harry!'

She is delighted to see him but Nora is fussing, twisting her hair up into a loose bun and fumbling for a pencil from the pen-pot which she will shove through her hair to hold it in place and proceed to pull out five minutes later, only to begin the process all over again.

'Greetings!' Harry looks wonderfully cheery today. He's caught the sun and is ruddy with health. Even better, in one bear-like paw he grips two bottles of dry Prosecco, in the other, a bulging and slightly soggy paper bag. Nora appears to be barring his way.

Ada makes a show of stretching out her arm and turning her wrist to the light to check the time. 'Aren't you just on your way out, dear?'

'Yes, Harry. Bad timing I'm afraid. I'm just off out teaching.' Nora has picked up her cello and with it she obstructs Harry's entrance. They look at each other and something passes unspoken between them. Harry's expression drops from cheerful to crestfallen.

'I've brought cherries for Rook,' he says. 'Peaches to make Bellinis for your mother.'

Seeing Nora's jaw grow firm, Ada clears her throat and draws herself up. She rests her chin on her clasped hands. 'Oh Nora, for heaven's sake give the poor man some space and make way for him to come in.' She arches one eyebrow for Harry's benefit.

Nora bangs out through the back door with her cello and is gone.

'IT'S INTOLERABLE. A television programme will encourage the hordes to the village.' Daphne Johnson's voice has a strident edge, announcing her views to the entire post office rather than Nora and Steve, who are in the queue beside her. In front of them a group of children fight over which penny sweets to buy from the jars on the shelves behind the counter.

'Litter everywhere, chewing gum on the pavements, queues in the shops.' Daphne nudges Nora's arm to get her attention. 'I hear from Ada he's called several times, the television man, especially to consult her, because of your late father's work.'

Daphne makes Jonny sound like an alien. *The Television Man.* Nora nods and half-smiles, sucking sticky raspberry juice from her fingers so that she doesn't have to reply. She has no desire to have the detail of Jonny's project winkled from her by Daphne's probing tongue; there are other things on her mind. She holds up the punnets of raspberries and checks the bottom of the containers, where red juice oozes from holes punched in the plastic.

The parish council has unanimously agreed to put forward a request to the bishop for permission to exhume what they are calling the 'Godwin Grave'. If the Saxon princess story is shelved in favour of the discovery of Harold II's burial place, Elsa Macleod will take centre stage in Ada's place. Ada is furious with Nora. Daphne obviously doesn't know any of this yet.

Steve's eyes are red and swollen, his fair hair sticking up at the back as if he's just rolled out of bed, late for everything. 'My feeling is, Daphne, in this village we are lucky enough to have a church of great romantic beauty and steeped in history. There's much to be said for sharing that richness with others.' He glances at his wristwatch.

'I can get these bits if you need to be elsewhere,' Nora says, nodding at his basket of groceries. 'I'm in no hurry, just on my way home.'

'Thanks, Nora. I'm fine for time, just keeping track.' Steve rubs his nose between his eyes. 'Hay fever,' he says, seeing her look. 'Comes on when everyone else has stopped suffering.'

'They're harvesting the peas. Frightful black dust.' Daphne wrinkles her nose in distaste, but doesn't allow herself to get sidetracked. 'I hear the television people want to dig up the body, take it away and film the entire process. Surely that won't be allowed, Vicar?'

'As yet, we don't know. Respect for human sanctity and the consecrated church will be a prime concern, but we will remain open-minded about scholarly research.'

From the foreshore echo the chimes of Giovanni's ice-cream van: Camptown Races, high-pitched and fast. Heads turn as one towards the doorway of the post office, where there's nothing to be seen except sunlight on the purple velvet of the petunias in Eve's courtyard garden across the road.

Daphne purses her lips. 'It's that Spaniard.'

The veiled racism makes Nora snappy. 'Which *Spaniard*, Daphne?'

Ada glides past the doorway, holding Zach's hand, pointing back down the road to something out of sight. Benjie trots by with his lead dragging along the tarmac. Nora piles her raspberries on top of the nearby stack of Coca-Cola cans. 'Sorry!' she says, and squeezes past Daphne.

Outside, Ada stands in the road, stroking Zach's blond cap of hair with the same deliberation as she'd stroke a cat. Zach's attention is focused on his melting ice cream, from which creamy rivulets run down to his elbow. Benjie sits beside them both, tongue lolling as he pants in the heat.

Nora squints in the sudden brightness of the sun after the darkness of the post office. 'What's going on, Mum?'

Ada watches her hand on the shine of Zach's blond hair. 'Since, once more, you were out, I called on Eve and now I'm looking after this beautiful boy. His mother is—'

Eve appears round the corner, a newspaper pinned beneath her arm and two more ice creams, one in each hand. She nods towards the front door of the cottage, above which Stavros has painted a sign saying 'Bosham Castle' to confuse the tourists who pause to comment on the quaintness of the terrace of cottages and to peer through the front window, straight through Eve and

Stavros's tiny living room and out of the window on the other side to the water. Eve pushes the door open with her foot and they all pile inside.

Ada sinks on to the sofa.

'Nana Ada?' Zach clambers up beside her. Behind Nora's ribcage something contracts. Zach glances at Nora and Eve, before cupping his hand to whisper in Ada's ear. She nods. He removes a hairpin from her chignon and holds it up to the light, inspecting it like a jewel before running a finger along the waves and bumps of the hairpin's length. He stabs at his fingertip with the pointed ends. Ada's hand rests on Zach's chubby foot where it lies on the sofa with the sock half off. Zach combs the hairpin through his hair, looking up at Ada, who nods and smiles, so he places the pin with care on the sofa arm and reaches up for another. Ada, meanwhile, closes her eyes, and smiles blissfully.

In the kitchen, Eve hands both ice creams to Nora while she fills Benjie's bowl with water.

'I wanted to talk to you about your mum,' she whispers, pushing the door to. 'She's been calling by a lot recently.'

'She's got funny about being left alone in the house.'

'She nearly drowned, Nor. It brought home to her that death is not far off, and she's frightened. She doesn't want to be on her own.'

'Frightened? My mother's never been frightened of a thing her entire life!'

'Fear can show itself as anger.'

A soft scratching comes from the other side of the kitchen door.

'Mummy?'

Nora steps over the dog, moving to make room for Eve, who opens the door and crouches to hug Zach. 'I'm here, sweetie. It's OK. I'm here.'

Zach's fingers reach round to stroke the hollow of Eve's neck. Eve takes the kitchen cloth and wipes the ice cream from Zach's face and hands.

In the living room, Ada is asleep on the sofa, the white bristles of the baby's hairbrush on her lap almost the same colour and texture as the hair falling straight and fine around her face. Zach lifts a finger to his lips and looks fierce. 'Sshh!' he whispers, 'Nana Ada sleeping.'

Nora and Eve exchange glances.

'She was up half the night,' Nora says.

The clink and rattle of ice in a glass had woken Nora, followed by the sound of the front door opening and closing. 'Her body-clock is all askew.'

'Let her sleep. Come out the back for a bit. I want to talk to you.' Eve takes hold of Zach's hand. 'Sshh!' she says, finger to her lips, copying Zach. The three of them step outside and Eve closes the back door with a soft click.

From the high terrace at the back of the cottage, they climb down on to Shore Road via the steep steps cut into the sea wall. Nora watches Eve on the uneven steps, worried her balance might be affected by the bulk of her belly. Tiny flies leap and settle on heaps of drying seaweed washed up by the last high tide. At the water's edge, Zach paddles his feet up and down in slick mud, picks up a stick and pokes at weed and flints.

'You know the story of the church clock, I expect?' Eve says.

Nora nods. After the Second World War, a memorial clock was proposed for the south wall of the ancient belfry. Some villagers considered it an act of defacement to insert a clock mechanism and place a modern slab of Portland stone on a Saxon tower, especially where it would partly cover a previously blocked-up Saxon window. Meetings were held, letters written, posters displayed outside the post office. In the pub and along the foreshore where the dog-walkers met, there were arguments as to the rights and wrongs of the proposition.

Nora knows about the clock because her father and grandfather, while in favour of a war memorial, fiercely believed the clock should not be allowed to deface the Saxon tower. They, alongside a few other opponents, petitioned against its instalment. It was a story her father loved to tell his girls, an argument which caused neighbours to fall out over garden fences or cross the road to avoid speaking to each other. Feelings ran high and took many years to die down.

It's not the church clock Eve wants to talk about. Nora stoops to pick up a length of rope lying in the weed and flings it. The rope snakes through the air with Benjie bounding in pursuit, spattering mud.

'Tell me you haven't slept with him.'

It's all right for Eve, pregnant by a man who adores her, living in her own house, following her own dreams. 'I take it from that comment you have strong feelings against the exhumation?' Nora says.

'The idea of Jonny digging up the dead for a TV programme has upset a lot of people.'

'It has?'

'He's just a front man, a smooth talker.'

'He knows he's no historian, he's consulting experts.'

'He told me his *experts* will extract DNA from the teeth, if the bones are found to be contaminated by handling. He'll find that hard without a skull, won't he?'

Nora picks up the rope which Benjie has brought back and toys with the frayed end before throwing it again, hard and far. She wasn't aware Eve and Jonny had even met. It seems impossible Jonny can have forgotten there is no skull in the tomb.

'DNA would be needed from both of the men who handled the bones,' Eve says.

'My father's dead.'

'I know, but there was another man, wasn't there? It has to be the male line, a male relative.'

'I didn't know you knew so much about it all.'

'Your mother brought her fifties photos to show me. She's very upset.'

'She's upset because she's been dropped. And angry with me. You are too.'

'No. I'm not. You love all the history of this place. I can see why you got involved. But I know the bishop won't give permission for this thing so I'm not angry.' Eve's strokes her belly protectively. 'Anger is a very negative energy.'

'This *thing* is going to be a substantial historical programme centred on a centuries-old mystery. It's a wonderful idea.'

'Nora, it's a TV programme. You're deluded.'

Benjie has returned with the sodden piece of rope and stands in front of Eve this time. He drops it at her feet, looking up at her with his paw on one end.

Eve is always so sure that she's right about everything.

'My grandfather was convinced they'd say no to the church clock, you know.'

Just above Eve's eyebrow the skin puckers around a piercing like a steel nail sewn through the side of her head. Close up, the punctured skin is disconcerting, the pull and stretch of flesh over metal.

'They said yes.'

But Eve is not listening. She grabs the rope just as Benjie pounces, ready for a tug of war. He grips the other end with his teeth, which are bared. Eve mimics his mock growl as the rope shakes and twists between them.

Laughter floats across the water from three people splashing in wellingtons as they wade along the path which, when the tide is right out, provides a short-cut across the inlet. However, water is fast covering the mudflats and the final stretch of their short-cut has already vanished beneath murky ripples. Nora and Eve lean against the sea wall and watch the waders' slow progress.

'Harry's given me five paintings to sell, to raise cash,' Eve says.

'Cash?'

'Yeah, to help get one of our projects off the ground when the café opens; Stavro's graffiti-teaching sessions.'

'Will anyone buy his paintings?'

Eve turns towards her. 'Are you serious? Have you *seen* them?'

Nora hesitates. 'No.'

She's not sure why she's lied, except for the complex mix of intrigue and guilt connected with looking at Harry's painting when he wasn't there. Also, she feels awkward around Harry. Her body had reacted of its own accord when he kissed her, pushing back into his, a frisson shooting through her hot as a blade. She's been avoiding him whenever possible; they haven't really spoken since she snatched the pickaxe from him and locked it in the shed.

'He's a man of hidden talents,' Eve continues.

'We argued.'

'You and Harry?' Eve studies her face. 'Really?'

'About the alcohol he brings to the house. He and Mum are always drinking.'

'Look what I found, Mummy, look!' Zach sways towards them with his stick, grinning and waving a dripping mop of green slime.

Eve licks her lips. 'Ooh yum! Green candy floss, my favourite.' She takes the stick of dangling slime, rubbing her stomach. Zach jumps up and down, shrieking and shaking his head when Eve mimes pinching pieces of green algae and pretends to pop them into her mouth. Zach's chin wobbles and his eyes grow round. 'No, don't eat it, Mummy, not in real life.' He clings to her arm to stop her.

Eve claps her hand to her mouth, rolls her eyes and wilts, as if falling dead to the ground. Her feet thud and bounce on the pavement. Zach's used to these baiting games, but Nora thinks he's not completely certain when his mother is playing Let's Pretend, unless she announces it.

He rubs his eyes and bends down to put his cheek against Eve's, where she lies 'dead' on the road. 'Just 'tend, Mummy? Just 'tend?' he whispers.

EVE WHEELS AN elderly man into the room. His hands and feet are trembling and he has huge, old-fashioned hearing aids in both ears.

'Where do you want to sit, George?' Eve asks, very loudly.

'I want to sit on your lap,' George replies, his head wobbling a little as he twists round in his wheelchair.

Eve laughs, and rubs his shoulder. *This is the lively group*, she'd said to Nora as they unpacked the car earlier. *Not so drugged up, so they're full of beans.*

One man is asleep, the woman next to him, perhaps his wife, plucks at his sleeve. 'Wake up! Wake up! She's here!'

Over by the door stands a woman on her own, bone-thin, her face like a crone's.

'Come on, Phyllis.' Eve's white-blonde plaits tumble over each other as she bends to hook arms with her.

Phyllis is the only woman in the room whose nails are not

varnished with a garish pink colour, which Nora takes as a sign she will not be cajoled into a chair or persuaded to conform.

'Get your hands off me,' she mutters. 'Don't you touch me, don't you dare!'

Her body is twisted with fury at being brought to this room with its circle of chairs, her back so hunched by age or arthritis she can only glare downwards at the floor. Yet she's as frail and slight as Ada.

Last night, waif-like in her pale nightdress and her silver hair in disarray, Ada stood by the French doors in the sitting room. Her back was towards Nora and she held the handle of the croquet mallet in both hands, the mallet's heavy head resting on the floor. Two or three of the panes of glass in the French door were ragged with broken glass, part of the wooden frame splintered. Ada rocked back and forth on the balls of her bare feet, unaware of Nora's presence. She heaved the mallet up, cradling it with both arms across her body until the weight began to topple her. The head of the mallet thudded down to the floor. Nora heard a low vibrating sound, feral. Ada straightened her back. Her shoulders swayed as she breathed hard and prepared again to lift and swing the mallet down on the window like an axe. The growl came from deep in Ada's throat.

Eve smiles at Nora over Phyllis's bent spine and shoulder blades. 'Where do you want to set up?'

'Don't you dare!' Phyllis lashes out with her stick.

Nora opens her cello case and glances round. The air is like soup, the room stuffed with an assortment of winged chairs and mismatched side tables on castors. In the far corner, a man with

244

the face of an ageing matinée idol sits upright and motion-less, his hands linked on his lap. His trousers are immaculately pressed. He stares at the floor with a dreamy smile, not at the repeated swirls and lurid colours of the carpet, but into the privacy of some inner space, his isolation in the crowded room due to drugs or sorrow.

Eve has backed away from Phyllis and moves round the circle of chairs saying hello, talking about last week's quiz, the weather, what they can look forward to for lunch. Every now and then she stops and straightens, putting a hand to the small of her back. Zach's face was pale and serious when Eve fell to the ground pretending to die, her feet bouncing on the tarmac while he hovered over her. She has been asked back for another scan, to check the unusually large size of the baby's stomach. The doctors at the hospital have told her it's probably nothing to worry about, but how can she not be anxious? She doesn't take enough care of herself. Here she is, in stifling heat, smiling and talking, bend-ing to make eye contact with each person in the circle as she says their name, crouching or putting a gentle hand on a shoulder; smiling, talking and touching.

'MUM!' Last night, Nora had yelled at Ada to get her attention.

Ada swung round, her eyes narrowed to slits. 'It's locked!' The words spat out.

'Use the key.'

'How dare you?'

'It's night time. Most people ...'

'I am not—' Ada stamped her bare foot. Nora darted forward as she swung the mallet again '—most people!'

Her mother's grip on the mallet was surprisingly strong. They glared at each other, both clasping the wooden handle. Sweat prickled Nora's forehead. With a blink, Ada's expression softened. Her hands fluttered and dropped. She frowned, lifting her hands to examine the palms as if they were dirty or unfamiliar and chafed them together. She was trembling. Nora let go of the mallet. Just in time she moved close to support her mother's weight and save her from crumpling to the floor amongst the shards of glass.

'Darling,' her mother leaned into her, 'Might I lie down for a moment?' Her voice passed over Nora's skin like a feather.

Eve has plugged in her CD player. 'Is everyone here? Where's Norman today? Is he still in his bath? And how are you, Clara?'

The woman next to Nora begins to hum, drumming her fingers on the chair arms. Every now and then she tugs her polyester dress down to cover her age-splotched knees. Her legs are naked. 'Down at the Old Bull and Bush,' she belts out, full vibrato, and chuckles to herself.

'A song for every occasion, haven't you, Iris?' Eve says.

Iris gives Nora a bold stare, then sits back in her chair and beams around the room. Nora looks away. Her cello rests between her thighs. When Harry kissed her, the bulk and weight of his body pressed against hers. She straightens her arms, pushing the cello upright and away from her body. She'll make a decision soon about whether or not to go back up to London. A few weeks from now the pavements outside the Academy will turn yellow and brown with a filigree of fallen leaves from the plane trees. If she does go back to London, she'll be able to see more of Jonny.

She brushes some dust from the polished wood. Her cello's formal curves and curlicues are artificial and out of place in this room; it doesn't belong here and nor does she.

Eve passes around photographs of wedding couples in church doorways, pictures of balloons and cakes. It's a session on anniversaries. Eve plays a recording of Happy Birthday and sings along at full volume, conducting with exaggerated arm and body movements. When Iris interrupts, warbling, 'To tell you the truth I'll be lonely,' with a doleful expression, Eve moves swiftly on.

When the time comes for Nora to play, Phyllis has seated herself on a chair to one side of the circle. Nora pulls the cello to her. During the Bach Prelude in G major Phyllis cranes forward in her chair, fighting the severe hunch of her back to get a better view of the cello, to look higher so as to be able to watch Nora's fingers. She taps with her stick on the carpet, keeping time, and her body – with the eager, forward stretch of her neck, the yearning of her jaw line – uncurls a little. Her head jerks upwards. Looking directly into Phyllis's faded eyes, Nora remembers her own face forced upwards by Isaac's hand on the back of her head, the shock of his roughness. She was playing Beethoven to a lecture hall of students. 'This, for the public!' he bellowed, 'Not for yourself!' He believed the cello to be an instrument with the power to influence, to transmit ideas and hypnotic images, spiritual states of being, to affect the human mind in ways as yet unknown. Nora lifts her head, keeps it raised as bars of semiquavers run beneath her fingers.

When Nora stops playing, the matinée idol with the crinkly hair swivels his gaze around the room. He hasn't said a word for the entire hour, but he has leaned forward and watched everything with a serene smile on his face. Now, he sinks back down and stares at his hands. He twiddles his thumbs, first one way and then the other. Phyllis is straining forward in her seat, but when she sees Eve has begun to pack her CD player into the plastic crate along with all her other bits and pieces, her face falls, her body slumping as the hunch returns to her spine.

NORA WAKES TO the smell of burning. In the instant of recognising the taste in the back of her throat, she's up, crashing into her father's study, her mind seeing the bookshelves on fire – but there's only darkness. The curtainless window shows a cusp of moon, a starry sky. Déjà vu washes over her. Somewhere in the night, her mother will be up and smoking, that's all. The house is still.

Without switching on the light, Nora walks one step at a time like a child, down the stairs. In the kitchen, the fridge hums. No movement from Rook's basket, but the smell of smoke is more pungent. She checks the oven and finds it cold. The acrid taste in her throat is stronger and she has a sense, now, of something stirring in the house.

From behind the closed door of the dining room comes a low-level noise like paper being screwed into balls. No one goes in there any more. Do they? With an unreasonable surge of premonition, she stops with her hand on the glass door knob. A flicker of light and movement gutters along the bottom of the door.

When she turns the handle, the door falls open to a room wild with the heat and roar of flames. She slams the door shut again, leaning back, pulling on the handle to hold the door closed against any suck of air which might force it open. A glimpse was all she'd had. So many licking flames: flames climbing the sides of the chimney breast; flames racing along the curtain pelmet; flames transforming the old raffia wastepaper basket into a spiky bush of orange.

Water. Bucket.

No, too late, too many flames, their darting image imprinted on her retina as her mind registers the shock and reaches for half-forgotten warnings about water and electricity.

If the curtains catch, the fire will take hold, become all-consuming. She must find a rug or floor mat before that happens. She must try to beat back the flames. Her eyes prick in the smoke leaking out under the door and around the hinges. Fire drill: teachers with shrill whistles hustling them out of the dorms. Do not stop to save valuables.

Do not stop. Her mind crawls.

A movement at the edges of her vision: Ada wafts down the hallway, silent as a ghost. Pausing, she draws on a cigarette held in an ebony holder, the silver of her hair doubled in the hall mirror behind her head.

The sight of her mother galvanises Nora into action. From the dining room comes the crack of wood. No time. She grasps Ada by the shoulders and turns her around, feeling the fragile jumble of bones beneath her hands as she guides her mother's feather-light body towards the front door.

'Out!'

The front door slams behind them, knocker banging. Outside it's cool, silent and still. Under the vast starry sky, shut outside Creek House in her nightdress, Nora feels exposed. In a macabre mimic of dance, the pulsing light from the dining-room windows strobes orange across the damp lawn and into the shadows of the shrubbery. Ada's cigarette holder gleams.

There's a shout, and Harry appears, jogging across the grass in his dressing gown, his arms wide, reaching for her. Nora leans into him, the thud of his heart. Momentarily, she is reeled in. Then she opens her eyes. His stubble scrapes her cheek as she wriggles away and reaches out for Ada.

'Look after Mum. Keep hold of her.' Nora pushes her mother towards Harry and dashes back to the door. Phone the fire brigade. The phone is in the hallway. Flames writhe against the glass of the dining-room window. Nora shields her face from the heat's intensity and daren't, after all, go back inside. She turns on her heel to race in the opposite direction, hitching up her nightdress to skin over the wall into Arthur's garden and tear up the path to his house. Her fists bang on his door. In her mind, the flames prowl and leap.

She should have gone back inside. She should have grabbed the cello, in its hard case in the hallway.

Humphrey the Great Dane gallops to and fro inside, bellowing, until the noise of his barking and clattering run brings Arthur to the door. Humphrey's weight nearly knocks Nora to the floor, his paws on her shoulders. In Arthur's hallway she hears her own voice rise in pitch as she gabbles an address into the telephone. 'Be quick; be quick.'

★   ★   ★

A cluster of neighbours huddle together outside the house, awed faces like pewter in the cold of the fire engine's blue light. Nora can't quite recognise any of them. She shakes, though she is not cold. The grass is wet under her bare feet. The fire hose, monstrous and black, snakes up the front steps, in through the door, down the hallway and into the dining room, where firemen, shadowy and huge in their helmets and uniforms, stamp and call to each other. The orange glow has died down. Someone has put Harry's heavy waxed jacket over her shoulders and rubs her back, but the hand is too small to be Harry's. He, she realises, has disappeared. His jacket holds the strong smell of tarry rope.

'It's mostly smoke damage. Don't worry. It looks much worse than it is,' a woman's voice says.

Nora's mind is blank. She has forgotten something vital, and the absence nudges at her mind. She can't think what it is until she sees Harry come running round the side of the house from the back with Rook's basket. She flies across the lawn and whips off the black towel. In a stretch of wing and claw, Rook flaps up on to the side of the basket and launches himself at her. The surprise of his movement knocks her backwards and she finds herself sitting on the grass with Rook treading her lap with his claws, wings outstretched.

The ambulance arrives and Nora watches, as if from a great distance, as Harry helps the paramedics persuade Ada to be gently led into it. They come for Nora, who refuses to get up from where she sits on the damp grass. Rook screeches and thrusts himself at the paramedics. The woman shields her face with her forearm and steps back behind her male partner, even though Rook can't lift himself higher than a few inches from the ground.

'Bloody hell!' the male paramedic mutters.

In their reaction Nora sees how much Rook has grown without her noticing. No longer the loose bundle of feathers he once was, he's a big, powerful bird with a vicious-looking beak and claws, and coordination of movement.

'C'mon, Miss. Just to check your breathing,' the male paramedic coaxes, recovering himself.

Harry squats and reaches out with his square hands, but Rook flaps and flutters, beak open, at his fingers.

'Don't!' Nora scrambles up. 'He doesn't like hands coming at him. Let me.'

Nora is silent in the back of the ambulance, thinking of the paramedics and Rook's shriek of fury. It's the loudest noise she has ever heard him make. She managed to settle him in his basket in the kitchen, with Harry promising to stay and keep him company until she gets back. The house is safe. She closes her eyes, overcome with weariness, bracing her body as the ambulance turns a corner. Her hands are linked in her lap, where Rook has taken to sitting every evening. Until now, because of his silence, she hasn't worried too much about whether or not he has imprinted on her, but if he's found his voice, he may now try to leave. She wonders whether he might soon discover he can fly up into the sky and join the circling cloud of rooks winding down over a copse at dusk, his heart beating fast as he soars and dips, the air around him filled with the caw and call of hundreds like him.

THE MORNING AFTER the fire Nora wakes late, to the smell of wet plaster and ash. She's alone in the house apart from Rook, yet from downstairs comes a noise she can't quite place, a creak or an echo. She strains to listen. The sound is like a swollen door opening. She sits up, suddenly alert: it can only be Rook. Rook cawing from the hallway, his caw cracked and wavering, his throat dry from disuse.

Sure enough, he's there, waiting for her at the bottom of the stairs, pacing to and fro, bowing and calling. She feels a rush of pleasure; his greeting is for her. Sinking down on the bottom stair, she watches the now familiar origami positioning of the fold of his wings, the angle of his neck outstretched, the lowering and raising of his head as he struts and bows in front of her.

Eventually his movements slow to a halt and he fluffs his feathers, regarding her, head at a sideways tilt. His white lid blinks slowly; it's her turn to be polite. She rises and inclines her head in return.

'Morning, Rook.' She dips her head again before following Rook's swagger and bounce, the leathery flap of his wings, along the hallway to the kitchen, drumming her fingers along the banister rails as she goes. Passing the hall mirror she catches sight of her face. She's smiling to herself.

She peeks through the half-open door of the blackened dining room where wallpaper sags in sodden strips from the walls and the polished gloss of the mahogany tabletop is singed, a black hollow where a pile of letters caught. Gone up in smoke. The sun shines on sooty dust. It could have been much worse. Nora shuts the door on the debris. The clearing-up will keep. She's starving and wants a celebratory breakfast with Rook. She can't wait to tell someone he has at last cawed.

Rummaging in the shadow of the larder for the cherries she's bought for Rook, she hums the Paganini Caprice. She tries Jonny's mobile number but it goes straight on to answer phone. He will be busy. She'll try again later. The only person who'll really be interested in Rook's new accomplishment will be Harry. The thought tightens something inside her gut, a twist of tension, like vertigo. Avoiding Harry has become almost a habit. She counts five cherries in to Rook's saucer and licks the red stain from her fingertips. The cherries are overripe.

Rook struts and putters around Nora's feet as she makes tea. Every time he passes the patch of loose plaster by the chimney breast, he stops and plucks at the flakes and edges of wallpaper until a bit more peels or crumbles away. The lathe and plaster of the wall's inner structure is clearly visible now. She'll have to check there for Rook's hidden morsels – the pieces of cheese, cherries.

He has so many hiding places for his food caches, under rugs, in curtain hems, between floorboards. She sniffs the air to see if she can smell any of his secret stores, but all she can smell is charred paper. Then she remembers her cello.

In the hallway, the cello case has been knocked sideways and lies half under some coats which the firemen must have brushed off the hooks as they bundled into the house with the hose. To her surprise the cello is not inside its case after all. Mentally, she retraces her movements yesterday afternoon: she remembers answering the phone on the way back up from the cellar, carrying her cello. It was Flick phoning, a long conversation about changing the dates for her visit. Something had come up, she was coming on her own, she said, without the girls. Nora propped her cello against the wall near the dining-room door and, for Ada's sake, had worked on persuading Flick to change her mind.

Then what happened? Harry came in from the garden. She'd made him tea but, not wanting to be alone with him, left him to drink it while she busied herself upstairs in her father's study, reading about the Bayeux Tapestry. Ada's always nagging about it cluttering up the house, she must have moved the cello out of her way.

Nora pushes the door of the dining room open wide and steps in. The cello lies half underneath the table, knocked over during the fire. On the table and around the cello lie the charcoal remains of burnt letters or perhaps photographs, the remnants reduced to black rectangles, edges and corners, tissue-paper thin. They disintegrate at her touch. At some point burning paper must have fallen on to the cello and lain there as the wood caught fire. A large area of the curved back is charred, the wood layered like black feathers.

She lifts the cello by its neck to examine the buckled wood. The cello's body is completely ruined but, though she has no money to buy a replacement cello, nor enough to get this one repaired, even if it were possible, she feels nothing. If this cello had been her beloved Goffriller, she'd be weeping.

LATER, AFTER WASHING down walls and sweeping up burnt debris, Nora has showered and is ambling barefoot in the garden while Rook bathes in the old enamel basin. The tinny tango tune of her mobile, still upstairs in her bedroom, rings out, building rapidly to a crescendo. At the same time, footsteps clang on the ladder up from the creek and Harry's head and shoulders, the bright Hawaiian fabric of his shirt, appear from the shoreline below. She acknowledges him briefly with a wave but turns to run in to the house for her mobile.

As she takes off across the lawn something 'pops' in the back of her right calf, the impact so severe she stumbles on to all fours, thinking she must have been hit by an air-rifle pellet. Tentatively, with a hand on the garden bench, she tries to stand again, testing her weight. Something has struck her, hard, in the calf, but there's no mark. Her flesh feels badly bruised and the pain when she puts her weight on the leg is excruciating. From upstairs, through the open window, her ring tone sounds out once more. It might be important, Ada or Jonny. Rook is cawing a rowdy greeting to Harry, who shouts something as he reaches the top of the ladder, but she continues to hobble across the lawn and into the house as the ring tune builds to a demanding fortissimo. She's got as far as the hall, leaning on the walls and hopping, when the strident ring tone abruptly stops again, cut off mid-phrase. A sob of pain escapes her and her legs fold.

The sound of Harry's crocs approaches, scuffing into the house and through the kitchen. On the tiled floor, Nora gingerly draws her legs up beneath her and tucks her dress around her knees. She closes her eyes; the pain is deep.

In the kitchen, the fridge door opens and closes, the freezer drawer scrapes. She hears Harry's breath as he crouches beside her and opens her eyes to find him offering her a bag of frozen peas.

She can barely speak. Sitting a little more upright, she tries to put her foot flat to the floor, but it's too painful.

'Can you phone the doctor for me? Where's Rook?'

'Sure. Let me?'

He kneels in front of her and lifts her heel on to his lap.

'Is Rook OK?'

Rook is out in the garden alone. The wild rooks might attack him.

'No worries. He's on his way. Takes him a while, that's all.'

Harry turns her foot gently in both hands and some of the tension of pain eases. Her eyes have closed. Her breath's shaky as a child's again, as when her father took a needle tip to a splinter or whisked the corner of his handkerchief against her eye to remove a piece of grit. Although Harry's hands are warm on her skin, through the thin cotton of her skirt creeps the chill of the black and white floor tiles.

'A sting?' he asks, head bent to examine the sole of her foot.

'No, no. It's more my leg. Here.' She points to the back of her calf. He places one hand around her leg and at the same time applies a light pressure to the ball of her foot, studying her face. As her toes are pushed upward, extending her calf muscle, the pain makes her gasp.

'Let's get you somewhere more comfy.'

'I can manage.' She levers herself partially upright, using the wall as a prop, but it's a relief when he slides one arm behind her legs and scoops her up. His hair or his clothes smell of meadow hay. An involuntary shiver runs through her as he sets her down on the sofa and slides a cushion under her right foot. His expression calm, he rubs both her calves with his hands, warming her goose-pimpled skin as he tells her she must press the frozen peas against her calf, 'To slow everything down', while he fetches a blanket.

'Where's Rook got to?' she says. 'Can you check?'

Harry disappears outside into the sunshine. Nora shivers again and draws the blanket up to her chin. Her calf, under the frozen peas, grows numb.

Harry has brought Rook, her laptop, woollen walking socks, made tea, phoned Ada at Daphne's to explain about Nora's injury and to suggest she stays with Daphne another night. Harry carried out an online Google diagnosis and came to the conclusion Nora has 'tennis calf', a torn ligament, common to runners too. She must rest it, elevated, with ice, as Harry has already done. Now, he is cooking something, frying onions and garlic, whistling in the kitchen. The smell makes her mouth water. She should phone Jonny and tell him about the fire, but she's very tired. She rests her head on the cushion Harry's put on the sofa arm and closes her eyes. Rook flaps his way from the floor to her lap and up to her shoulder, the pads of his claws cool on her skin as he treads from side to side before settling down.

Her tango ring tone jangles from upstairs. Harry fetches the phone, but too late for her to answer it. She's about to see if there's a number she recognises in Missed Calls, when it rings again.

'Hiya, is Dad there?' The voice sounds girlish and there is some sort of rap music playing in the background.

'Dad? No. I don't think so. Who is this?'

'Chelsea? Only this is his work mobile and he's left it at home.'

It's a young voice, with that confusing upward intonation at the end of each sentence as if everything is in question. It could be a pupil, but she doesn't give out her mobile number and she doesn't recognise the voice. 'I think you must have the wrong number.'

There's a sigh and the sound of rapid gum chewing. 'Reckon? Well this number comes up, like, a zillion times in his History?'

'This number? You're sure?' Nora begins to repeat her number, slowly, but the voice interrupts her.

'Yeah? Anyways, so I reckoned it must be a work number or whatever, y'know, for his new project?'

'No, I'm really sorry.' Nora presses the red button to end the call and checks the number of the incoming call. It's Jonny's. She chucks the mobile on the blanket, wondering why she has been the one to apologise.

'I'M SO HOT,' Eve complains. She cups each breast, lifting them and peering down with a grimace. 'These are getting way too heavy to lug around.' She is sitting on the paving of her back terrace, legs akimbo, a sarong loosely wrapped around her swollen belly. Her marbled breasts are half-out of a halter-neck bikini top.

'You know your front door's wide open?'

'Through breeze. The house needs cooling down as much as I do.'

The tide is out and an underground smell wafts up from the drying mudflats. Nora limps across the terrace to admire the row of jam jars lined up on the wall, painted with fish and shells, curling waves and flying gulls. The colours, cobalt and emerald green, royal blue, turquoise, are transparent and intense.

'Paint one yourself if you like. Watery colours only. They're for the café, in case you hadn't guessed. Like everything else in my life.'

The opening of Café Jetsam is only days away.

'Where's Zach?' In the corner of the terrace, Zach's teddy bear sits on a child-sized chair with a broken cane seat and the two back legs unpegged.

'Walking the dog with Stavros. I hope they all come back exhausted.' Eve looks up. 'Sweet, isn't it, the chair? We're going to have a go at recaning it. Harry brought it round. He's house-clearing for Daphne. Her mother's just died.'

Harry has found all sorts of treasures in the attic, Eve says, and Daphne doesn't want to know about anything unless it's in pristine condition. She's given him the job of disposing of everything else.

Nora sits beside Eve on the ground. Because of her injured calf she's been unable to run for days, and it's making her restless, fidgety. She picks up a jam jar from the pile and begins to pick off the sticky remnants of the Robertson's Lemon Marmalade label. Eve clears her throat.

'He was a rat. I'm so glad you finished with him.'

'I'd never have guessed.'

The focus of Jonny's eyes had shifted, that was all, when she told him about the phone call. They were sitting in his car, about to drive into town for a meal. He made an attempt to take her hand, but she folded her arms. 'Oh God, Nora, I didn't mean you to find out in this way, but . . .'

'*The time was never quite right to tell me the truth?* Listen to yourself, Jonny.'

Jonny, inevitably, started to talk. His wife Kimberley is older than him and has run a successful catering business for years. He'd left university to marry her and play a role in her business. He cracked his knuckles, pulled the sun visor down and slammed it back up again.

Money is the problem. Kimberley is obsessed with it. She has kept hold of the business purse strings. He has to ask her for handouts when he's strapped for cash. He tapped the car key on his thigh and his voice dropped as he dwelt on the lack of sex, *Almost from day one*.

He raked his fingers through his hair as he talked, and lifted his eyebrows in an upturned V of appeal when he turned to her and explained the Godwin Grave Project might be his chance to break away from Kimberley, to set himself free. She found herself wondering if he had practised the look in front of a mirror.

'I discovered there wasn't much to finish,' Nora says to Eve. Selecting a tube of transparent cobalt paint and a short wide brush, she paints a blue line around the base of the jam jar. Her attraction to Jonny had been as fleeting as a schoolgirl crush.

Having decided to talk things over in the pub, they got out of the car, Jonny tugging at his cuffs to adjust the length of shirt-sleeve showing beneath his jacket. Nora wondered how she hadn't noticed, up until then, that he was vain.

From the church came the clang of the bells: Thursday evening bell-ringing practice. The hesitation and tumble of chimes drowned the music from the bar and distracted Nora from what Jonny was telling her. He'd soon moved off the subject of his money and wife to tell her about a commission from a prestigious series for the Godwin Graves Project, an hour slot. *Perfect*. He waved his arms around as he warmed to his theme. He'd submitted the proposal. Once they had permission for the exhumation, that's all they were waiting for, any day now and everything would be *squared away*. But news had come in a phone call as they sat in the little garden at the front of the Anchor Bleu.

'You were right it seems,' she tells Eve. 'About the bishop. Permission for exhumation was refused.'

Jonny had answered his phone, leaving Nora alone at the table as he paced up and down the lane. The church bells pealed. Nora's thoughts drifted to Flick's wedding at Bosham church, adjusting Flick's tiara and shaking out the long ivory train as they stood in the porch together before walking down the aisle. They both missed their father that day. Flick had chosen a friend from university to give her away.

Bloody unbelievable. It's outrageous. Jonny was tight-lipped and frowning when he returned to the table.

'Did they tell him why?' Eve asks.

'They mentioned lack of a credible academic framework and valid research aims.'

Nora had tried to ignore Jonny's foot knocking to and fro against the leg of the wooden picnic table, but in the end she put a hand on his leg. Jonny stood abruptly and walked to the wall, hands rammed into his pockets. He scowled towards the church, just visible behind the yew.

'A few floorboards, a few fucking fifties' stone slabs, for God's sake,' he jabbed his finger in the direction of the bell tower. 'A few inches of sodding mud.'

'He said he could take a trowel and dig the body up himself in less than an hour.'

'He wouldn't, would he?'

'Come off it, Eve. He's arrogant but not stupid. No. He's been told they can take the matter to court, if the parochial church council supports an appeal. He's not giving up that easily.'

The cobalt blue paint transforms the jam jar. For the sky, Nora selects turquoise. With a candle alight inside, the colours will glow like stained glass, dance with light.

Isaac used to say a musician paints with sound. He'd recite the names of forty or more paint colours, proclaiming the words like a monologue in a different language, just a list of colours, to a lecture hall full of students. When he reached the end, he'd pause to neaten the pages of his notes on the table in front of him before looking up at the tiers of seats. *Sound is an infinte spectrum of colours.* The difference between an instrumentalist and a musican, he said, is the development of an acute inner hearing which allows the musican to distinguish the subtleties of different sounds. Far more than the bow's basic sound production, nuance and hue and shade must be produced by the left hand through an immense variety of vibrato. To create colour, musicians use their imagination, search their own memory of experience for image and sensation. It is this, in part, from which Nora still shies away and which prevents the synchrony with music which once came to her instinctively.

She describes to Eve how the sight of the feathery charred wood of her burnt cello gave her a sense of opportunity. She's hired a cello so that she can continue to play in the retirement homes over the summer, but has handed in her notice at the school. She'll be paid until the end of the school holidays and then she'll have to decide what to do.

'I needed to stop,' she says, 'There was only one pupil I enjoyed teaching.'

And Rachel, her star pupil, would soon be moving on to other teachers. In York, when the judges of the festival competition read out their reports, it was immediately clear Rachel had won. They praised her dexterity and fervour, the rich and burnished string tones, the full-throated eloquence of the Largo opening of the Eccles Sonata she and Nora had chosen as her individual piece. In her summing-up, Lady Fisherton talked of the extraordinary emotional transparency, the rhythmic clarity and tonal vigour in Rachel's playing. Backstage, Nora took the cello from Rachel, hugged her and gave her a gentle shove back on to the stage as wave after wave of applause surged from the depths of the auditorium.

'Couldn't you get a job in some Paris conservatoire? Is that a French word? Or Russian? Just give master classes to the most talented students? The hot ones?'

'I don't think I have what it takes.'

'What you *have* is a gift going to waste.'

Nora is no longer sure of this. 'Before, I felt guilty all the time, never switched off.'

The cello possessed her. When out with friends, she was never fully there, always distracted, her head occupied with the music, a phrase she couldn't quite get right, or a particular technique she needed to improve. A large part of her only wanted to be practising, but if she turned down too many invitations to go out, she felt guilty about neglecting her friends. Her practising grew rigid, days strictly timetabled to fit in a certain number of hours: cello practice between seven and ten in the morning, two and four in the afternoon, nine until eleven at night.

'My life got too unbalanced. Some of the instinct and intuition had gone. Trouble is you can always be better. When I wasn't playing, it was as if every experience in my life had to be translated into something which could be put to use in my interpretation of music.'

'Kind of living back to front, or inside-out?'

'Yes, exactly like that,' says Nora, surprised at the clarity of Eve's understanding. 'It's all you think about, the desire to play better.'

'Question is, can you live without it?'

Nora doesn't know the answer.

'Tell you what, though, if your leg doesn't hurt too much would you be a dear and limp off to fetch me a bowl of cold water to put my poor aching feet in?'

'Eve, how can your feet be aching? You've been sitting there all day doing these tea-light jars.'

'There speaks someone who's never been fat and pregnant.'

ADA KEEPS HER back to the room. The ivories of Café Jetsam's piano are badly stained, the colour of nicotine on a pub ceiling. She runs her tongue along her front teeth. Since the fire, Nora has grown high and mighty about not smoking in Creek House. Without touching the keys, Ada holds her hands over the piano in the playing position. The brass candle holders on either side of the music rack are blackened by tarnish. She is surprised Eve has not given them a quick clean and put in fresh candles for the opening of the café. But then Eve has been busy with preparing food and making the gay floral and pastel-striped bunting that is pinned in zigzags from the boathouse high ceiling beams. And she's pregnant, so bound to be muddle-headed.

Ada doesn't want to think of her own muddle-headedness the other morning at breakfast when she was talking about the finely tooled Horsham stone of the larger coffin and said to Nora, *Your father will know the answer to that,* meaning Robert. Only when

Nora's face softened with sentiment did Ada realise her mistake. Nora's father, as far as she is concerned, is Brian. Was Brian. *Of course I mean Harry.* Ada had tried to gloss over her error. *Harry will know the answer.*

Behind her, chairs scrape and feet shuffle. She will not glance over her shoulder to see the chairs fill with people, the majority of whom she has known for years. Hell or high water, here they all remain. The tiny flags on the bunting are fluttering in a breeze. Nora and Stavros climbed up tall ladders to hang it yesterday. Prettier than the old-fashioned stuff one saw once upon a time at fairgrounds.

The café begins to smell of dog and ancient waxed jackets, clothes as stale as their wearers. Ted, tweedy in a jacket and flat cap he has worn since the fifties, is trying to catch her eye, but Ada dips her head to adjust the height of the piano stool and pretends not to have seen him.

The velvet on the seat of the stool is worn to a shine and holds the smell of greasepaint. The piano must have belonged to some theatre and been kept backstage for years.

Eve has given her a list of songs on a piece of paper propped on the music rack. 'I'm Forever Blowing Bubbles' is top of the list. Ada has no recollection of ever memorising songs like this, but nevertheless she has them all by heart. 'Roll out the Barrel'. Meaningless ditties, all of them. She adjusts the paper on the music rack. On one holder, a dribble of wax once molten, brought to life by the flame's heat, trickling down the candle to cling to the underside of the holder and ready to drip, is now cold and hardened. Paper and wood: one scratch of a match and *Pfffff!* Letters and papers curled and blackened, floating on a current of air. Layers of polish and the chemicals which make up the shiny skin of varnished wood are more flammable than one might imagine. The whoosh of flame: a fierce heat.

The candle holder with its dribbles of wax is lopsided. Ada pushes it upright but the fitting is loose and when she takes her hand away it slips to a tilt again. If a candle were to be lit in that holder, hot wax would dribble all over the keyboard.

The Hoover hums a middle C, middle C, Nora would sing out. Dance around Ada as she hoovered, getting under her feet until they went to the piano in the playroom to find middle C. Nora was always right. Ada told everyone she possessed perfect pitch, though she had no real idea of the meaning of the phrase.

Mixing egg whites for meringue, the Kenwood whined. *High E flat,* Nora piped up. The little finger of Ada's right hand hovers over the ebony key, a stretch, more than an octave above middle C. With a fruit cake, the Kenwood would strain low, bass clef, D. Little finger, left hand.

Nothing ever got done. Nora heard a note in everything: the wind whipping round the corner of the house by the coal bunker; the fog horn at dusk – even the ring of the halyards on masts. Between them, she and Nora used to fill that old house with music. Brian would come in and find them both at the piano, Nora on Ada's lap, the scent of Pear's soap on her skin.

A sing-song round the piano, all three of them.

Where was Felicity in this memory? Had she already been sent away to school?

Well, just look where they all are now. Ada feels for the hand-kerchief tucked at her wrist. In no time at all, Nora was able play the piano better than her mother and, once the cello took over, she was like a wild thing possessed. This last year or two, music seemed to have lost its hold, until recently. Recently, it's back with a vengeance, all hours of the day or the godforsaken night, angry, tuneless stuff winding up from the foundations, sawing through the fabric of the house. No sleep for anyone.

She had stubbed her toe on that ugly lump of wood just once too often. Twitched out a foot and kicked it back. A satisfying muffle of echoing notes and the instrument lay like an upturned beetle on the floor.

'Johnny's so long at the fair.' She's courting disaster with him, her daughter. All mouth and trousers, promising to pay the bills the church has run up what with this, that and the other, trying to get his Godwin Grave Project off the ground, astronomical legal bills and archaeologists' fees. Never answers his emails, according to that nice young vicar, never answers his telephone. Only clap eyes on him when he's after something. In all likelihood Nora will up sticks and follow him, go waltzing off back to London and that will be that.

The murmuring behind Ada has grown steadily louder, but it now ceases and plump little Eve is at her shoulder, asking something about sheet music. A reflection of the two of them moves on the dark facade of the piano. Behind their reflection the strings are stretched taut, the hammers at rest, ready to strike. In the shiny lid of the piano, curved like a fairground mirror, Eve's body is squat and distorted. She makes no attempt to cover the shape of her pregnancy. Whereas Nora has always been so angular, has never possessed womanly curves.

Ada feels for her handkerchief again. She will not allow her emotions to get the better of her, not before the entire village on this special occasion. 'This candle holder is a fire hazard.' She points out the lopsided holder, but Eve has gone, moved away already, only her oily perfume remaining in the air. Ada's question is mistimed, has interrupted Eve's welcome address.

'I'd like to welcome you all to Café Jetsam's opening celebrations,' Eve says to the listening room, which is stuffed full. All those people breathing. Don't think of Brian trapped in that underground chamber. Ada's vision telescopes; she sways on the piano stool.

'All right, Mum?' Her daughter is beside her, a big, capable hand on Ada's shoulder. 'Want some fresh air?'

In answer, Ada strikes a chord or two on the piano, and begins to play the sedate opening bars of 'Greensleeves'. 'Alas, my love, you do me wrong . . .'

NORA WATCHES ADA from the doorway. Daily she seems more confused, uncertain and unsteady on her feet. On the other hand, she might simply be nervous about playing to such a crowded room. Although everyone in the village was invited, more people have come along for the opening of Café Jetsam than Eve and Stavros were expecting. All the seats are taken. People stand along both walls and are gathered at the back of the room. As Steve introduces the first song, Stavros appears beside her, his breath smelling of garlic.

'Feta in the oven.' Stavros offers an arm. '*Ella*. Come.'

She follows him to the boathouse kitchen, where she's surprised to find Harry, Eve and Jonny, in heated discussion, the three of them crammed into the narrow space. Eve is flinging clean cutlery into a drawer.

'In this day and age, how many people in this village go to church or believe in God?' Jonny says.

'Consecrated means,' Eve waves a fork at Jonny, 'associated with the sacred.' She rams the emptied cutlery holder back into the dishwasher; Stavros raises his eyebrows at Nora, grabs a tray of crockery and heads off to lay up the tables in the shaded downstairs room of the café ready for when the music session is over.

'The church council have agreed to appeal,' Jonny replies. 'A unanimous agreement, I'd like to point out.' He loosens his tie and undoes his shirt collar. His shirt is sticking to his back.

Harry looks up from the orange he is peeling. 'Human spirituality takes many different forms. Anything consecrated should be considered worthy of spiritual respect, whatever your beliefs.'

'I'm an atheist. I have no beliefs.'

'But you have a soul, a spirit,' Harry says. He pauses as his eyes search Jonny's face. 'Don't you think?'

'Besides all this,' Eve waves a hand to hurry the two of them along in their discussion, 'I'm not sure of your motives, Jonny. Bosham is a family village where people have lived for generations. The church is already enough of a tourist attraction because of the connection with the Bayeux Tapestry and the story of Cnut's daughter. The lanes are narrow and many of the houses are old with front doors opening straight on to the road. Tourists take up all the space in our car park every day from April or May onwards. Do we really want more outsiders with cameras, rolling up in coachloads to ogle at a grave in our little Saxon church, even if it does belong to a king?'

Nora can hear the barely suppressed anger in Eve's voice. She wonders how long they have been discussing this before she arrived. Harry sits on a stool, relaxed, apparently absorbed with separating the segments of his orange, but Eve and Jonny stand with their heads thrust forward like teenagers confronting each other.

Harry sighs melodramatically. 'No seats in the Anchor for the locals.'

'How will we all cope with the media interest that will descend, if it does turn out to be Harold II's grave?' Eve wraps her loose shirt protectively around her belly. 'Worse, what if they start charging us entry to our own village church?'

The church door under the broad stone arch is never locked. Anyone, at any time, can push the weathered wood and step down in to the church.

'Come off it, woman!' Jonny's usually malleable face is unsmiling. 'You can't tell me tourists won't be a valuable source of income for you and your new café, as well as for many others.'

Eve crosses her arms and opens her mouth to reply, but Harry starts speaking first. 'They do that at Rosslyn.'

'Do what?' Nora asks.

'Charge entry. Used to see that church from miles away; beautiful, it was, across the fields, part of the landscape.'

Eve nods. 'You can't get anywhere near it since Dan Brown wrote that book. All scaffolding and screens. They don't want you to catch a glimpse unless you have paid the whacking great entrance fee. No photos allowed, of course, because they make money from selling postcards. A church should belong to everyone. We shouldn't have to pay to enter.'

'Portaloos,' adds Harry, nodding.

'All you can see is the hideous ticket office like something at Disney World. Me and Stavro turned around and drove off. Way too sad.'

Harry smacks the counter top and they all look at him, but he's gazing off into the middle distance. 'Man,' he shakes his head, 'I've just got to wondering what our loss will be if we find out for sure Harold does *not* lie buried in the church?'

Jonny looks exasperated. 'And your point is?'

'My *point*—' Harry looks up at the ceiling, rubs his chin and sighs, 'is the mystery. Way too big a loss, the mystery.'

Eve nods and flushes. 'All for a TV programme.'

'The stories which beguile us, take us out of ourselves. We need them. And those stories about Harold would be lost.'

'Some people prefer the definite. Facts, not fairy tales.' Jonny lifts his eyes, staring at Eve again.

'Facts, they have a habit of changing,' Harry says.

'It's not *just* a TV programme, is it?' Jonny says quietly, as if speaking only to Eve, and it dawns on Nora he may be trying to flirt with her. Not a good move. Eve, with her blue eyes and blonde hair, is used to men flirting and skilled at caustic put-downs.

'What is it for then? To get your name in the headlines, you pretentious prick? And excuse me,' Eve adds, before Jonny can retaliate, 'but I have more important people than you to attend to.'

ON THE GROUND by the back wheel of Harry's caravan lie several creased, bent tubes of paint and a piece of board covered with smears of colour. *Raw Sienna*, Nora reads, *Indian Red. Ultramarine White, Mars Orange, Rose Madder.*

She knocks on the caravan door. Blue and white striped fabric shifts at the open windows, and the rooflight is thrown open. This time of year, the heat must get unbearable. She wonders what he does for warmth in winter.

Harry's unlaced work boots and a few rags which smell of turpentine and something oily like linseed sit on the bottom step of the caravan. She knocks again, wondering if it is perhaps not after all today they arranged she would come to help carry his paintings to Café Jetsam. The door falls open towards her. Although it is mid-afternoon, Harry is cleaning his teeth, the toothbrush still in his mouth. He has no shirt on and white paint streaked across his forehead. From the bottom of the steps, Nora can see a painting – the paint applied in thick slabs – on an easel behind him. Toothbrush between his teeth, he gives a nod, standing aside to indicate she should come in.

It is the first time she has visited him in his caravan. The double bed at the far end is made up and covered with a patchwork quilt, tucked under at the corners. On the bed lies an old scout blanket with badges from different countries sewn on to it, wrapped around something bulky. An enamel mug and bowl have been rinsed and left on the draining board. Overlapping on the floor are two or three rugs which might be prayer mats, dark red and sage green. The caravan smells like hay on a warm day, the smell she associates with Harry.

While he bends over the sink, rinses his mouth and spits, Nora takes a closer look at the painting on the easel. Harry has applied the paint to the canvas in such a way as to suggest a contrast in textures, capturing both the chalkiness and the sheen of the flint in the wall. Creamy climbing roses tumble through a high hedge, behind which rise the wooden shingles of Bosham church spire, the weathercock gleaming gold on the top. She knows these cream roses, opposite the beer garden of the Anchor Bleu. They flower, full and heavy-headed, in May.

Harry has added an upper and lower margin, instantly bringing to mind the margins of the Bayeux Tapestry. The lower margin is edged with a long row of stylised waves, as a child might draw, and a line of tiny naked human figures, their backs to the viewer as they walk into the sea. Now she is closer, she can see the figures are dancing, arms in the air, feet stepping over the waves. Something about the mood of joy and expectation reminds her of the woollen figures wading out to the dragon-headed longboats in that early scene on the Bayeux Tapestry. Harold and a few of his men, falcons on their shoulders and hunting hounds in their arms, their elaborate tunics hitched at the hip, their moustaches sprightly as they embark on their journey.

In the upper margin, a pale duck-egg blue, Harry has painted fifty or sixty motes of black crowded together in the shape of a tornado which swirls sideways towards a group of trees. These specks, she guesses, are rooks, although individually they are too small to tell. When she narrows her eyes and squints in the way she did as a child trying to look grown-up when her father took her to art galleries, the black specks become smoke, rising in the sky.

'Coffee?' Harry asks.

Nora turns towards him to answer and catches sight of the painting she's seen before, stacked with other canvases on the floor against the wall. A bunch of palette knives stand in a bucket and a sheet has been thrown over the paintings, not quite covering them. All she can glimpse is a corner showing the tips of a woman's hair.

'Harold must have known Cnut's daughter, mustn't he?' The painting has made her think of the Lady of Shallot and the drowning of the little Saxon princess. 'They'd have been about the same age, growing up in the same village. Don't you think?'

The Bosham church scene at the beginning of the Bayeux Tapestry shows the horseshoe shape of the chancel arch, below which Cnut's young daughter already lay buried. Had lain for thirty or more years, by 1064.

When Harry doesn't answer, she looks up from the half-covered painting. Forgetting she has not filled him in on her line of thought, she continues. 'They prayed there, didn't they, Harold and his men, just before they went to France?'

Harry is lifting the flapping lower edge of a rip in the T-shirt he has just pulled on, as if the rip can be sealed up again through his effort.

'The custom before a journey.'

'And then the wind took them in the wrong direction. Because they can't have wanted to end up as hostages of Guy of Ponthieu.'

'No.'

'In the tapestry, Guy's soldiers have swords and lances.'

'Harold has only a dagger.'

'He wasn't prepared, so he wasn't going to France to fight.'

'Wreckers.'

'That's what Elsa says. She says they were famous for it on that stretch of French coastline.'

'You both have your reasons for wanting the bones to be Harold's.' Harry's face is serious.

'Who?' His statement takes her by surprise, coming as it does, sideways into the conversation. He must mean her and Jonny, grouping them together, as a couple.

'Sometimes wanting something to be makes it seem so.' Harry sits down on the end of the bed. 'All I'm saying.' Sometimes his sentences telescope into riddles.

'It is an important part of English history,' Nora says. 'Jonny is right to pursue it.'

'He wants his programme very much indeed.'

Nora doesn't know if she wants the TV programme to be made or not. What she does want is the coffins to be opened again. Or, at the very least, she wants someone else, another archaeologist, someone who knows what they are doing, to take up the story where her father left off.

Harry leans to one side and tugs the sheet from the stack of paintings. 'They are for Café Jetsam.'

Nora is embarrassed; she must have been staring.

'Is it Edyth?' she asks, too quickly, when the painting of the woman's hair is revealed. 'The swans? Is that why she's so white?'

Harry begins ripping pages from the telephone directory to wipe white paint from a palette knife. 'It is and it isn't.' He doesn't look up. 'Can that be fixed?' He nods in the direction of the scout blanket, still wiping paint from his palette knife.

Irritated by his evasiveness, she gets up. When she lifts one end of the blanket, she sees a broken headstock and stops in surprise.

'In the attic – it was Daphne's grandmother's.'

Nora lifts the blanket away from the cello, which is in pieces, the soundboard loose and splintered, the fingerboard warped. The upper bout has cracked off and lies separated from the body of the cello.

'What happened?'

'I think all the pieces are there, except the strings.' Harry shrugs. 'Spanish, Daphne said. She has no use for it.'

Nora laughs, and runs her hand over the worn finish on the sound board. 'I think she means Italian.'

'It fell down the stairs when they were putting it in the attic.'

A glissando of excitement runs through Nora. The Italian restorer who fell in love with her Goffriller had talked to her at some length about how restorative wood is. She sits down on the bed and carefully lifts away the loose soundboard to look for a maker's mark. 'I know just who to ask about it.'

Harry nods, smiling to himself as he begins to clean another palette knife.

THE DOOR BELL rings. Jonny stoops in the porch under the tendrils of honeysuckle, one arm balancing a sheaf of flowers, tangerine and red buds of gladioli. Nora's mind is elsewhere, she wasn't expecting him. In fact, she wants to put more distance between herself and her entanglement with Jonny.

'Good news!' He places the gladioli ceremoniously into her arms. 'A date has been set for the consistory court. Things are moving again. No hard feelings? I thought we could celebrate the Godwin Graves Project.'

Rook appears at the kitchen doorway, his beak stained with cherry. Jonny steps in, muttering, 'This place stinks of bird shit,' and turns to close the front door. Before Nora can say anything, Rook launches himself down the hallway screeching, the crown of feathers rising on top of his head. Neck arched and wings outstretched, he rears and prances towards Jonny's calves, beak thrust forward like a spear. He lets loose a pile of guano on Jonny's smart London shoes and hops away again.

'Bloody hell!' Jonny swears and, pulling out a tissue, bends to his shoes.

Rook rears back once more. He hurls himself higher and higher into the air, claws raised, until he's shrieking and swooping above Jonny's bent head and shoulders. Battering the walls and ceiling of the hallway, he knocks the mirror frame crooked with his outstretched wings. He is an explosion of noise and movement – the flap of his wings, the scrape of his claws – he ricochets up and down the hall like a loose firework. Jonny cringes and backs away, his arms over his head to protect himself. 'Christ! Get that fucking thing off me!' He swings back a leg, lashing out to kick.

'Careful!' Nora grabs at Jonny, too late to prevent his foot connecting with Rook's body. Kicked mid-air and knocked sideways, Rook tumbles downwards only briefly, screeching, before he rises up again, his wing-beat wild with fury.

'Fuck. I'm out of here.' Jonny fumbles at the door latch.

Rook has dropped to the floor and lies in the corner, a jumble of feathers, breast heaving and beak half-open. With his feathers puffed he appears three times his normal size. Nora approaches him tentatively, reaching out her hand.

'Hey, gorgeous, what did you just do?' she murmurs. 'Did you just fly?'

A car pulls into the drive, a taxi. Nora hopes Flick has not decided to make an impromptu visit. She offers Rook her arm and he sidles on to it. In the kitchen he huffs his feathers and begins to preen.

'Back soon, you clever boy,' she says, as she closes the kitchen door.

Their heads bend together and they stand so close in the front porch, for a moment they are one person, Jonny-and-the-girl. Her hand lifts as she says something in a low, urgent voice; Jonny murmurs a reply. His shoulders shift towards her; the angle of his neck. At the click of the closing kitchen door, Jonny-and-the-girl turn as one to stare at Nora, their faces blank. The girl's cheeks are tear-stained; Jonny's hand drops from her elbow. He steps away from her and smiles at Nora.

'Nora!' He spreads his arms in an expansive gesture. 'This is Emma, my PA. First time in this neck of the woods – she's a London girl through and through.'

Emma brushes a hair from her face.

'PA?' Nora's mind is glassy, opaque. The girl, it's true, is clutching what could be a filofax – bulging and floral-covered – but she can't be more than eighteen.

Jonny's fixed smile confirms everything. 'At last you two get to meet!'

Emma has bunched her fingers to her lips. The tips of her nails are brilliant white and thick. They must be false.

The three of them stand in the porch. A smell of mud and decomposition rises up from the creek.

'Anchor Bleu?' Jonny asks. The taxi is turning round in the drive.

Nora shakes her head at him.

'Jonny, the train?' Emma looks at her watch and stands down a step. 'Got to go, sorry.' She's already shuffling sideways and giving a little wave. 'Call me later?'

Emma says nothing to Nora, doesn't even look at her. That's how the realisation settles, fully, on Nora. She leans in the porch, her hand on the flint wall, the rounded pebbles fitting her palm as they fitted the palm of the stonemason who placed them there, more than a hundred years ago. Traditional lime mortar keeps a wall alive, her father explained to her, whereas a wall built with cement is dead. He'd shown her the differences in the laying of the stones, how you could tell whether the stonemason had been left- or right-handed, the different styles and colours and patterns of the stones in every flint wall in the village.

Emma's high heels sink in the new gravel where it's too deep, her progress towards the waiting taxi as slow as if she was making her way barefoot down a shingle bank. Not an outdoor girl. Emma is dressed for a carpeted office with a desk broad enough for impromptu sex. Nora will laugh, later, at this whole scenario.

'Nice girl.' Jonny ruffles his hair with both hands and they stand, side by side but not together, in the porch. He turns towards Nora. Tiredness drags over her. He will want to eat and drink; he will want to talk about the Godwin Graves Project; he will tell her more lies, or perhaps just not tell her the whole truth. It's a relief not to want him any more. The bright sun highlights dry skin flakes between Jonny's eyebrows, the downward pull of lines around his mouth, and she feels a wave of pity for the professional and personal muddle in which he's embroiled – the possible failure of his dream to gain permission to make the TV documentary of the decade, perhaps the century; a wife he wants to escape, a teen-age daughter and very possibly, if she can read him at all, another lover: this young girl, Emma. And Nora: the tricky 'ex' he needs on board for his Project.

Just 'tend: Zach's phrase. Nora rehearses a sentence. She might manage to stick to chit-chat, but already she can sense Jonny's preoccupation as he looks back down the drive.

Harry ambles out of the shed and heads for the orchard with his spade on his shoulder.

No, she can't spare any time or energy for Jonny. 'Aren't you going with her?'

For a moment it seems he will argue; he opens his mouth and hesitates, trying to work out whether or not she has put two and two together. If nothing else, Jonny has great ability to believe in himself. He smiles, gives her a peck on the cheek. 'Sure?'

She nods.

He saunters down the drive, jacket slung over one shoulder. As he opens the door of the waiting taxi, he swivels on a heel, waves and blows a kiss.

AUTUMN

ADA HAS PACKED Cheddar and Ritz biscuits. She should have done this long ago because she would like him to talk to her again, more than anything, the way he used to when he dressed in the mornings, telling her about his day ahead as he wrenched his belt buckle tighter – he always bought his belts too long, took his Swiss Army knife to them to stab an extra hole in the leather.

In the dark, Ada trips on an uneven plank in the boardwalk. The picnic case knocks her ankle. She has teabags and boiling water in the thermos, slices of Eve's fruit cake wrapped in foil. Though Brian had been a much bigger man when he was younger, in later years his appetite was only for his books.

She puts up her hands to cover her ears. They ache, from the lack of his voice or the whipping of the wind she can't tell. The roar of her blood or the sea drags her into a tornado of thoughts and memories twisting inside her skull. *What was the point?* Nora had cried. *I didn't tell you, because I knew you wouldn't want anything to do with it.*

She tried to feed him up, cooked Beef Wellington, steak and kidney puddings, roast dinners with Yorkshire pudding – all his favourite meals – for him when he was home between trips. Not through guilt because she'd been seeing Robert, but because she wanted him back: she wanted Brian as he was before.

Sand whisks up, vicious as gravel on Ada's face. She grips a stake in the fencing while her stomach heaves and she tastes bile. How she could do with an invigorating sip or two of Harry's *sol y sombra*.

Ada had wanted to start a conversation. 'You never tell me anything,' she said, needing Nora to stay and talk, wanting her to listen to what she had to say instead of locking herself away with that instrument for hours. She wanted them, mother and daughter, to chat companionably over the kitchen table, instead of which, between them, they brewed an argument.

The day had been miserable, the chill of a damp autumn just beginning, mist and rain rolling in from the sea. In the afternoon Ada made herself a hot toddy and was sitting down just as Nora came in from a run, the plaited length of her hair beaded with moisture, tendrils curling round her face as they had done when she was a child. She tugged at the band which held the strands wound together and shook them out, lifting the weight of hair, letting it fall like a cloak below her waist.

The argument was about Ada's reasons for selling the house. Or it was, to begin with, but became snared with questions about the disappearance of Nora's handbag, her missing cash, questions which Ada turned into accusations about Nora earning only enough to support a flea. At any moment she knew Nora would start on about the afternoon drinking, so Ada was pleased to be able to pre-empt this discussion by mentioning the bottle of gin secreted in Nora's wardrobe. One thing led to another, Brian's shoes, Brian leaving, until finally they arrived at the very heart of the matter: why Nora came home last spring and had never left again.

'I want to know what happened,' Ada demanded.

Nora had a foot up on the kitchen stool – her long legs must have been cold, all that bare skin in those shorts – one of her gym shoes, hideous things which cost a fortune, fell to the floor with a thud.

'I didn't tell you, because I realised,' Nora said – shouted, to be precise, startling the ugly bird on her shoulder into a hop and flap. It opened its beak to contribute a racket of its own to the mayhem. 'I realised *you* wouldn't want to look after a baby.'

Ada's mind swam. Since the boat accident, creek water silted in the nooks and crannies of her mind and sometimes the sense of what she wanted to say or even think had washed away or sunk.

'You got rid of it.' This was not a question, no. A mother knows these things, and she'd known all along, there was a baby, once upon a time, and then there was no baby, no happily ever after, only Nora with her pent-up misery – never communicating, never writing home when she was away, shutting herself in her bedroom for weeks on end when she *was* home, wrapping packages in newspaper to hide in her wardrobe. Brian's shoes, for pity's sake!

'Him, Mother, not *it*; my baby was a little boy.'

At that, Ada sat down. A cherub, an angelic baby grandson with the white blonde curls and blue eyes Nora was born with, both of which came from Robert. She put down her whisky glass with care; picked it up again to swill the ice cubes; put it down again.

She could only whisper the words: 'You mean you gave your own son away?'

Nora slumped to the kitchen floor, one gym shoe still on. She shook her head but she didn't speak. The creature was making an almighty racket, feathers flying, knocking into things as it danced to and fro, edging towards Ada's feet, vicious claws clicking on the flagstones.

'His name was Noah.'

Ada could barely catch Nora's words because she was addressing her knees.

'I did not give him away.'

'Where is he then?'

'He was ... taken from me.'

What she meant precisely, Ada has no idea, because at that moment the phone rang and it was Stavros, his Greek accent obscuring the sense of the words he spoke but not the urgency. Ada handed the phone to Nora, who pulled on a coat over her shorts and left.

The bird fluttered up on to the back of a kitchen chair opposite, folded its black wings and balefully blinked one white eyelid at her. Outside, the mist obliterated trees and fields. The landscape had disappeared. Robert, Brian, her mother, Felicity and her girls; a baby grandson called Noah – all gone – leaving her where she has been for seventy years or more, at Creek House, and with no one but a bird for company. The blasted thing stole the last of the cherries. Nevertheless, she would mix herself another whisky sour.

Hours later, when Nora still had not returned – goodness knows where she could be, wearing that ridiculous get-up – Ada could bear to be alone no longer. It was time. She considered the bottom of her glass – lead crystal, the best – where the orange slice lay juiceless and squashed. It was time for Brian, as was his right, to be involved in the Godwin Grave Project.

When Ada can walk no longer against the drag of sand into which her feet sink with each step, she slumps down in a hollow where, mercifully, the wind is less vicious. Grains of wind-blown sand have stuck to her skin, to her scalp. Edges sharp as glass in the roots of her hair, beneath her fingertips, in her mouth, between her back teeth. The Ancient Egyptians sometimes walked out into the desert, Brian told her, to die in a cave, the life scoured out of them by sun and wind, their skin leathered and preserved by rapid desiccation.

For a moment she'd forgotten why she was wandering the dunes. She has lost Brian. When they told her the news of his death a part of her mind switched off: Ping! The noise a bulb makes when it blows. She should have tried to discover what happened to him and why, but there's only so much one can bear to dwell on at the time. All the same, she should have come looking sooner.

THE SWOOPS AND curves of Ada's handwriting make Nora picture her mother as a girl in school, hair in plaits, laboriously tracing over the lines and loops, each 'y' and 'g' joined to the following letter, but when she reads the words themselves, the message written there, time halts.

This note must have been on the kitchen table when she came in last night, because the ink is smudged by a circular mark from the empty milk bottle Nora picked up, rinsed and put out on the front step before she turned off the lights. All of which means Ada has been out all night.

The police officer who answers the phone has a Welsh accent, the gentle musicality of which makes Nora want to weep.

'And what is it which makes you concerned about her absence? Will she not have popped out to the shops?'

'She's been out since last night.'

'Were you at home?'

'No, I went out, to babysit for a friend.' Nora left the house in the middle of the row with Ada, driving in the grip of a white-hot fury. Eve had been taken into hospital. On the telephone, fear had exaggerated Stavros's heavy accent.

This is not the right time, Nora, is too early for our winter baby.

'When I came home, I thought she'd gone up to bed,' she tells the police officer.

'She doesn't usually take herself off of an evening, or decide to stay over at a friend's house?'

'No. Yes, she does take herself off, but not . . . She's in her seventies. She left a note. It doesn't make sense.' Nora hesitates. 'She may have been a little bit tipsy.'

Gone to look for your father. Nora begins to explain the note: her father's death, years ago, what few details she knows, the accident, underground. As she recounts a version of the story she has created for herself, the familiar desert images play through her mind and it occurs to her she knows where Ada might have gone.

She bangs out through the back door and runs down the road to the Anchor Bleu. Yesterday's mist has cleared, it's a sunny midday and the pub is full. She slams her hand down on the bar, aware of faces turning, blurred, towards her. Jason looks up from changing a beer barrel.

The thought of the sand has dried her mouth, so she points out of the window, towards the creek where sea-scum froths with the incoming tide, covering the mud. 'My mother is missing!'

She's already heading for the creek path down to the dunes by the time Jason stands in the open door of the pub, jangling his keys as he shouts, 'Everybody out!'

★   ★   ★

Later, Nora would find pinpricks of blood on her shins and her forearms where the marram grass had needled. On the top of a high sand dune, buffeted by the wind, she scanned the miles of sand and grass, the stake and wire fencing, the vast stretches of wet sand to the south, sweeping towards a scribble of sea in the far distance. Ada might be anywhere, lying in any dip or hollow, out of sight. She wouldn't hear Nora's shouts, snatched away on the breeze.

Dogs, police, a helicopter, holidaymakers, people from the pub and village, everyone dropped what they were doing and joined the search for Ada. Dr Robertson's daughter set off on horseback along the shoreline. The sea had by now reached the edge of the pebbles and shadows stretched over the dips in the dunes, where sand flew like spray lifting off water.

Nora kept running. Though she was wary of sudden stops or starts, her calf injury of a month ago had healed and she felt no twinges. She left the line of searchers who moved slowly across the dunes and jogged back inland through fields of harvested rape, following narrow footpaths she hadn't crossed since childhood, hidden short-cuts familiar only to those who'd grown up nearby. Ada could have headed for the dunes last night, but she might not have reached East Head. Or she might have turned back for home and fallen. Nora beat back the undergrowth with a stick. Brambles caught at her arms and hair; rabbit holes trapped her feet and turned her ankles. She moved like an automaton, breath jolted from her with each step. If she stopped running, she would cease to breathe. As if from a high summit, she watched her body make laboured progress across the fields.

The day after Noah's birth she had run upstairs, taking the stairs two at a time, because she'd heard his cries from downstairs in the kitchen though the doors in between were closed and Ada was chopping carrots with the radio turned up full volume. She was out of breath when she lifted him and kissed the top of his head. *Noah.* He was quiet. She unwrapped his tiny limbs all the same and climbed into bed with him, holding him close, skin to skin, as she had when he was born. Then, the two of them had lain in the bathwater until it cooled and her teeth began to chatter. She'd swaddled him in the hand towel and was on the way to her room with him when she felt another contraction, and looked around for somewhere safe to put him down. In the bottom of the wardrobe was the Italian leather bag Isaac had bought for her months ago, before everything changed. The bag was wrapped in tissue tied with slim ribbon, slipped inside a red and black plastic carrier bag, exactly as it had been when Isaac passed it to her over the table at Fortescue's. Another contraction made her pant and fold at the waist; she thought about climbing straight into bed with her baby but was worried the pain might mean she would not be able to hold him safely. *What shall I do?* she asked her absent father, seeing him in his study, head bent under the circle of light from the Anglepoise. *What shall I do?* She spoke the words out loud.

The handbag smelled of new leather but was supple, with a silk lining, and as big as a holdall. The opening was easily long enough to allow her to place Noah, wrapped in the hand towel, inside, without scraping his head or toes on the ends. She placed the bag on her bed near the wall. Later, she wrapped her placenta in another towel and put it in the red and black plastic carrier bag. Without the energy to wash or finish undressing, she crawled under the covers and fell asleep. When she woke in the morning, the night's events were wiped from her mind until her hand crept to the looseness of her belly. A sticky soreness between her legs, and when she lifted her hands to her face, a metallic smell. A little blood had dried around the thumbnail of her right hand.

The whole village is out, including Steve, Eric the Swan-man, Daphne and Terry, Jason from the pub and the waitresses from Mariner's teashop, searching along the shoreline and moving across the flat arable land behind the dunes. At the far edge of the wheat field, a part-time fireman, the father of one of Nora's youngest pupils and the son of a man who'd grown up with Ada, thrashes the bulrushes at the throat of the rife, shoulders burly with rage. Above, a skylark flutters and falls in the blue.

When the heartbeat thud of the helicopter's blades recedes, Nora can hear other searchers in the far distance calling her mother's name. *Ada. Ada.*

She is no longer running. The footpath cuts through a field of ripe wheat, rustling, waist-high and rippling with shadow and light. Here and there, flattened by the recent rain which has delayed cutting, the wheat appears trampled. The farmer, Ted's son, has begun to harvest the field but abandoned his combine to join the search. Nora's strides have taken her into the field's centre, walking over the cracked mud where the footpath is the width of a single tractor tyre, a right of way for hundreds of years; all those feet passing. In the private, swaying warmth of the wheat, Nora's voice sounds hoarse from calling. Her stomach churns. Through the pale stalks she can just make out the line marked by the other tractor-tyre; tramlines, the farmers call them. Shadows move near the unwalked tramline, a blot of shade squatting in the wheat stalks. Her pace slows. A boy is there, a toddler, not fair-haired like Zach, but with a cap of hair, dark and sleek as an animal pelt.

Nora folds her arms against her body. Not this again. This was finished months ago, seeing him. She concentrates on a slow breath, on the reassuring rise and fall of her ribs beneath her forearms. She turns her mind from the memory resolutely, the way she has taught herself to do. It is possible. Eventually, she opens her eyes to look again. There is nothing, only a sense of movement in the sway of shadows.

Hands on her thighs, Nora crouches to ease the stitch in her side. The wheat stirs again, a breeze eddying over the ears in sudden swirls drifting to stillness. She puts her hands to the ground where the earth's surface lifts like a scab. Between the lines of stalks, weeds with tiny red flowers and heart-shaped leaves spread their tendrils across dried fissures of mud. The wheat stems hold back a silence, rippling with something waiting.

A cry goes up. *Coooeee!* In the field's entrance, Mary, Steve's childminder, has raised both arms, her forearms scooping the air to beckon them back, her pink mobile phone clutched in one hand. 'She's safe, Nora!' She points at her phone. 'Harry's found her!'

'I THOUGHT YOU'D be at the hospital with Mum.' Flick rubs at the lower part of her bare arms and Nora's reflection jiggles up and down in the mirrored surfaces of her sister's sunglasses. Behind Flick's back, Eve pulls a face like a gargoyle.

'Are you cold? Do you need a jumper?'

Flick's wearing a white, closely fitted sundress with killer heels which make her about five foot four. Her tanned calves and forearms are pimpled with cold but she shakes her head and reaches up for one of Ada's old coats on the hooks by the front door.

'No, but I do need a fag. Back in a tic.' Her heels click down the tiled hallway and out through the French doors.

Despite having spent the night in a hollow in the dunes, Ada is suffering only mild hypothermia, the doctor says. The coat she was wearing is an old heirloom, a full-length beaver fur coat which once belonged to Nora's grandmother. Without its protection the hypothermia would, in all likelihood, have been severe. In the morning, in a shaky and confused state, the doctor says, it seems Ada might have fallen as she tried to scramble up the steep slope of a dune. Her hip is broken. She will be in hospital for a while.

Eve, however, is out of hospital, sent home the next day while everyone was out searching for Ada. A false labour. Eve reaches up to give Nora a kiss. She checks her watch. 'Right, I'm off. Don't let her bully you, sweetheart.'

'Thanks for driving all that way to pick her up. She should have caught the train from Gatwick.'

'I enjoyed the trip – got me out of the house and away from Stavros and his fussing.'

Benjie spots Eve's approach and leaps to and fro over the seats of the 2CV. When Eve stops mid-stride Benjie stops too, tongue lolling and a paw poised up at the closed car window. Eve has scooted back to whisper in Nora's ear. 'Only one topic, so be prepared.'

'Money?'

'Nope – husband, soon to be ex.'

'Oh no.'

'Oh yes. She plans to nail him with those stilettos.' Eve fishes in the pockets of her denim jacket for her car key. 'Prime candidate for anger management classes.'

Nora laughs.

'I'm serious.' Eve jabs the air with her car key. 'She'll gnaw away, chew up the kids at the same time and still feel self-righteous about it. Forgive me, she's your sister but she's a money-grabbing cow.' She opens the car door and Benjie scrambles all over her, licking her face.

In the kitchen, Harry is washing up. He rinses a glass under the hot tap and holds it up to the light. Polishing fast and with a flourish, he turns the glass expertly, lifting it to the light a second time for inspection before placing it on the shelf. He plunges his hands back in the water.

'You must be Harry,' Flick says, stepping in the back door from the garden. Petite as a child beside him, she offers her hand, high and straight-armed, as if intending Harry to kiss the back. He gives a shrug towards his hands, covered with bubbles in the sink, but smiles and nods.

'Those are lead crystal. They mustn't go in the dishwasher.'

Harry smiles and over the top of Flick's head his eyes meet Nora's. He slowly raises the submerged glass from the bubbles in the washing-up bowl.

Flick's neck flushes.

'Harry, this is my sister, Flick.' Too late, Nora remembers she hates her name being shortened. 'Felicity will be staying for a few days.'

At breakfast, Felicity scraped butter on to toast, edge to edge, crust to crust, and said she wanted Rook moved out.

'Out?'

'Out of the house, out of the way.'

'Out of the way.'

'It's just a bird, Nora. It won't feel excluded.'

'How would you know?'

With exaggerated care, Flick put down the slice of toast and marmalade and rested her wrists on the table. 'You've heard the expression "bird brain"? It won't work out what's going on, will it? It'll just be in the shed instead of the kitchen.' She picked up her toast again and delicately bit off a corner, her rosebud lips moving round and round with the chewing movements of her jaw.

They argue most of the time, but manage a united front in the hospital for Ada, visiting her together once or twice. More often they take it in turns. Felicity's talents lie in getting things done with speed and efficiency. She is adamant Ada cannot be left to live alone and, since Nora is vague about her future plans, it is agreed Ada will go out to Spain for a month or so once she is discharged, to recuperate and to see how she likes the expat life. Nora cannot argue against Ada's obvious enthusiasm for the idea. Flick and Ada draw up a list of jobs to be done by a 'handyman', and Flick even suggests Harry. Now she has met him she apparently no longer finds him a threat to her inheritance. By the time Flick leaves at the end of a fortnight, Creek House has been valued. They have started to fill packing cases for storage and Nora is exhausted.

NORA SITS ON the floor in the hallway of Creek House, a bowl of cold porridge on her lap. Outside, Harry whistles 'Sweet Sixteen'. His ladder scrapes the crazy paving. She's left money for the window-cleaning in an envelope with his name on it, poking out of the letter-box. Sitting here, she cannot be seen, because the only windows in the hallway are stained-glass panels set high in the front door. Unless he lifts the letterbox flap to peer in, he will presume she's out.

Last night she got back late from dropping Flick off at Gatwick. After she'd put Rook to bed, because the road was still with her, lines and lights streaming towards her vision, she wandered out with an apple into the cool garden. It was high tide, the creek frilling against the retaining wall at the end of the garden where the lawn drops to the shoreline. From the millwheel came the sound of water rushing. She looked out over the harbour at the lights on the boats. Only when she turned back towards the house to go in did she see it, and the muscles around her heart contracted.

Harry has finished digging the vegetable patch. The area, freshly dug-over with manure, stretches right up to the overgrown hedge on the left-hand side of the garden. Right up to the apple tree. Fleetingly, she imagined climbing straight back into the Wolseley and driving away.

They did talk about Ada's vegetable garden, she and Harry and Flick; she remembers that much. And it was agreed Harry would finish preparing the ground, perhaps even do some preliminary planting before they put Creek House on the market, but Nora hadn't thought things through. As usual, she hadn't been thinking straight at all. Last night, not knowing what else to do, she took the hired cello down to the cellar, where she played for hours: Dvořák, the final coda; its intense, yearning *ppp* as the cello slowly glides from the heights.

This morning, Harry had left a message for her in the kitchen. After cleaning the windows, the note announced in sketchily printed capital letters, he will prepare the ground for the path round the vegetable area.

Harry improvises as he whistles – warbling trills and extravagant cadenzas. Her memory dredges up words to fit the repeated musical phrase: 'I love you as I've never loved before'. Nora prods at her porridge, an island floating on milk. The edge dips under as she prods with her spoon, but bobs up again. She's been sitting so long the porridge is too cold to eat and under her buttocks the chill from the floor tiles has spread into her hip bones.

Harry would stop and come in, if she asked him. Sit with his chipped-knuckle hands around a mug of tea. Talk with her about – anything – help fill her mind with something other than the memories, half-formed and fragmented, which now insist on rising to the surface.

Last night she stood under the apple tree and placed both of her hands on the cankered bark. She thought about how time has passed since Noah's birth, the days and weeks and months and seasons since she last held him.

This May the apple tree had very little blossom. Since her childhood, it has borne no more than a handful of apples and the branches have a lopsided look through competing for space and light with the vigorous growth of the hebe hedge. One branch, which should have been pruned back long ago, stretches out low and far into the garden and here Nora hung the wind chimes she'd remade after the spring gales. Underneath the tree, grass is beginning to recover from the summer drought. Last winter a flattened track across the grass led from the house to the tree, showing the path Nora walked at night. Ada never once commented on the trail, which looked much like an animal track, a fox or a badger on its nightly travels along the edge of the lawn.

The capital letters of Harry's message make it very clear what he is about to do. She has seen the plan for the vegetable patch, studied the drawings spread out on the kitchen table. She knows where the path will run around a low box hedge, and she knows that the space between the hedge and the dug-over area is not big enough, at the moment, to make any room at all for a path. Today, when he's finished the windows, Harry is going to prepare the ground for the path. To do that, he will have to cut back the hebes, just beginning their autumn blooming. She could use this fact as an excuse to stop him. She knows she won't.

Across the skin of Nora's sloped thighs, lozenges of red and blue light fall from the stained glass. The hallway at Creek House is long and narrow as a timeline. Her legs are too long, now, years too long to be sitting here on the tiled floor with her back pressed against the wall, her bare toes gripping the rim of the skirting board opposite. Harry will soon start digging.

Even now her mind skates away. Before she left with Flick for Gatwick, the hebes were taller than a man, shaggy and dense, but by the time she returned, Harry had cut the glossy leaves back to reveal skinny knobbles and kinks, their inner branches deformed by lack of light. Now, in the open, hangs the wire she once threaded with holed pebbles, bending the wire into the shape of a heart.

Nora puts down the bowl and hugs her knees. Fifteen years since he left and one of her father's trilbies still hangs on the hat-stand. The breeze of her family's comings and goings lifts the hairs on her arms, their busyness in other rooms, at other times. Not any more. And not here, where she sits, halfway between the front door and the kitchen.

Her father's bee-keeper's veil and gloves are piled on to the shelf above the coat rack where layer upon layer of the family's coats hang on scooping hooks of wrought iron. None of her father's shoes are here. Nora doesn't know whether he took them, or whether Ada gave them to charity or chucked them out with the rubbish. The only pair of her father's shoes left in the house, as far as Nora knows, is upstairs, in a newspaper-wrapped package at the bottom of her wardrobe.

That May night she wrapped her beloved baby tight and held him close for the last time. She took him down the garden to the orchard. Masses of forget-me-nots covered the ground beneath the trees, the blue of thousands of tiny flowers hovering over the earth like a mist.

Harry's whistling moves with the clank of his buckets along the side of the house. She should call out and ask him to come in now. She imagines herself going to the door and shouting his name, sees her hand on the latch opening the door, leaning out, her mouth open wide to call out to him but her mind stutters and fails to follow thought with action. She whispers another name: *Noah*.

Harry's footfall passes back along the side of the house to the front. Perhaps he's leaving, had enough for one day.

A window must be open somewhere in the house because a breeze carries the watery sound of the poplars, the chime of halyards against masts.

Strapping man, Ada always says, *built like a barrel*. Harry has physical stamina. Cleaning the windows won't have tired him.

The blue hand towel was embroidered with a border of swans. Nora tucked the corners of the towel under the swathes of fabric so as to hold her tiny baby safe. She kissed the top of his head. She couldn't say goodbye.

She hunches over her arms. Rook sidles along the hallway, head on one side. With a sandpapery rustle of feathers, he places a cool foot over her toes.

The poplar leaves are lapping. The submerged drift of her mind has registered the sound of footsteps, boots approaching on the brick of the garden path, but her body is no longer part of her. Her mind is frozen. The kitchen door falls open. Harry stands there, a red sky behind him, warmth from the low sun pouring in. Sparrows squabble in the hedge. Harry stands with his legs apart, breath heavy from digging. His shirt is undone. In the crook of his elbow, against his chest, he cradles a mud-covered, raggy bundle.

Nora feels her body rise from where she is sitting at the kitchen table. Her face is dry.

'Look what I've found, Nora,' he says, still looking down, his voice a murmur.

She sways over to Harry and holds out her arms.

THE POLICE OFFICER closes the door into the garden. He is Welsh and his voice is both comforting and familiar though she doesn't know why, or what he means by waiting for SOCO.

'We mustn't touch anything else now,' Harry had said, after he'd phoned the police and repeated to them everything she'd told him.

The police officer puts a hand on her shoulder then briefly touches the top of Noah's head, wrapped in the hand towel. Nora would like to get up and wash the towel so that it is the right shade of blue again, so that the border of swans shows white and clean, but she doesn't move.

Blue and white tape festoons the garden: POLICE.

Her arms around Noah hold him close, against her body warmth.

The police officer makes tea for himself and brings Nora a mug too, although she shook her head when he asked if she wanted one and shakes her head again when he lifts the mug into her line of vision before setting it on the table. Lights are bright in the garden, the shadows of people moving in and out of lit-up areas. Someone is taking pictures, a flash bouncing light off the glass in the window. Then a camera flashes, twice, and the rumble of Harry's voice travels to her from somewhere at the front of the house. Nora looks in the direction of the hallway. She doesn't want Harry to go anywhere.

The police officer says something to her which includes the words *witness* and *questions*, and which doesn't make sense.

'There were no witnesses. No one else was there,' Nora says to the policeman. 'No one else knew.' Not quite accurate, because Isaac knew and Ada had guessed at something, but no one knew about Noah's birth or his death and that is what she means.

She wants to tell the truth so she must be sure not to forget anything, not to leave anything out. Impossible though, because already she is not certain what she remembers and what she has forgotten and whether, between those two extremes, some details are those her mind has invented.

'I hadn't even met Harry then.'

'Don't worry.' The Welsh police officer's neck is too thick for the stiff collar of his shirt; he pulls at it with a forefinger and says something about an unexplained death.

She would like her baby's death to be explained. Whether he had died because she fell on the stairs after drinking gin or whether it was something she did wrong or failed to do. She would like to ask the kind policeman what he thinks about this, but she is too exhausted, scraped out. She closes her eyes.

She rocks to and fro, curled around her baby. The police officer puts his hand on her shoulder again, and his touch helps her mind focus. She keeps her eyes closed. She keeps thinking about the heart-shaped cockle shell, its two halves shut together, the spines pricking her hand. Inside, the shell was bone-white and empty.

'Do you think he drowned in the bath?' Nora's voice croaks. 'They can breathe underwater when they're born, can't they?'

He doesn't answer, perhaps because a woman has entered the kitchen. Nora didn't hear her come in, but she can smell perfume or body lotion and the woman's heels clack on the floor. She says something in an undertone to the Welsh police officer about securing the scene then comes nearer and pulls up a chair. Nora opens her eyes. She holds Noah closer, lifting her hand to protect the side of his head. The woman's face fills her vision. Particles of face powder cling in the hair above her ear, close to her cheek. She has put on her make-up in a hurry.

After all this time, everything is happening at once. Nora sits up. A constriction scrapes her throat. 'You're going to take him away from me, aren't you?'

The woman glances to one side, down to the floor, and then to the other side, out through the window at the lights and movement – and she could be shaking her head, she could be saying *No, we're not going to do that*, but then the woman looks down at her hands in her lap and Nora knows the answer is *Yes, we are*.

She's choking then, the constriction in her throat building and building.

The woman begins to talk rapidly and while she talks Nora wails, *No, no, no*, over and over, thinking of nothing but the tide retreating, mud and weed exposed, water held stagnant, the smell of Salthill Creek.

'YOU CAN HAVE Noah back later.' Another woman, nearer her own age, holds Nora's hand as she says this.

The room at the police station has no windows. Nora does not remember how she came to be here. The lights in the ceiling pulsate. Rook, a starveling, his tiny body pulsing with each beat of his heart. She had saved him.

They have taken Noah away for a post-mortem, the woman explains as she rubs her thumb to and fro over Nora's knuckles. 'We need to find out why he might have died.' The woman's hair is pulled back from her face in an unbrushed ponytail and she wears no make-up. This honesty makes Nora feel safer.

'Can we turn off those lights?'

'Of course we can.'

The darkness is comforting. She will be able to talk into this darkness.

'I ran a bath. I'd had some gin. I wasn't thinking.'

The woman's thumb continues to move across Nora's knuckles, stroking. She tells Nora her name is Clare and she is a family liaison officer.

'I was frightened,' Nora says. 'I hadn't told my mother. It was all too soon. I thought he would be born at the end of the summer, not at the beginning. I didn't know what the pains were. I got into the bath.'

Clare explains it is an offence to conceal the birth of a child, but Nora does not understand what she means.

'What happened to you was not a miscarriage,' Clare says. 'We think your pregnancy was too far on for that. Which means Noah was stillborn.' Illegal disposal of a dead body, Clare goes on to tell her, carries a prison sentence. They have to collect the evidence. If it is in the public interest to prosecute, there will be a court case.

A police officer had fetched the gin bottle and the red leather bag from the bottom of her wardrobe and brought them downstairs in clear plastic bags that are on the table in front of her.

Almonds and lemon juice from Spain, cassia bark and orris, grains of Paradise from West Africa: exotic ingredients from far-flung places and the drink she associated with Isaac, the beginning of their love affair. She had twisted off the cap. Aromatic fumes flowered at the back of her nose and throat.

Juniper and liquorice. She drew the bedroom curtains across the dark window and eased off her jeans with a sense of relief. The button had been undone all day, the zip's teeth catching on her flesh and biting a raw place on the fold of her skin. All day there'd been a dragging sensation in the small of her back which made her weary. Her mother fussed over lunch and supper. *You're not eating properly. No wonder you're skin and bone.* She'd gone to her room wondering how she could stand living like this. The neat gin burned her lips; she needed to fetch tonic water.

She listened out for the click of her mother's bedroom door, then tripped on the hem of her nightie on the way back up, her foot missing the stair so that she had to grab for the banister to prevent herself from tumbling all the way down. She found her shin skinned from the carpet burn the next day.

She had woken some time later, her stomach churning. A cramp squeezed the hollow of her back and she thought her bowels were about to open. Stooped double, she crossed the landing to the loo. As soon as she sat and leaned forward on her thighs, her muscles unclenched and liquid gushed from her in a watery flood. She felt momentary relief until a cramp squeezed at her bowels again and forced a grunt of pain: less liquid this time. The pain was familiar, like period cramps, but stronger. She peered between her legs into the toilet bowl. Another cramp wrung the small of her back and spread fingers of pain, muscular and demanding, round to her womb, squeezing the breath from her. She lowered herself to the floor to inch across the smooth linoleum to the high-sided bath, where she turned both taps on full. Her mother might wake at the emptying gurgle of the hot tank, but warm water would help her relax. She thought the neat gin had made her sick.

Grains of Paradise.

Noah's head was like a pomegranate, his skin red and wrinkled. Wisps of dark hair lay flat against his head and his eyes were closed, the lids pressed together as if sealed. He didn't make a sound. She kissed his minute, translucent fingers. He did not stir. She wrapped him in the blue hand towel but unwrapped him again to study his chest. He was not breathing. She cupped his tiny body in her long hands.

WINTER

Hinetone, mid-eleventh century

IN THE DEEP of winter, what remained of his bones was brought to her in a fishing creel.

The horse's flanks heaved and the salty scent of wet dog told her the broad-shouldered stranger had travelled hard and fast. When he dismounted, though the light from the fire inside had scorched her vision, she saw a gathering basket slung across his body beneath his furs which he took time to unstrap. It was too late in the day for a fisherman to come selling, no silver-bodied fish slithered at the basket's opening. The unfamiliar shape and size and the manner in which he cradled the basket gave her pause. She obeyed his gesture to step outside, but her hand shook as she protected the flame of the lamp.

The stranger showed respect and stood more than a stride away, straight-backed as a warrior, the basket at his chest shielded by his crossed arms. A blade had slashed one forearm in the recent months; the wound was puckered, still livid. The basket he clasped had a dense weave of rush. Her heart, brittle as a wick snuffed, pinched with unease.

On that night in October, the stranger said, young men, a group from Harold's village in Sussex, had disguised themselves in garments stripped from the Norman dead. Their fathers, whose bodies lay for the women to reclaim, had been Harold's playmates, and one among them had been schooled in the French language. They followed William Malet through the glōm, and heard Guillaume le Bâtard order him to bury the Norman dead. The digging and shovelling would take all night and more so. At the second command, Malet's shoulders slumped. He was required to reassemble Harold's corpse, wrap it in purple linen and return to the camp at Hastings to bury the remains on the white cliff's crumbling edge. In this way, le Bâtard jested, Harold was to be granted his wish made in arrogance, and be left to guard for ever the sea he had so desired to rule.

As the pattern and purpose of the stranger's story became clear, Edyth pulled her furs round her shoulders. Her mind shied from the remembrance of Harold's corpse.

The Bosham Boy had dreamed a plan which he spoke to Malet in French: Harold's body hauled in a net, far out to sea, a burial place impossible to discover. Malet hesitated. The Boy spat on the purple-wrapped body of the king then smiled up at Malet. The impermanence of the sea would allow no shrine. With that, Malet was persuaded.

Edyth pictured the boys taught alongside her sons by the elders of the church at Bosham. One of them?

'No names,' the stranger said.

Malet's horse tossed his head and high-stepped on the cliff top as the Boy rowed out to sea with the purple wrappings. As soon as the net splashed overboard Malet, impatient, turned his horse to leave without witnessing the marker which bobbed to mark the place.

The Boy had family in that village, fisher folk. A few days later, wanting to pray forgiveness to Harold for his disrespect, he rowed out to the marker and transferred the royal remains to a fishing basket to allow the fish to clean the bones. The basket was checked regularly, changed often for another of tighter weft and weave, each basket made anew, woven with prayers for the king.

Edyth reached out to touch the rush woven neat as cloth. The basket gave off a smell brackish as a joined shell from the seabed cracked open in dry air, like the oysters she had shared with Harold twenty years since, their wrists tied in the binding knot of their hand-fasting.

'All flesh has gone,' he said.

Of this she was glad; his remains would be clean and strong. And there was no head. She was glad she would never gaze into the empty sockets of his skull. They will not return to her the heat of the man but these bones might be a different memento. Her children's children chanted a rhyme as they played their hand-games of chance, gathering and counting and throwing small stones and bones. Her game of chance lay in the latticed dark of woven rush.

As the stranger placed the basket in her arms Edyth thought of the canons who had visited from Waltham not long ago. They told her Guillaume le Bâtard had allowed Harold's mother to bury two of her sons at Bosham and also gave permission for Harold's remains to be buried at the religious house he had founded at

Waltham. She did not believe them. The canons' true desire was for the abbey to become a shrine, a place of pilgrimage to which a throng of pilgrims would bring offerings of money to King Harold's resting place.

Edyth told the canons she would not search for Harold again, knowing well that even if they did not find him, they would spin an untruth to suit their purposes. She allowed the dogs to unsettle their horses before whistling them to her.

The broad-shouldered stranger mounted his horse and left her standing in the doorway. At first light, she must ride with the hounds on the other side of the moat where the rooks swirl a cauldron of black over a stand of trees. She could keep him here, where he had ridden with her; bury his bones like twigs in the forest. Harold loved these broad horizons, had thought them not dissimilar to the flatlands of his Wessex manor. She could bury him where the rooks gather as the light thickens, a place where the men would not hunt boar because it was too marshy for the hooves of their horses. Even the dogs whined and cowered at the earth's suck.

She turned towards the doorway and the fire beyond, the basket in her arms light as the winter air.

HARRY SWERVES INTO the gateway of a field and gets out, leaving the engine running. They must be lost. Nora stays where she is, huddled in the van. The fan heater, turned to the highest setting, whines frantically as it whirs. Harry pulls on his woolly hat and gloves and gazes out across the flat fields towards the west, where the white sky has flattened the sunset into a rose-coloured smudge across the horizon. They are in the middle of nowhere. Harry walks round the van to the passenger side.

The door drops on its hinges as he opens it. Straight away, though she can't see them, she hears the cacophony of rooks.

'We're here,' he says.

She tugs the zipper on her fleece up to her neck. Outside the van the air is raucous with coarse croaks mixed with higher chirps and squawks, a clash of sound like the orchestra tuning before a performance. Her eyes fill with tears. Freezing air dries the back of her nose and throat as she takes a long breath. She has not ventured out much since Noah's funeral; weary from inactivity, she thrusts her hands into her pockets and steps slowly towards the gate. Her body is stiff from the long drive and tractors have carved deep ridges in the mud at the field entrance, making it difficult to walk on. Harry reaches into the back of the van to grab her bundle of warm clothing – hat, gloves and scarf.

She has never seen so many rooks. Across the ploughed fields towards the distant trees, the furrowed earth seethes with black. She leans on the metal bar of the gate. At her feet, slabs of mud glisten in light from a low sun.

The hole they dug for Noah, though deep, was not much more than a foot long. She dropped a sprig of holly on to his wicker casket. Behind her, the churchyard was crowded with people from the village, who stood in quiet groups, their presence behind her a comfort though she was unable to look anyone in the face. In the end, though there was no court case, Nora had been cautioned, the criminal offence formally recorded; her fingerprints, photograph and DNA taken.

Clare, the family liaison officer, was right: when Nora thinks of Noah now, she sees the holly with its berries resting on basket weave. She sees the faded blue hand towel with its border of swans. And she sees the three photographs taken by Clare before the funeral. *A memory, of you and Noah*, Clare said. They were sitting on Eve's terrace with the creek flowing past behind her, Noah in his wicker casket on her lap. Eve had threaded holly sprigs into the basket weave.

'You'll need these,' Harry says. He holds out an extra pair of socks along with a pair of wellington boots he has fetched from the back of the van. She doesn't answer. The air is filled with the noise of rooks, and she stands on the edge of turbulence. Harry nudges her elbow with the bundle of warm clothing, so she peels her fingers from the frozen metal, takes the extra socks from him and swaps her shoes for wellington boots.

With his hat pulled down over his ears, Harry looks different; the spray of lines at the outer corners of his eyes more noticeable. He is thinner.

Harry had washed the blue hand towel for her, pegged it out on the line to dry in the sun. Many mothers find keepsakes are important, Clare explained, as a focus for memories. We all grieve differently, she said. Just do what you feel you need to do.

Nora didn't need to see soil thrown on Noah's casket. She felt the spin of vertigo, saw herself on all fours, clawing back the dirt, until Harry offered his arm and they left the churchyard together. He turned right at the church gate, towards the millstream and she allowed herself to be led away from the village and the people heading home along the narrow lane. Jason was opening up at the Anchor Bleu, pushing the anvil doorstop into place with his foot. Others wandered between the gravestones in the winter sun, visiting their own dead. A man in a long dark overcoat held on to his hat as he ducked beneath the yew tree and she thought of Isaac. She dreams of him rarely these days.

She pushes her hands back into her pockets. Silhouetted on the skyline is a stand of trees where rooks cluster thick as black blossom. Those on the ground swagger and bound, spike at the earth with their beaks. More fly in to land on the telegraph wires slooping low under weight of numbers as the birds shift sideways for room, wedged together.

She and Harry walked for hours the day of Noah's burial, until she was exhausted. He didn't talk much, and said nothing to her about the consistory court proceedings held in the church a few days before Noah's funeral. Permission for exhumation of the Godwin grave had been refused. She knew from Eve there was standing room only, the church filled with villagers who gathered to listen to the experts give witness. Though there were many differing viewpoints, translations and interpretations of various historical documents, Elsa Macleod was a minority of one in believing Harold to be buried at Bosham.

Eve said that when Elsa was called, a slant of light from the west window fell on to the stone slabs under the chancel arch, just where the stone coffins are buried. Elsa's voice rang out as if she was preaching from the pulpit. She described the swans depicted in the margins of the Bayeux Tapestry, how she believes many clues lie hidden in the woollen stitches, coded messages she is determined to decipher. 'Hers was the best performance,' Eve said, 'ten out of ten. It was magical. She had my full attention.'

High above, streaming towards them across the sky, twists a sooty skein, the exuberant chatter of the approaching rooks building to a crescendo as they funnel downwards on to the fields.

'There are so many.' Her voice wavers. Harry cups her hands in his and rubs them briskly.

He places her gloves in her hands. 'I came here with my wife.' He turns away to rest his forearms on the gate and lifts the binoculars to look out over the field of rooks. She stares at his back, at the ill-fitting jacket made for a smaller man, one pocket half-ripped off and flapping loose. He has not mentioned a wife before.

Rooks begin to leave the trees and telegraph wires, funnel and dip in the sky before coming down to land in the fields, along the furrows, causing other birds to peel up and back to resettle. Nora hugs herself, shrinking into the downy warmth of her coat, and wonders about children.

'Warm enough?' Harry says.

'Yes.'

Their space disturbed, another group lifts, a mounting wave, soaring higher to curve back and land elsewhere.

They had to clip Rook's wings after he'd knocked himself out. His flying is too haphazard, seeming to take him by surprise when he is angry or frightened, the flurry of his wings beyond his control, sending him crashing into walls and ceilings, or up into trees, stranded. Nora took him to the man with mermaid tattoos at the bird sanctuary and was reassured when he said wing clipping was not permanent. 'It'll need to be done again in the spring,' he said, as he showed her which of the long feathers to clip. 'Unless,' he looked up at her briefly, as if to judge her likely reaction, 'unless, that is, the instinct for flight comes to him fully and he makes up his mind to go.'

Gradually the movement of the birds lessens. Fewer new birds arrive. It is almost dark. The rooks grow quieter, their murmurs simmering. Nora rubs her arms to warm herself.

'C'mon,' Harry says, startling her. He sets off down the lane at a brisk pace.

Her toes are lumpy and stiff with cold, but she wants to stay until the rooks finish roosting. 'Can't we stay and watch?'

Harry points across a flat field towards a copse of alders. 'That's where they go. We'll guess at their flight path.'

They sit together, their backs against a tree, not talking. One side of Nora's body, the side next to Harry, is warm, the other cold. The sun has disappeared and all movement in the fields has ceased. Harry is scanning the almost dark sky.

'Is it over?' she asks.

He puts a hand on her forearm.

And it starts: a whisper of feathers, a disturbance of air rippling into an explosion of sound as rooks rise in ragged clumps from the fields with the jubilant clap of wings beating, wave after wave. Nora's stomach flips, like the lurch of love. A blizzard of clamour, the sky teems black as birds bank and roil, funnelled clockwise one moment, sucked back the next, eddies and spirals blurred against a glimmer of sky. Nora, shivering, barely registers Harry's touch as he slips his coat around her shoulders.

The two of them get to their feet, surrounded by the applause of wing-beats, exultant as a standing ovation.

ACKNOWLEDGEMENTS

I'D LIKE TO thank my agent, Hannah Westland at Rogers, Coleridge and White, and all at Bloomsbury, especially Helen Garnons-Williams, Erica Jarnes, Audrey Cotterell and Greg Heinimann, all of whom gave me inspiration, support and help with producing this book.

My thanks are also due to the following people: Kathy Page, Vicky Grut, Renate Mohr, Ann Jolly, Melanie Penycate, Maria O'Brien and Karen Stevens, who were early readers and offered suggestions; David Knotts, Heather Harrison, Cecelia Bignall for allowing me to listen in to cello lessons at the Royal Academy; Erica Stewart from SANDS for sharing her story; Chris Dennis for help with the Waltham Chronicles; Joan Langhorne, for coffee and biscuits as I poured through church archives, more than once; Jo Phillips, for rook information; Jill and Karl Campbell for advice on police procedure and the law; Sharon Martin, for the visits to retirement hotels and for her wonderful session about Burns Night;

Yvonne Herrington, for help with smudge sticks and auras; Jackie Buxton for tips on running; Sue Bisdee, for midwifery advice and anecdotes. Any mistakes I've made with all this generously given information are my own.

John Pollock's work on the history of the stone coffins of Bosham church in 'Harold: Rex - Is King Harold II Buried in Bosham Church?' (Penny Royal Publications, 1996, with 2002 supplement) first captivated my imagination. For further research, the following publications have been indispensible for both inspiration and information: 'A Guide to Holy Trinity Church, Bosham' by Joan Langhorne; *Crow Country* by Mark Cocker (Vintage, 2008); *Corvus: A Life with Birds* by Esther Woolfson (Granta Books, 2008); *1066: The Hidden History in the Bayeux Tapestry* by Andrew Bridgeford (Walker & Company, 2006); *Mstislav Rostropovitch: Cellist, Teacher, Legend* by Elizabeth Wilson (Faber, 2007).

I'm very grateful to my daughter, Natalie Miller, for sharing my passion for rooks and taking photos on rooking trips. Thank you to all my family for their support, most especially David for his love and patience with all the 1066 and rook talk, as well as with the hours I spend writing.

What inspired you to write Rook?

Writers sometimes describe the earliest stage, when something haunts your mind and you're not at first sure why, as a 'gift' from the unconscious. My gift was rooks - birds I'd never particularly noticed properly before. They were nest-building in trees arching over the road as I drove to work, and I began to look out for them every day.

At around the same time, the untold side of a tabloid newspaper story piqued my interest. By chance I came across another, very similar case, and was niggled by the one-sided telling of both. I didn't want to write about these 'true life' events: what happens to Nora is not something I have experienced myself, plus sensationalism was a danger. One day when talking to a friend about my preoccupation with these stories, in one of those weird moments of synchronicity, I learned she'd recently been involved with a very similar case at work. So my resistance in the end gave way and Nora's story began to grow.

The moment when several apparently disconnected threads came together was during a wander around Bosham church. There's a bird etched onto the memorial stone for King Cnut's daughter and, though I'd seen it many times before, the etching suddenly appeared to me to be very much like a baby rook. Eureka! I knew then that the village traditions, mysteries and myths surrounding the ancient stone coffins in Bosham church would provide a frame around which to weave the various narrative strands which were the chaos of my first draft.

You 'bookend' the novel with two vividly imagined episodes featuring real historical figures – are you tempted to write a full-blown historical novel?

The brief battlefield scene which opens *Rook* was written very early on and the process absorbed me for days. The imagining of such a savage scene forced a focus on concrete imagery which links love and loss, a theme which was to be central to the novel, though I didn't know it at the time. I later wrote more of Edyth Swan-neck's story which was cut right back during redrafting to leave just the two episodes. *Rook* wasn't the place for it. I had an inkling this was novel three surfacing but again resisted the idea (this seems to be part of my creative process!) because the voice which came so powerfully when writing Edyth's viewpoint is intense and would be difficult to maintain for a whole novel. However, the hidden histories in the Bayeux Tapestry remain a preoccupation, as does Edyth's story and what happened to her after the Norman Conquest. I'm now planning a trip to West Stow Anglo-Saxon village. So, yes, I'm more than tempted.

Both your novels explore secrets and hidden stories. Is this a preoccupation of yours?

Yes. Untold stories fascinate me, the power they hold over people/ characters who, for whatever reason, can't at first voice them. The 'underside' of things draws me: the secrets people choose to keep;

a point of view which may go unstated in a newspaper story; mysteries which can't be solved because we don't have enough information – but we try to solve them anyway. More than a preoccupation, the unfolding of a story which is at first hidden is very much part of my writing process. Michèle Roberts talks of 'writing into the dark' with a first draft and that's how it is for me: both exciting and frightening. The sense of the story about to be discovered, as if it already exists somewhere, is what drives me.

You write about Rook so convincingly. How did you do your research into birds?

I began with *Crow Country* by Mark Cocker, a glorious book which sent me off on an exuberant quest to Norfolk to watch thousands and thousands of rooks come into roost – one of the most uplifting experiences of my life. Rook himself grew from information gleaned from my husband and his sisters about a pet rook their mother kept for years in the casing of an old television in their kitchen. I also learned a great deal from *Corvus: A Life with Birds* by Esther Woolfson, who writes with captivating detail about a baby rook she reared. I've never had a close encounter with a live rook, but when editing during one early summer I often ate my lunch outside in the company of a semi-tame female blackbird. Watching the blackbird watch me, the way she moved and the way I felt when she eventually took food from my hand, all added to my understanding of Rook and Nora's relationship, and helped me appreciate the fragile balance between what is wild and what is tame.

Both The Devil's Music *and* Rook *are closely tied to the landscape of Sussex where you live – do you think you would be a different writer if you lived in the city? Do you think writers are products of the landscape they grow up in?*

Details of landscape and my response to it have become part of how I understand and see myself, but it's not as straightforward as being a 'product' of where I grew up, since my connection with landscape has deepened through writing. Simon Schama suggests that landscape is 'the work of the mind. Its scenery built up as much from the strata of memory as from layers of rock', and it's true my attachment to the seascapes of Sussex is rooted in memory. I grew up in Bexhill, East Sussex, where we had a beach hut. Often we'd be there in all weathers, from breakfast until bedtime, and my childhood memories are mostly of being outside, barefoot under broad skies; of running on pebbles, climbing breakwaters, exploring rock pools, building huge sandcastles with crowds of other children. I also lived for thirty years in the Witterings in West Sussex, writing *The Devil's Music* in a house just across the road from the sea.

I've learnt recently that the word 'landscaef', brought to Britain by Anglo-Saxon settlers, meant a clearing in the forest with animals, huts, fields and fences; a place carved out of the wilderness; a place made 'home'. Choosing a Sussex beach as the primary setting for *The Devil's Music* was, I expect, a way of providing myself with a place to feel at home when everything about the process of writing my first novel was challenging and unfamiliar. *Rook* ventures a little further inland, along a creek path, across wheat fields. With novel three – which looks as though it might be set in forests on the Downs – I'm getting really adventurous!

Who are your key literary influences?

I began to love the idea of writing when I was about nine or ten after reading Catherine Storr (*Marianne Dreams*) and Alan Garner (*The Owl Service*). Since then, I've continued to be influenced by each encounter with a writer whose work thrills me in some way. There are many, so this list is not exhaustive, and I have to include poets: T. S. Eliot and D. H. Lawrence when I was a teenager; contemporary poets such as Vicki Feaver, Helen Dunmore, Stephanie Norgate, who I came across in my thirties. Later, fiction writers like Jeanette Winterson, Michael Ondaatje, Maggie O'Farrell, Julie Myerson, Patrick McGrath, Jon McGregor and early Ian McEwan; more recently, Evie Wyld, Sarah Hall, Katie Ward, Deborah Levy and the poets Philip Gross and Esther Morgan have delighted me with what they've achieved with language and form.